Penguin Books

THE DOGSBODY PAPERS

Eric Oakley Parrott was born in 1924 in London, well within the sound of Bow Bells, and so is technically a Cockney, but was brought up in Shoreham-by-Sea, Sussex, where he attended the local grammar school. After winning that school's most coveted academic award, the Gregory Taylor Scholarship, in 1939, he went to Brighton Technical College, where he studied for a BSc in Mathematics and Geography. He then spent twenty years as a cartographer with the Hydrographic Department of the Ministry of Defence, and while there edited the Admiralty List of Radio Signals. He began to write seriously in his spare time – articles, plays and entries in various literary competitions. He has always taken a keen interest in the theatre and was both an amateur actor and a producer, becoming an Associate of the Drama Board in 1961. He has had a number of his plays produced and his radio plays have been performed by the BBC and in Germany, Canada, Australia and New Zealand, among other countries. In 1976 he resigned from the Civil Service, and, after a year at Garnet College, Roehampton, taught English and general studies at Havering Technical College, Hornchurch, Essex. Here he compiled a number of Units for the Longman's General Studies Project. Failing eyesight forced him to retire from teaching and he has now begun a third career as a full-time writer. His books include *The Penguin Book of Limericks*, *How to Become Ridiculously Well-Read in One Evening*, *Limerick Delight* (Puffin), *Imitations of Immortality* and *How to Become Absurdly Well-Informed About the Famous and the Infamous*, all published by Penguin. He lives on a converted Dutch barge on London's Regent's Canal with his wife and son.

Also edited by E. O. Parrott

The Penguin Book of Limericks

Limerick Delight

How to Become Ridiculously Well-Read in One Evening

Imitations of Immortality

*How to Become Ridiculously Well-Informed about the
  Famous and Infamous*

The Dogsbody Papers

or 1066 and All This

Compiled and edited by E. O. PARROTT

Illustrations by W. F. N. Watson

PENGUIN BOOKS

For Bob Lindop

PENGUIN BOOKS

Published by the Penguin Group
27 Wrights Lane, London W8 5TZ, England
Viking Penguin Inc., 40 West 23rd Street, New York, New York 10010, USA
Penguin Books Australia Ltd, Ringwood, Victoria, Australia
Penguin Books Canada Ltd, 2801 John Street, Markham, Ontario, Canada L3R 1B4
Penguin Books (NZ) Ltd, 182–190 Wairau Road, Auckland 10, New Zealand

Penguin Books Ltd, Registered Offices: Harmondsworth, Middlesex, England

First published by Viking 1988
Published in Penguin Books 1989
10 9 8 7 6 5 4 3 2 1

Filmset in Linotron ITC Galliard by
Rowland Phototypesetting Ltd, Bury St Edmunds, Suffolk
Printed in Great Britain by
Richard Clay Ltd, Bungay, Suffolk

▌ *Table of Contents*

Table of Contents

The Parrott File

Pterodactyl Publishers
Lemming Place
Bloomsbury
London WC1

19 January 1986

Dear Mr Parrott,

I am given to understand that you have already edited a number of books, and I am wondering if you would be interested in doing a volume for this house.

I believe Willoughby Dogsbody instructed his son, Winston, that he felt the time was now ripe to make a start on publishing extracts from the Dogsbody Papers, a monumental task as you possibly realize, but one that could be, to coin a phrase, 'the publishing sensation of the century'.

If you would care to discuss this, please ring my secretary's secretary for an appointment.

We are a small, rather old-fashioned publishing house so we do still allow authors on to the premises, although we prefer them to use the side entrance in Lemming Mews.

We look forward to adding *The Dogsbody Papers* to our History List.

Yours sincerely,
Julius Wotherspoon

WILLOUGHBY DOGSBODY (1905–85) *Head Librarian at Ardleigh Green Public Library. Hon. Archivist to British Council (1945–65). Married Artemisia Crusshe-Liteley; one son, Wilkins, born 1940. Died in a fit of apoplectic rage when the ferrule of his umbrella became trapped in the floor of the Humour Section of the London Library.*

Lammas College
Oxon.

15 February 1986

Dear Eric,

I've done my best, though I'm no history man.

Dogsbody is, of course, quite a common surname. There are a few living near here, notably in the villages around Stratford. There are a few pamphlets in the Bodleian by one Mortimer Dogsbody, a rather dull archaeologist. Quite unreadable. If this is the standard of their papers I do not envy you. Nor your readers.

Lewis just came in. He says Dogsbody is a common enough working-class name. There are lots in South Lincolnshire, which is his home patch. They even spill over into North Norfolk, which is just what one would expect of a Dogsbody, I suppose.

Yours ever,
Ian

Chichester

25 February 1986

Dear Eric,

The news about the next book is good. Many of the contributors (did I understand you to say we are nearly forty strong now?) will welcome the change to historical research. I presume a similar system will operate, in that we choose the material, and then translate, edit, etc., ready for press, and you then select out enough to make a book . . .

Yours, as ever,
Martin Fagg

Ipswich
28 February 1986

Dear Eric,

I have struck gold, or rather, I have spoken with one Adam Dogsbody, and even peered into the dark recesses of the archive, or a portion thereof, for the Dogsbodys are obsessive about collecting. Their family motto would seem to be: 'An Englishman's home is his dustbin'. Papers! You never saw the like! Diaries and journals going way back. Just about every Dogsbody there ever was must have kept a diary, and they are all there, every single one of them . . .

Regards,
Paul Griffin

Extract from a letter from Mrs Mary Holtby to E. O. Parrott:

. . . when I mentioned Sir Max Dogsbody and Theophilus, he became quite choleric – red-faced and choking over his empty tankard. The landlord signalled to me that I should buy him another pint. 'It's the break with family tradition that gets old Ezra. It's them getting famous and going on the box. That's never been the Dogsbody way. It's as well you didn't mention Sir Mortimer. He gets quite ill if he hears that name.' Old Ezra gave a shudder, and I ended up buying him a large brandy as well.

But it was worth it, as he took me round the archives, which are in an old barn, like the lot that Paul saw. The condition of items is variable, but there is a great deal of material here.

Extract from a letter from Bill Greenwell to E. O. Parrott:

. . . what is becoming clearer is that we should select items which illuminate history as we know it and shed new light on events or people.

Incidentally, I asked old Miss Emily Belle why no one had ever attempted to get the archives published before, and she simply said: 'No one's ever suggested it afore. Why should anyone want to read our silly old bits and pieces?' I told her lots would, and that the bits and pieces were fascinating . . .

MI6
Ministry of Defence
c/o 10 Downing Street
W.C.1

16 June 1987

E. O. Parrott, Esq.
c/o Pterodactyl Books
London W.C.3.

Dear Sir,

It has come to the attention of the Ministry that you are to edit some of THE DOGSBODY PAPERS for publication. I would point out that many of the documents in this vast collection are known to be Secret, MOST SECRET, etc., and were in fact unofficially purloined. Many members of the Dogsbody family were civil servants, members of the Armed Services, etc., and although, in most cases, such service pre-dates the Official Secrets Act, nevertheless it remains an offence to communicate to a potential enemy any information which might be useful in time of war. It may seem far-fetched to designate information about our forces as top secret, especially when the details date from the time of, say, the Battle of Trafalgar or the documents themselves have appeared in *Pravda*, but the law must be enforced.

I am
Your obedient servant,
A. Potterton-Smythe, D.D.C., D.C.S.

Extract from a letter from Wilkins Dogsbody to E. O. Parrott:

. . . I am glad to hear from Winston that you are getting it all together and the omens are promising. The archives are in a mess in places. Not all family members have been as meticulous as Winston and dear old Willoughby. In some cases we have no idea how items were acquired. In a few instances items conflict with one another, so there may be a few 'frauds' around . . .

Extract from a letter from Pterodactyl Books to E. O. Parrott:

23 June 1987

. . . It is a pity you did not tell us before that you had an agent. Had we realized you had expert advice, we would have made a more generous offer. It is, of course, our duty to our shareholders to maximize our profits.

Not that we shall be able to improve much on our contract. As I often tell authors, publishers do not have the aesthetic satisfaction that comes from writing a book, nor do they experience the joy of knowing that you are bringing untold pleasure to your readers. Compared with that, the paltry monetary reward which publishers receive is very small beer indeed.

Extract from a letter from John McLaughlin, literary agent, to E. O. Parrott:

. . . as for Dogsbody, there is nothing from Wotherspoon. He's in Venice for a Conference on Religious Books. Pterodactyl do not publish any, but that wouldn't bother Julius.

On the other hand, I have had a reasonable offer from Viking, though you still have that three months' delay in the payment of royalties. Why this should be necessary in these days of computers, nobody will ever explain. It just means that there is a delay in authors getting their money (and their agents, too!), during which time the publishers get the interest on the author's money. If it's any comfort, it's worse in the USA.

On the other hand, the good news is that Viking want two more books, at least, after this one. Opera and poetry are suggested as topics . . .

E. O. PARROTT
November 1987

The Dogsbody Family:
An introductory romp

Dawdle with Dogsbody,
Peeking at History,
Through lenses quizzical –
Or with a grin!
See how the family,
Quasi-ubiquitous,
Seems to get into things
Up to its chin!

When great events unfold –
Hastings, or Runnymede –
Dogsbody's lurking there,
Note-book down hose;
Flirting in Kenilworth,
Courtesan-cognizant;
Chatting with Cromwell, re
Warts on the nose!

Charge of the Light Brigade,
Relief of Mafeking,
Roses, the, Battles of –
Dogsbody's there;
Writing from Waterloo,
Uninhibitingly
Telling a cousin just
What, when and where!

Soon you'll be into these
Recitals recondite:
Things never heard before,
All in one book;
Historiography,
Anecdote-Armagnacked,
Served with a piquant sauce,
By a sly cook!

PASCOE POLGLAZE

The Dogsbody Papers

EDITOR'S NOTE: These extracts from the Dogsbody family's archives have, in most instances, been arranged chronologically. However, in a few cases, such as a group of documents concerned with one individual, a single event or a relationship, other arrangements have been adopted.

FRONTISPIECE: The annexe to The Vicarage, Woddlestone, the 16th-century listed building which houses part of the Dogsbody Archives and Dogsbodleian Museum.

c. 15000 B.C.
The Discovery of the Wheel

STONE SCRATCHED by Ugg Dugg Budd:

Was chipping a flint in the cave when young Mugg came rushing in, very excited, and shouting that he had made a great discovery. Not again! What will become of the lad I do not know. He is continually messing about with bits of trees, earth of different colours and things, instead of gathering berries and beetles like anyone normal of his age.

Well, what was it this time?

'Round things roll,' he blabbered.

I patiently explained that everybody knew that – otherwise we wouldn't have a word 'roll' in the vocabulary. You can't have words for things you haven't discovered yet.

PREHISTORIC ART: Images incised on part of a mastodon's scapula, discovered in 1949 by Professor Philemon Dogsbody at Cimbel las Corta-bolsas in Andalusia. They clearly show that Dog's Body the Wheel-maker was the first viniculturist and alcoholic orgiast. This is also the earliest known representation of the Dog's Body image.

Oh yes, he knew that, he said, but what he had in mind was somehow to get three or four round objects, and put a flat object on top. You could then sit on this, or put heavy things on it, and so move about more easily.

Still patient, because you can chip a flint and talk at the same time, I explained that he had evidently forgotten one important fact. What was that? It was that round things roll, right enough, but only downhill. So what happened when you got to the bottom with your contraption, even if you ever managed to fix it together? Did he expect it to roll back up again? Of course we didn't know why round things rolled downhill and not uphill, but that was beside the point. It was just nature, that was all, and we would just have to live with it. Like, well . . . like having to live with bare feet. So his idea was preposterous.

He hadn't an answer.

Pressing home the advantage, I gave him a long lecture about wasting his time on fantasies, instead of doing a useful job for the community, like keeping the food coming in. I ended up with the most absurd example I could think of, to show him the error of his ways.

I put it to him: did he think it reasonable to expect that one day we would be able to make a fire right here in the cave, when we wanted it, instead of having to trudge all the way up the bloody volcano in bare feet to get it?

That really finished him.

But you can't win, with the young. He is still not out gathering with the others, but sits twiddling about with two bits of wood and handfuls of moss.

The weakness is on his mother's side. She had a cousin who went raving mad, and tried writing on dried animal skins. We did our best to explain to him that they would rot down in no time at all, so that posterity would get precisely nothing from us. But he couldn't see it.

W. S. BROWNLIE

1500 B.C.
The Building of Stonehenge

HERE IS AN EXTRACT from *The Dying Testimony of Crwg Dwgsbwdi*, Section V of the epic poem *Crwg's Saga*, one of the undisputed masterpieces of early British literature. Unhappily, as in the work of Sappho (who may in fact have been a contemporary), only fragments remain.

This translation, the best we have, is by Ezra Shilling (the U.S. poet and critic). It is far better than Dante Gabriel Dogsbotti's rather wishy-washy attempt, or even Alexander Cardinal's, the opening of which we give you, for the sake of comparison:

> Speak not to me of stone, for I was left
> When Dewi Dugsbuddy of life was reft,
> A quarry to myself, which pleased me not;
> 'Twas not as good as what my brothers got.

We may spare you further quotation.

Ezra's translation, although flawed in some respects, has something of the rough-hewn alliterative vigour of the original. The opening passage of part V is almost complete in the original, although some parts have been eaten by sheep. Crwg Dwgsbwdi, a tough, independent man with a dishonest streak, is shown here in a state of deathbed repentance.

> My brudeman, Dewi the Dolmen, now dead,
> Left me a large quarry of lumpish stone
> Starkly standing beneath the starry sky,
> Small earnings for a stalwart son,
> While my brothers had broad fields of breadwheat,
> Downcast I delved .... dug .... dung ....
> .... swearing .... miserable sod ....
> Till of a sudden .... a scheme ....
> .... on the proven proverb ....
> Whereby the Wiltshire dumbwits will believe anything;
> The more unlikely the lie, the better they like it.

Trusting their dupehood I trumped up a trick,
Sold them my whole supply of stone
And blueprints for a blithe block-ring
Of jimcrack geomancy and of gigantic girth.
Then came they to hand like hound to ham-bone.
Not only on the stones did they squander their savings
But payed precious pence for porterage and purveyance
(Eleven pence per long land-league) ....
Then hoisted we into place a huge Henge,
Claiming for it use as calendar and cultureplace
And pretending all sorts of peculiar powers.

Now that I die on this drear deathbed
I regret my rascally ....
For the thing must have toppled and tumbled these twenty
    years.
'Twas a dire and dirty doing, but droll.
Long did I and my louting labourers loudly laugh
As we fled with the fundings before it fell flat.

Elsewhere in the Saga is an account of Crwg's somewhat ingenious method of conveying vast megaliths over long distances and through water, but it is too technical to be worthy of inclusion in a work of this kind.

GERARD BENSON

*c.*1500 B.C.
The Discovery of Woad

ONE OF THE MOST remarkable discoveries of the late Dr Theophilus Dogsbody was the solution of the early inscriptions in the Wookey Hole Caves at Cheddar in Somerset. It was he who realized that this apparently random series of scratches was, in fact, the earliest example of graffiti known. Not only did Dr Dogsbody manage to translate this primitive picture-writing, but he was able to show

---

D R THEOPHILUS DOGSBODY (1870–1958)
Director of Ethnic Studies at Oswaldtwistle Institute of Ling-uistics. Younger twin of Philemon. Special interests: Middle and Far Eastern folklore. Self-taught expert on hieroglyphs and other ancient writings. Tragic death in 1958, much reported, when the lid of a sarcophagus which he was inspecting fell, decapitating him.

---

conclusively that the messages, which appear to be in four different hands, form a sequence in which later messages comment upon or answer earlier ones. The Doctor, in a typical stroke of originality, has labelled the separate writers of these messages *A*, *B*, *C*, and *D*.

A I have discovered woad.
B What the hell is woad?
C Ugg was here.
A Woad comes from a plant.
D So do the other nuts.
A Woad dyes you blue.
B Who wants to be dyed blue?
C Ugg was here again. I saw someone dyed blue. He looked nice.
A That was me. It is very fashionable to be blue.
B Who cares about fashion?
D I fancy blue men. They are sexier.
C How do you know?
D How do you think?
A Who is scared to be blue?
B All right, but how do you get this blue off?
A Why do you want to get rid of your woad?
B A man does not want to go on being blue.
A Hard cheese.
D Blue men are getting even sexier.
C Ugg was here yet again. How do you get woad from these plants?
B I am now one for the woad.

The final inscription covers one whole wall of a second cave on the third level, a short distance from where the previous inscriptions were found. The characters are, for the most part, much larger.

B If you are feeling blue, WOAD will change all that.
Buy URK'S WOAD now! It dyes the parts other woads never reach.
D Blue men are sexier.
C I like being blue. Yum-yum!

E. O. PARROTT

c. 1300 B.C.
The Fall of Jericho

A SCROLL DISCOVERED near the Dead Sea, an alternative version of Joshua 6:1–27. It was written by a scribe whose name is interpreted as Dogsbethel or Dagsbod. The latter is more likely (see Ichabod). The translation is for a Supplement to the New English Bible.

1 Jericho was bolted and barred against the Israelites. The Lord said to Joshua: 'Behold, I have delivered Jericho and her king into your hands. It is for you to finish what I have begun.'

2 So Joshua the son of Nun made his plan. This was for seven priests with seven trumpets of ram's horn, and seven priests with seven drums of stretched skin, to march in front of the Ark of the Covenant, and make the circuit of the city. The men drafted from the two and a half tribes would march also in front of the Ark. The rearguard was to follow behind the Ark. Meantime the camp followers dug sulphur from the rocks, burned wood into charcoal, and boiled goats' dung, skimming the nitres from off the top. All was mixed together. Many pots were gathered. And the women made strings of blue cloth which they soaked in the nitres. Then those who were smallest in stature began to dig under the earth towards the city of Jericho. The drafted men and the priests and the Ark of the Covenant and the rearguard began to march round the city. Such was the noise they made that the digging by the smallest in stature could not be heard by those in the city. And the soil from the digging was taken away by night in the pots that had been gathered.

10 So it continued for six days. And each day the smallest in stature dug further, and the priests blew and drummed louder, and the noise that they made became greater, and the army grew wearier. And those within the city of Jericho looked in wonder from the walls, for they had never seen the like. And they mocked and said one to another: 'What fools these Israelites be! We are here within our stronghold with corn and water enough for many days, and they make music and walk in circles. Truly they are as the pitcher that goes longest to the well.' And they rejoiced.

15 On the seventh day the seven priests blew the trumpets, and the seven priests beat the drums, and they and the army marched seven times round the city. The while, the smallest in stature filled the pots with the mixture that they had made and bore them under the earth towards the city. And when they were set, they lighted the blue strings that the women had made and retired immediately.

18 Then Joshua said to the army: 'Shout! The Lord has given you the city. No one is to be spared except the prostitute Rahab and every woman who is with her in the house, for I have need of them. And all the silver and gold shall be holy also; they belong to the Lord and they must go into the Lord's treasury, the charge of which he has given me.'

20 At this, the army murmured and said: 'This was unknown to us before. We have marched many leagues in the heat of the day, while Joshua has reclined in his tent. Is it not the custom of old that rape and pillage should be the prize for the taking of a city? Why should we not have our reward?' And the courage of the army melted and flowed away like water, and they did not shout as Joshua had commanded them.

23 And the smallest in stature murmured also, and they returned immediately and snuffed out the blue strings that they had lit.

24 So it was that the city of Jericho was spared.

25 But Joshua had it told in Gath, and published in the streets of Askelon, that he had slain his thousands and his ten thousands, and had brought down the walls of Jericho. And so it was written, and many were disinformed.

27 And his fame spread throughout the land.

W. S. BROWNLIE

·7

*c.*1300
The Plagues of Egypt

FROM THE JOURNAL of Tut Degsbhudi:

Ra be praised, I have been given a sabbatical by my Master. I am to study climatic conditions, that our crops may be grown more successfully. To this end, I have resolved upon practical seclusion for three months. May our rye and our wheat, our flax and our barley prosper. Also, I think we should diversify into beansprouts. Ra.

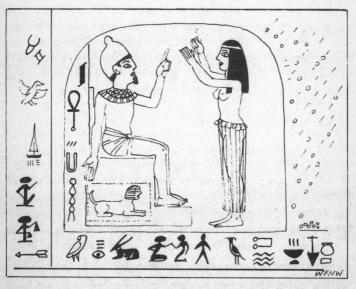

EGYPTIAN TOMB PAINTING (Tel-el-Imshi-Igguri, *c.*1300 B.C.): The so-called 'Sphinx' depicted, which is in reality the Dog's Body, identifies the grave as that of the scribe and diarist Tut Deghsbudi; his account of the plagues is here illustrated, and shows his connection with the Pyramids at Gizeh, which are presided over by the well-known giant figure of the Dog's Body symbolizing his family. The tomb was unfortunately blown up by Ordnance Artificer Faroosh al Cloomsi in 1950.

I have been working upon the portents. Esther, my Hebrew slave, nice girl but bangs endlessly on about milk and honey, has just brought me an extraordinary drink. Left it without a word, and yet all I requested was a cup of fresh river water. Instead, she has given me something thick, viscous and scarlet. It is perhaps a tomato-juice, in which case I have made a genuine discovery. Whatever it is, it tastes bloody good. Ra.

Esther is not as dim as she looks. Everyone is drinking the stuff! So bang goes my scheme quietly to corner the market. I looked out from my windows and saw half the town pie-eyed with it. It appears to have alcoholic content. I ordered up a couple more, but I am patently impervious to its wiles. Refreshing! Perhaps it may prove a good fertilizer. Ra.

There is a chronic water shortage, but ample supplies of Esther's Crimson Special. I planted some bulrushes in it, and they are growing like wildfire. Ra.

The red stuff has proved merely a passing craze. It has also all vanished. If I know Rameses, it has probably been confiscated and kept for him in a special cache. I have today tested various sorts of mud. Esther is unusually quiet. Ra.

These mud experiments are a phenomenal, unexpected success! Without warning, the house filled with frogs, all burping excitedly, and mating left, right and centre. The Nile's banks have been known to breed serpents, I know, but this is proof positive. And tasty. I shall send word to Pharaoh: a frog economy is what we need. Corn is yesterday's commodity. Ra.

Think again, Tut! After a week, my laboratory fast-food frogs developed fever and croaked their last. Back to the drawing-board. Ra.

Lice! My latest fertilizers have created lice! They are pleasantly crunchy if fried in a little butter, but devilishly hard to catch. I will change the ingredients. Ra.

Wonders shall never cease. I have now discovered the growth potential of flies, although this is hardly an achievement calculated to win me friends, and will need considerably careful marketing. I have beaten off a swarm all day, much to Esther's amusement. They do not touch her, interestingly. I put it down to the appalling diet these Hebrews hold to (no frogs, for a start!). Ra.

No more flies, but Esther's activities continue to agitate me. Whilst I was busy with my calculations, she brought me news that all the cattle have died (except in Goshen, where the Hebrews have their huts). This sort of exaggeration is typical of the Israelis. However, if half-true, I must redouble my researches into soil technology. Meantime there is steak, steak, steak on the menu. Ra.

I thought something was up with that meat. I am covered in repulsive, purulent boils. Esther severely reprimanded. Ra.

I was awoken by a rattling on the roof. Called Esther. 'Hail, my Lord,' she replied mysteriously and buzzed off. I resumed my research – the boils have gone – but the noise was deafening. And it was then redoubled by thunder. I called Esther in, and she told me that, so terrible has the weather been (more secret Hebrew smiling), all the cattle left in the fields were killed outright. I picked her up on this. Only the other day, I said, you said they'd already snuffed it, didn't you? The fibber. She pouted and pushed off. Ra.

More rain and thunder. Bad for the barley and flax, but the wheat and rye should do rather well as a result. Ra.

As I was sitting down to my investigation of the relationship between tidal currents and the propagation of root vegetables, the room filled from top to bottom with locusts. My experiments are ruined. They have eaten all my seeds, my cuttings, my roots, my leaves, yea even my lunch. However, much to Esther's chagrin – that girl is forever smirking in the most uncivil fashion – I have always been partial to raw locusts as a delicacy. I feel quite gorged. It has almost taken my mind off the inevitable hiccup in my research. Ra.

More locusts! Yum yum! Ra.

I have gone blind. I cannot see. It is all dark. I blame it on the locusts. Bitter. Ra.

Joy! My sight is returned! An even greater joy is that my elder brother is reported dead, which means that the pyramid business passes to me. Apparently, so Esther informs me, a number of firstborn have come to sticky ends. Doubtless Rameses is embarked upon yet one more of his purges, or even one of his loopier genetic experiments. A human cull is just the sort of thing he'd go in for. It all seems to have pleased Esther and her friends – that is, when they have not been decorating their lintels with red stuff (it seems to have turned up again). I do not think it will catch on as a fashion for exterior decoration. Ra.

TUT DEGSBHUDI *Scribe and general factotum at the court of the celebrated Pharaoh, Rameses, Tut was the second son of Argal Degsbhudi, the first successful seller of pyramids to his compatriots, often years before they were built. Later in life he patented the Rhomboid, a new design of sepulchre, but it never caught on and he died of a broken wallet.*

Esther has done a bunk! It seems, according to the proclamations that waft up from the street, that she and her lot have nipped out of Goshen, and headed off for the Red Sea. Word has it that they have turned and encamped before Pi-hahiroth, between Migdol and the sea, over against Baalzephon. Nice little resort. I am joining the posse. Ra.

What a day. First of all, my nag goes lame. And then, when I catch up with the riders, I find the whole army has attempted to ford the channel. Ford it! The new Pharaoh is to be installed tomorrow. Let us hope he is not as mad as Rameses. It seems unlikely. He has made me his Chief Enchanter. It will make a change from crops.

BILL GREENWELL

1300–1200 B.C.
From *The Attic News*

AMONG THE FAMILY treasures of Kuondemas of Athens was a wax tablet, which appears to be part of the 'script' for the local equivalent of a Town Crier, an official charged with announcements, news, etc. Apparently the service, as all good services, was privatized and supported by 'small ads'. One decipherable piece dates the tablet as coming from the period immediately following the fall of Troy:

FOR SALE, LARGE WOODEN HORSE: Only used once. Good condition. Would make ideal playroom for Pony Club addict or conversation piece for LARGE banqueting hall. Cheap, as owner going abroad. Apply Odysseus, Ilium.

KUONDEMAS (448–398 B.C.)   *Greek slave. Served the Clerk of Works at the Acropolis. Given his freedom in 401. Great collector of records, most of them scratched on to stone. Self-appointed disseminator of news and gossip to the people of Athens, to whom he would read his gleanings, standing in the gutter.*

E. O. PARROTT

1300–1200 B.C.
Songs of the Sea

PROFESSOR PHILEMON DOGSBODY (1870–1959)   *Son of Victor Dogsbody, Latin Master at Oswald-twistle Grammar School, and Athene née Blott. Twin brother of Theophilus. Sometime Professor of Classics at Slough. Toured extensively in the Mediterranean region. Last heard of in Sicily, in the remote village of Porca Miseria. He had been engaged in research for his posthumously published* Treatise on Hand Laundering Methods Around the Mediterranean, *and it is thought that his enthusiastic questioning of the women of the village during their communal washing sessions on the banks of the river Cosanostra may have given rise to suspicion and jealousy among their menfolk.*

TWO SAILORS' SONGS from the post-Trojan period, collected by Professor Philemon Dogsbody on his travels around the Mediterranean shores:

1 A rowing-song of impenetrable antiquity, yet used within living memory by sailors plying their oars off Italian coasts. This is only one of several versions, some of which, though similar in theme, are a trifle more forthright in expression. – P.D.

> Madam the Carthaginian Queen,
>   Di-did-do!
> Madam the Carthaginian Queen,
>   Di-did-do!
> Madam the Carthaginian Queen
> Ought to have kept the party clean,
>   Aeny-paeny, Di-did-do!

2 An interesting companion-piece, the original of which had been lost but surfaced in an 'English' version during the First World War. Though there are various alterations and accretions, it is recognizably the same song. Careful readers will note that the original is in the plural, the inference being that the sailor (definitely singular) was bidding farewell to a *group* of girls rather than a single sweetheart. (There is also a notable lack of the endearments characteristic of the English version.) I class it as a companion-piece because it was almost certainly sung by Aeneas' sailors as they left Carthage, taking 'a bowzy short leave' of their girls on the shore . . . It may be of interest for readers to learn that the expression *'mentum-mentum'* ('chin-chin') disappeared for several centuries before its emergence in the modern era and is quite unknown in classical Latin. – P.D.

> *Valete! Valete!*
> (Goodby-ee! Goodby-ee!)
> *Lacrimando, oro, abstinete!*
> (Wipe the tear, baby dear, from your ey-ee)
> *Separare est durum,*
> (Though it's hard to part, I know)
> *Ire tamen gavisus sum.*
> (I'd be tickled to death to go)
> *Siccate! Pacate!*
> (Don't cry-ee! Don't sigh-ee!)*

---

* More properly, 'Dry up! Shut up!', but the translation tends to be rather squeamish. – P.D.

Nubes argentiferas spectate!
(There's a silver lining in the sky-ee!)
Mentum-mentum, vesperascit dum
(Bonsoir, old thing; cheerio, chin-chin)
Clamo: Finis est, valete!
(Na-poo, toodle-oo, goodby-ee!)

MARY HOLTBY

965 B.C.
The Sculptor Pheidias

Death of a Dogsbody

A FRAGMENT FROM the Platitudes of Hepatitis Escalator of Semicolon:

It is related by the learned historian Herodotus that the great sculptor Pheidias was once arraigned before the Areopagus, charged with having murdered one of his slaves. This man, whose unpronounceable name in his own vile tongue was Doegesboddicc, here translated as Somakunos, was a native of the Tin Isles near the far northern land of the Hyperboreans and had been brought to Greece with his woman by Phoenician traders. An uncouth barbarian, his unsavoury body besmirched with crude designs incised in his hide with blue dye, he was employed in the sculptor's workshop to sweep and gather the marble chippings that fell from the skilful chisel of his master. The great Pheidias stated in evidence that on the fatal morning he had just finished a nine-month-long labour of carving for the Temple of Poseidon at Lemnos, a monumental and eye-delighting work of art representing mighty Hades, King of the Underworld, in the act of carrying off Persephone, lovely daughter of great Demeter. The unclothed Earth-Shaker was superbly depicted striding along triumphant and amorously ithyphallic, with the struggling maiden flung over his powerful shoulder. Having given a final polish to this

S OMAKUNOS (born Doegesboddicc) (*c.* 500–*c.* 460 B.C.) *Barbarian, probably Celt of Durotrices tribe in Tin Is. Slave to Greek sculptor Pheidias. Destroyed by Divine Wrath of the Olympian Gods.*

A SPHYXIA DOEGESBODDICCA *'Wife' to the above. Slattern and perjured virago; flogged for blasphemy, etc. No further details known.*

masterpiece of his divinely inspired art, the great sculptor ordered the slave Somakunos or Doegesboddicc to clean and wash the floor in readiness for the expected arrival of the Lemnian priests and elders. Thus instructed, the ignorant slave came with a large waterpot brim-full and, before the sculptor's horror-stricken eyes, hung it upon the marble god's virile person causing that exquisitely tooled portion, thus put to base menial use, to snap clean off (Exhibit Alpha). So much was beyond question.

The shrewish female slave Asphyxia Doegesboddicca vehemently swore that great Pheidias, in a transport of vicious rage, seized a heavy crowbar (Exhibit Beta) and struck her simple husband on his innocent head so that he fell dead, and in falling knocked down the top-heavy idol (so she blasphemously termed it) to smash on the stone floor into a thousand fragments (Exhibits Gamma to Omega millennia).

The honoured Pheidias, however, gravely assured the court that rather than suffer an example of his supreme art to survive mutilated and emasculated, or cobbled together, he, grief-stricken, smote it off at the knees (Exhibit Gamma) with the aforementioned crowbar so that the ponderous, maiden-carrying torso of the god fell to smash as described, but in falling merely brushed lightly across the ignorant slave's shaggy elf-locks, which nevertheless encompassed his instant death, undoubtedly at the express decree of the outraged god himself.

Having heard the evidence, the wise archon Anaestheseus gave judgement, with the entire Areopagus concurring, that the only matter of consequence was the obvious displeasure of the gods that a work of genius and beauty solemnly dedicated to one of their divine fellowship had been destroyed by a worthless barbarian, whose death in any case, he being a slave, was of total irrelevance.

The noble Pheidias was therefore courteously dismissed with the court's heartfelt commiseration and a suitable compensation in gold drachmae for loss of income. The hag Asphyxia was ordered to be whipped once for wasting judicial time, and a second time for blasphemy.

W. F. N. WATSON

950 B.C.
The Dark Ages of the Greeks

DOGOSBODOI   *Son of Dogosbodoi* (960–920 B.C.). *A travelling bard based at Chios. Only one of his poems has been preserved and translated.*

A Year in a Poet's Life

Firm, it seems, is the offer from the King of Corinth,
And Thea has ordered an amphora of olive oil.

The King of Samos favours the hetaira Dioge,
So Rumour has it. She liked my last recitation.

Corinth has fallen through. Back to making verses.

In fish-smelling Pouros I met that blind Smyrnan
Whom I met on Delos. He's stolen my best epithet,
Wine-dark sea, which he uses every fifteen lines.
Sounds in the air, he said, could not be owned by anyone.

Before the harvest I made one more try at Corinth.
This time he's gone too far, the devious word-stealer,
One day he was to give the popular single combat,
I on the next the vengeance. The bastard changed it!
So Achilles won, and Hector lost, and gods, I was furious
At this nonsense-making of my piece, so I shouted at him:
'Hexametric whoreson, what are you doing, Homer?'

He answered: 'My best scene is that one of Hector,
Wife and kid – tear-wringing words. Can't you see
How poignancy-gaining it is if I kill off Hector?'
'Why not a wife for Achilles?' I said sarcastically.
'It won't work – you don't bring a wife to camp with soldiers!'
'You've left out the Phoenicians. They are the deciding factor,
To further flatter the Greeks.' 'Dogosbodoi,' he said,
'Stone-minded comrade, you're in the wrong market.'

At Mycenae's harvest festival I find that this Smyrnan –
He's cagey on his origins but he must come from Smyrna –
He's been there before me, for when I gave my *Iliad*
Someone blacked my eye for omitting Agamemnon,
Whose part he's been emphasizing, in Mycenae.

Autumn equinox, I am in despair. Naxos,
Lesbos, Thea is suggesting. But he and his followers,
Unscrupulous word-pedlars, may have the punters' ears
Tuned to their pitch. Crete, she says, is very far away.
The Cretans did applaud my usual recitation,
And in the audience who also should be clapping,
With constraint, with delicacy, so I wanted to kick him,
The blind bard himself. 'So you liked it then?' I said.
'Very well turned are those words of Cassandra.'
'You will have been forced to drop her altogether,
She doesn't fit in with the way you tell the story,'
I said, pleased, for Cassandra has fine speeches.
'That's true,' he said, surprised, and then he sat thinking,
Chin in his hand. I left him like that on the benches,
But passing by six hours later I found him there again.
He recognized my footsteps, cried: 'Dogosbodoi, Eureka,
I had this idea – her prophecies would be mistaken,
But that's a waste of verses, screeds of false futures,
No one could endure it. So what she says is true,
But she's never ever believed. A wonderful effect.'
'Why does no one believe her, if she's been right before?'
'Heavens, as for that I can cobble something together.
She once refused some ravishing god or other,
Who put a curse upon her. You can always do anything
With a lustful god and a curse.' I left him in disgust.

Having returned to Chios, able to pay our creditors,
I found Thea anxious. She told me there'd been a traveller,
A bard, and he had got a very good reception,
At the king's last banquet. 'What was he like?' I asked,
With a sick-feeling heart. 'You know my cousin,
That one who married a lord – she told me Blind as a Bat,
Bald as a Bone, a wine-red nose and a voice,
A voice like honey. His recitation was all about Cassandra,
Quite different from yours, she said, went down very well.
Now they'll want to hear no other version,
Like the children when I tell them their bed-time story.
Perhaps you . . .' 'Perhaps I could servilely follow his style,'
I shouted and threw down the lethykos I'd bought her,
On to the floor, which was muddy from the winter's rains,
So it didn't break, but over my head broke the amphora.

Well-received in Athens, I've got new cloth for Thea,
Priam and Achilles went down like frothing milk,
I just caught up with Homer, who is adding verses
On the dragging of Hector's body. 'After death, I hope,'
I said at the taverna. 'Before is over the top,' he said,
And he paid the reckoning. In the summer he's coming to Chios,
Thea must weave him a coverlet. We'll work together.

REM BEL

432 B.C.
The Building of the Parthenon

From the Clerk of Works to Macc Daoghsboadhe, Builder:

Most people are almost finished. Will your bit be much longer? We are
anticipating a bit of a 'do' to mark the opening and it would be a pity if
this were marred by scaffolding and suchlike spoiling the effect.

To the Clerk of Works:

You cannot hurry things like this. I would remind you that I done my leg in finishing off the top of a column and this slows a team down, especially when there is no talk of compensation.

To Macc Daoghsboadhe:

I am sorry about your leg. The paperwork on that one is going through. All the same, I feel there has been time enough for the finishing touches which is what you were brought in to do. I hate to bring up the subject of penalty clauses, but . . .

To the Clerk of Works:

Have no fear, squire. We'll be out by the end of the week. My lads have worked hard on this site, even though we have not always been kept in the picture. When we started we was told that we was working on a bus shelter, but, to my way of thinking, it has got out of hand. Even so, we would've been finished ages ago if we hadn't been kept waiting by others: sub-contracted plasterers and the like.

To Macc Daoghsbhoade:

Your involvement is much appreciated. Please, please can you be done by Friday. Personally I don't mind, but there are others who are saying some very cruel things about what will happen to me if there's so much as a chisel left lying around for the ceremony.

To the Clerk of Works:

I've got the lads sweeping up at this very moment so panic over, all right? A nice-looking job, though I say it myself. There is just one thing though. My mate reckons the frieze looks a bit dull so he's chipped out a bit of a horse. I don't suppose anyone ever looks up there but see what you think. I mean, we take pride in our work and it would be a pity to leave it looking half-finished. I know this means we'll have to work our way round the rest of the frieze – should've thought of that before we started, I suppose – but it shouldn't take long. It'll all be done by 5 on Friday. Promise.

N. J. WARBURTON

415 B.C.
The Peloponnesian War

KUONDEMAS ALSO LEFT us a few fragments of other tablets. They appear to have formed parts of a daily journal, *The Apollo*. They suggest that, despite all the changes that have taken place, there is nothing new under the Sun.

. . . ing heavily with the bouncy Danaë. 'Actually,' she said with a smile: 'it was a shower of gold.' And if you believe that you'll believe anything.

THE APOLLO SAYS: GO FOR SICILY!!

Haven't we been too gentle on Sparta for too long? Isn't it about time we started taking this so-called war to THEM? We say go for Sicily and go for Sicily NOW! The weak-willed and spineless say it's too expensive. Or do they mean too dangerous? Athens was not made great by backing away from danger. The gods are against it, they say. Whose side do they think the gods are on?!

MIND THAT CHISEL!!

Sicily is in the wrong direction, they whinge. Can you think of a better way of confusing those thick Spartans? But if you have no guts for a fight you'll come up with any excuse. The latest is that the rude bits have been knocked off certain religious statues. This is supposed to be a bad omen. Rubbish! It was probably the Spartans who knocked them off! We hear there's something of a shortage in that part of the world. (On the other hand, let's face it: have you ever come across a Spartan who knew what to do with his rude bit?)

OEDIPUS STARS IN DRINK AND DRYAD SCANDAL

Stars of the long-running drama *Oedipus* have confessed to *The Apollo* . . .

N. J. WARBURTON

400–49 B.C.
Marching Songs

IN THE COURSE of his wanderings around Europe and Asia in search of forgotten folklore, Professor Philemon Dogsbody has collected some extremely interesting examples of soldiers' marching songs, far older than any discovered by his predecessors in the field. In obscure shepherds' huts and crumbling tenements these ancient ditties have been orally preserved, no doubt in a debased form, but with the authentic ring of the distant days in which they were composed. They take us back in time as far as Alexander's famous march towards India in the fourth century B.C. – the invasion of Italy by Hannibal in 218* – the breathless days in 49 before the die was cast and Julius Caesar entered Rome with his army.

> Some talk of Alexander
>   As if the chap were sane,
> But our supreme commander
>   Is off his chump again.
> From General Inertia
>   His troops he can't defend;
> We had our fun in Persia –
>   The Indus is the *end*.

> It's a long, long way to Carthaginia,
>   It's a long way to go.
> Italee, it's blooming hard to win yer
>   When the Alps are deep in snow.
> Don't like elephants, chum,
>   (Don't like Hannibál)
> As well as being hard upon your pants, chum,
>   It's a long way to fall.

* A notable example of the Lili Marlene syndrome – a take-over from the enemy.

When Caesar's across the Rubicon
(Ave! Ave!)
We'll make up our minds what side we're on
(Ave! Ave!)
Of one thing there can be no doubt,
If Caesar's in, then Pompey's out,
And we'll all 'Ave!' when Caesar rides into Rome.

MARY HOLTBY

*c.*400 B.C.
Extract from *The Dogs*
by Aristophanes

THIS FRAGMENT FROM the Dogsbody archive – here roughly translated from the Greek – appears to be a chorus from a hitherto unknown Aristophanic comedy entitled *The Dogs*. It seems likely that the author abandoned it in favour of a more popular subject and it was only preserved because of its personal interest to the family, if to nobody else.

The Dogs

The gates of Hell. Several gibbering shades of both sexes are waiting for admission. Enter Diogenes, with a sour expression on his face, closely followed by his Dogsbody, whose expression can't be seen as he is carrying his master's tub over his head. As they approach the gates a group of miscellaneous dogs bounds out.

DOGS: *Bow-wow-wow-wow, woof-woof, woof-woof!*
    Woof-woof, woof-woof, woof-woof!
  O welcome to Hades, inanimate ladies,
    Inanimate gentlemen, shady and dumb!
  We're Cerberus' chummies with ravenous tummies –

You've brought him a cake, you can give us a crumb.
On earth we were noted as douce and devoted,
  As dogged in duty as deft in the chase;
Our patroness Artemis (hearty, not tarty miss)
  Trained us for hunting and taught us our place . . .
    Woof-woof!
  She certainly taught us our place.

Bow-wow-wow-wow, etc.
So some had to prey on the voyeur, Actaeon –
  They tore *him* to pieces while *she* had her swim;
And some sought the sky on the heels of Orion –
  At night they're allowed to be starlets with him.
Odysseus' arrival ruled out the survival
  Of Argos, who instantly dropped as he passed,
And Orthrus, once dreaded, was doubly beheaded,
  And Laelaps lapsed into a statue at last . . .
    Woof-woof!
  But all of them got here at last.

Bow-wow-wow-wow, etc.
And now we all greet you – delighted to meet you,
  The Dog and the Dogsbody, bound for the Styx;
We've got just the clinic for canine and Cynic –
  A hell for old dogs where we teach them new tricks.
By choke-chains suspended, we swing them up-ended
  Where triple-jawed Cerberus, slavering, hogs
Rich bones as he poses right under their noses:
  Now who wants a ticket to go to the dogs?
    Woof-woof!
  Dog-cheap for a day with the dogs.

MARY HOLTBY

55 B.C.
Julius Caesar's Landing in Britain

ONE OF THE TREASURES among the Papers is a new manuscript of Caesar's *De Bello Gallico*, with hitherto unrecorded passages. Here, lovingly translated from the Latin by Professor Philemon Dogsbody, is one:

Britain, like Gaul, is divided into three parts, each part dominated by one tribe – the Taurii, the Socii, and the Libii.

The Taurii dominate the south of the country. The men are mild-mannered and busy in the pursuit of wealth, many of the older ones being ex-soldiers who, as in the Roman system, have been allotted land and honours in recognition of their past services in battle. The women are far from mild, but gather periodically to demand stronger laws and bitterer vengeance on their traditional enemies, the Socii. All paint themselves blue in battle.

The Socii paint themselves red, and rule the northern and western part of the country. Legend says they are the descendants of former slaves who rebelled and shook off the yoke of the Taurii. In theory, these people hold their goods in common, thereby removing all cause of envy or bitterness; but in practice they quarrel fiercely. After a war with the Taurii, all accuse each other of treachery, and there are mock executions at great gatherings on the north-eastern and north-western coasts. One particular sect of the tribe is renowned and feared for its bellicose disposition. Other sects live in the mountains and underground galleries of the west and north, where the Taurii cannot reach them. One powerful group of Socii hold the city of Londinium in a state of perpetual siege.

The Libii favour an orange colour. They are a smaller tribe than either of the other two, and find it difficult to hold a large territory. Consequently, some concentrate in enclaves, where they devote their efforts to holding the balance between the other two tribes. Once, the Libii say, they dominated Britain; but eventually enormous numbers were enslaved by the aggressive Socii. But always they look to the time when they will recover their former greatness. Meanwhile, they constantly suggest strange projects, in the hope that the two great tribes will come to blows over them, and exhaust each other. Instead, they fail to agree over these projects, and themselves come to blows.

Since the language of these quarrelsome tribes is extremely difficult to master, and since they all loathe and detest foreigners, I see no point in colonizing Britain. Such a course would merely unite people otherwise occupying themselves happily in their own destruction.

PAUL GRIFFIN

55 B.C.
Early Advertising

CANISCORPORE FORTE

HIC

HABEO BONAM MENSAM

ET

IN VINO VERITAS

INCISED STONE, *c.*55 B.C., found in 1889 by Mortimer Dogsbody, then aged nine, on fossilling trip to Lyme Regis. (Similar, uncovered Budleigh Salterton 1903, now in Metropolitan Museum, New York.) Thought to be roadside catering booth, possibly oyster bar, in anticipation of Roman landing. Scant ground remains (*Archaeologist*, February 1934) indicate that poor market research and faulty intelligence led to failure of this enterprise. With the Roman landing at Deal, and subsequent march northwards, the Forte chain folded.

D. A. PRINCE

SIR MORTIMER DOGSBODY (1880–1949) *Archaeologist and renowned authority on Early Saxon doorstops. Son in old age of the remarkably vigorous Rev. Francis Dogsbody.*

BAS-RELIEF (Roman, 1st century B.C): Discovered in the ruins of the Temple of Mars at Brutum Fulmen, this bas-relief clearly provides proof that Boadicea was indeed a Dogsbody.

44 B.C.
The Ides of March

SUETONIUS: *Life of Julius Caesar*. Vatican manuscript, trans. Macaulay Dogsbody. (Other manuscripts omit this paragraph through faulty copying.)

81a

Out of the many soothsayers abundant in Rome the augur Caniscorpora had a popular following. Refusing to distress her suppliants or to deny her clients – for which weakness she had been expelled from the number of the Vestal Virgins at an unusually early age – she would give messages of unfailing good cheer. She it was who encouraged

Caesar to extend the boundaries of the empire to the 'tropical zones' of Britannia, ever urging him with prophecies of the rich lands, flowing with milk and honey, in Hibernia. These things she witnessed in the lentils, for she was a vegetarian. When Calpurnia sought counsel for black and violent dreams Caniscorpora blamed the cook, a trophy of the Gallic wars, persuading Calpurnia to replace his rich meats with onions and chicory for healthful sleep. She sent a message by her to Caesar:

> The Ides of March is your lucky day. Have a stab at a lottery, or get your friends together to back a winner. You can't lose.

It is thought that Caesar, much heartened, favoured her auguries above those of Spurinna, and set out for the Senate after breakfasting on carrots and figs.

There is a statue, much defaced, thought to be Caniscorpora (from the cornucopia of lentils and beans at her feet) in the Forum, recorded by Macaulay Dogsbody in his diary (11 October 1893) on his first visit to Rome.

D. A. PRINCE

ALEXANDER POPE sent the following translation from anonymous Greek and Latin poets to his friend Horace Dogsbody.

> Julius Caesar, far away from Rome,
> Conquer'd armies but was fell'd at home:
> His front 'gainst enemies he could defend,
> But not his backside from a treach'rous friend.

MARGARET ROGERS

STATUE OF CANISCORPORA (Roman, 2nd century): Sketch made by Macaulay Dogsbody, dated 1893.

31 B.C.
Cleo

IN THE PAST, a number of distinguished writers have been awarded the privilege of inspecting the Archives at first hand. This translation of a prized papyrus collected by Dr Theophilus Dogsbody was presented to him by the author, and, although fairly 'free', is a reasonably accurate rendering of the original:

I would meet Cleo in one of those huddled cafés that seem to have been there since Alexandria rose from the sea. Around us rose the cadences of all the languages and races that have, as Al Nasr wrote in his secret diary, grown like lichen on ancient urinals; and of those five sexes of whom the city's poet speaks.

I knew that Cleo had belonged to many people. How many I preferred not to know until a later stage in this profitable tetralogy. Perhaps Charmian will complete my work; often, as she has writhed in the extremes of sexual exaltation, I have heard her cry out long sentences in perfect classical Latin.

Cleo had had at least one child. My uncle always claimed to be the father, but Cleo said the truth was stranger than that.

'Look in the cup,' she would say, softly swirling the grounds of her sweetened coffee, with an inexpressibly bitter smile; 'there is the father.' Then, sadly: 'But do not tell my husband. He is only fourteen.'

I would go away for long periods, round the capitals of the world, fighting a little, talking a lot, seeing my uncle's inheritance frittered away, struggling with strange, strong girls in cold beds, but always I would come back to Alexandria, and to Cleo.

'You must go back to your wife,' she would say, as she dangled her perfect limbs in Lake Mareotis. I cannot remember which wife she meant. Perhaps Alexas will remember when he writes the next volume.

It is time to end. Cleo tells me the ships are waiting, somewhere over there, off a cape called Actium.

'[Dali*],' she says, yawning; 'I am bored. Let us go and fight.'

* This word was not completely legible.

I remind her my name is Antony. She seems surprised, but laughs. 'Then there is a sixth sex,' she breathes.

Alexandria, Alexandria, what music plays in the sweet secret hideouts of your heart?

PAUL GRIFFIN

A.D. 0
The Nativity

A ARON BEN DOGSBODIM (33 B.C.–A.D. 1½) *A simple shepherd on pastures not far from Bethlehem, who spent his youth wandering on a green hill without the city wall.*

EXTRACT FROM court records in Bethlehem, re the Roman Empire *v.* Aaron ben Dogsbodim, a herder of sheep, for malicious rumour-mongering, and withholding information from King Herod. Researched and translated by Dr Theophilus Dogsbody.

Q What happened on the night in question?
A Me and two mates were looking after the lambs.
Q And then?
A And then we saw a star. In the firmament.
Q He means the sky, Your Majesty.
A Oh no, no, no. Definitely the firmament. It was a big star.
Q How big?
A Well, at that distance, sir, it's hard to say, but I'd have thought it was as big as a ewe-dropping. But more . . . more luminescent.
Q Go on.
A Well sir, we went after that star.
Q You rose in the air?
A Oh no, it was definitely moving. We could tell that because Zach –

he's the dim one of us, sir, and no mistake, he makes the sheep look smart – had left the gate open.

Q Gate open?

A Gate open, sir, and the whole flock got out, while we were sitting round sort of seated on the ground. We wouldn't have noticed, I daresay, only this bright bloke dropped by and said we were . . . we were . . . in for a surprise.

Q And were you?

A *Were* we? Were *we*? Ho ho! Yes, sir. All the whole flock had followed this star, which we knew was moving, sir, see, because when we got a few miles down the road, it was still in the same place. Funny, that, eh? A moving star?

Q And did you find your lost sheep?

A Not lost, sir, strayed. Led astray. By Zach. They were only in Bethlehem (that's a madhouse) – in Bethlehem, mucking in with a few donkeys, cows et cetera, on some straw, and bleating all peaceful.

Q Whereabouts in Bethlehem?

A Er, by The Merry Phalanx, sir, in the stables.

Q And what was going on in there?

A Where?

Q You have heard that a few innocents have been, how shall we say, massacred just a little recently?

A Oh, *there*. Well, they were . . . just kipping down, on the straw, er, going baaa-baaaa-baaaa. Unseemly for sheep.

Q But what else was *there*?

A Oh, I don't know. Drinking trough. A few crates of empties, a manger. Three kings. Nothing out of the ordinary.

Q What about the baby?

A The baby? Oh, the *baby*. Er, bleating faintly, a bit shivery. We soon got her back to her mum.

Q The *human* baby. The child. What about the child? Was there not a child there?

A Child? Oh dear me no. Oh dear me, no. As Christ is my witness.

Q As who?

A Oh blast.

BILL GREENWELL

A.D. 48
Messalina

EXTRACT FROM THE remnants of a second-century scroll discovered by Professor Philemon Dogsbody in a funerary urn at Bovillae in 1920:

. . . moreover, during the divine Claudius's absence on campaign in Britain, the Lady Messalina challenged Rome's leading courtesan to an endurance contest in the practice of her profession, and outdid the woman by many hours and more gallants, as is well known to readers of Tacitus and Statius. Less well known, however, is her encounter four years later with the barbarian Pwlldhunigern Dogsbodius of the Trinovantes, as related in the Sermunculi of Pendulus Flatulens of Putrium.

This Dogsbodius had personally slain in battle a noted decurion and his entire decuria before being taken and brought captive to Rome. There, sent into the arena as a retiarius, he scorned the Trident and used the Net merely to cover the naked state in which retiarii customarily fought, and then with his bare hands killed his fully-armed opponent, the famous swordsman Ballisticus. This feat so impressed the Lady Messalina that she requested that next day, in martial imitation of her amatory exploit, he should be matched in unarmed contests against a succession of adversaries for as long as his strength should last. This proved to extend until darkness ended the day's games, with the Empress's doubts almost as completely laid to rest as were the twenty champions he had vanquished. Yet to avoid the risk of wasting her imperial time, she ordained, before herself venturing, that first he be pitted against females of less exalted rank than her own.

Accordingly, he was led next day to a noble villa outside Rome, bathed, and handed over to the attentions of a galaxy of shapely, shameless baggages. Not until the following noon, released at last from their labours by the tenacious Dogsbodius, were they free to attend upon their impatient mistress, to whose favours they recommended the Briton in glowing terms. So on the morrow he was brought to a fine apartment containing a sumptuous silken couch whereon the beauteous Messalina, most exiguously clad, was voluptuously outspread, to his clearly approving contemplation. Meanwhile her fascinated and detailed survey of the splendid, intricate designs etched in blue all over his superb form having not only whetted her appetite but actually ennobled it with an awakening of genuine love, she raised a beckoning finger . . .

Alas, words cannot describe the royal disappointment and humiliation. The base barbarian mutinously refused to approach, let alone embrace the lovely Imperatrix. To provocative wiles, inviting gestures, passionate pleas and heartbroken supplications alike, he obdurately returned only unintelligible Celtic monosyllables, until in fury she called the Duty Praetorian, who, in obedience to her hissed order, ushered the obstinate wretch from the bedchamber.

Now it had so happened that in the British campaign of 43 against these same Trinovantian Dogsboddii, the captives had included a tribal wise-woman called Llyngwnvrha Dogsbodia, deeply versed in Druidic lore. She had become a freedwoman in the household of the scholarly and divine Claudius, and since the learned work he was then engaged upon was his famous *Historia Britannorum*, he regularly consulted her. Finding her name unpronounceable, however, he called her simply 'Britannica', or, to be exact, because of his stammer, 'Brit-tit-tit-tan-tan . . .', by which time she had usually answered, and which in any case was a name not inappropriate to her bronzed and buxom aspect. The rest of the household, resenting her privileged position and boasted esoteric knowledge, usually called her in derision 'Encyclopaedia Britannica'.

Thus, on the day after the unfortunate tryst with Dogsbodius, the Lady Messalina, seeking someone on whom to vent her spleen, entered the divine Caesar's study, where he was questioning this Britannic Encyclopaedia about Celtic religious festivals. 'B-B-Beltine?' he asked; 'Imbolc, Lugnasad and S-Samain? C-come, t-tell me more, Bri-tit-tit . . .' 'Yes, indeed, learned Encyclopaedia,' sneered Messalina, 'pray enlighten our ignorance of your great British institutions.' Nothing loth, the Druidess began forthwith, saying: 'Know then, great Claudius and Madam, that yesterday, the Kalends of May, was our great festival of Cetshamain, or Beltine . . .' 'Yesterday?' Claudius inquired, 'But you kept no festival yesterday that I saw.' 'Nevertheless I did so, Caesar,' she said, 'as far as my duty to you permitted; a small bonfire in the garden, dawn prayers, and above all, total abstention from carnal congress, and . . .' 'Hades!' shrieked the Empress, rushing from the room and screaming for the nearest Praetorian. But of course she was far too late. The headless body of Dogsbodius had already been fished from the Tiber, a half-day's march downstream.

W. F. N. WATSON

A.D. 120
Hadrian's Wall

THE TRANSLATION of messages discovered on tabulae incorporated into Hadrian's Wall near Housesteads, believed to be between the Emperor Hadrian and Maximus Caniscorpus (A.D. 120). Found by Sir Mortimer Dogsbody during his last big excavation at this site in 1952.

To the Most Illustrious Emperor Hadrian.

Sir,

It is impossible to construct a wall on the scale you suggest. In the first place, Britain does not possess the material resources or human skills for this enterprise.

The wall will cost at least six hundred thousand denarii, and with interest charged at seven virgins per cent per annum, we will require forty-two thousand virgins each year to service the debt. It is unlikely that even the Roman Colonial Civil Service could readily identify an annual supply of forty-two thousand virgins in what is an extremely lecherous land.

As the natives are utterly devoid of art or application, perhaps you may care to implement a Youth Training Scheme, whereby we might motivate these worthless young people with very sharp sticks or the liberal use of boiling fat.

Sincerely,
Maximus Caniscorpus
Clerk of Works, Walls and Parapets Division

FRAGMENT OF TRIUMPHAL COLUMN (2nd century): This sketch by
Macaulay Dogsbody shows a fragment of the Column of Maximus Caniscorpus, from the Cloaca Exit at Porculaneum. Probably modelled on Trajan's
Column, that of Maximus apparently depicts the endless procession of virgins
supplied as interest on Hadrian's Wall building loan.

My dear Maximus,

The capital required for the proposed wall can be borrowed from the Bank of Sodom and Gomorrah, who, I understand, are prepared to accept ninety per cent of the interest charge in pre-pubescent Anglo-Saxon males, the transaction being secured by a deposit of ten per cent, payable in well-greased young sheep.

I am advised that there is an abundance of skilled building workers in the island to the west of us. These people can be induced to accept payment in generous and regular libations of dark fermented broth, and the opportunity of at least one good brawl each night. I will arrange for their foreman, Padraig O'Daoghsbhoade, to finalize arrangements with you.

Hadrian

RUSSELL LUCAS

*c.*A.D. 200
A Roman Soldier Dreams of Home

THE EXCAVATIONS at Housesteads have yielded a great many objects of archaeological interest, but surely nothing with more human appeal than these songs, scratched by soldiers on rocks close to the famous Hadrian's Wall, which overlooks the camp. We owe our knowledge of them to the distinguished archaeologist, Sir Mortimer Dogsbody, whose researches have taught us all so much about conditions in Britain under the Romans.

> There's a long, long wall a-winding
>   Across the land of the Brits,
> Where the rain falls cold and blinding
>   And our camp's the pits.
> There's no leave, no girls, no parties,
>   And I wish I was at home
> With the lares and penates
>   Back in dear old Rome.

> Curse the Wall!
> Curse the Wall!
> It's worse than Iberia or Gaul.
> Perpetual motion is Hadrian's notion
> Of keeping his troops on the ball.

> Keep the home fires burning,
> Soon we'll be returning
> Back to bread and circuses
>   In dear old Rome.
> Back to see our maters,
> Girls and gladiators;
> O what bliss to leave this dump
>   For the joys of home!

MARY HOLTBY

5th century A.D.
The Saxon Invasions

IN 1958, SHORTLY before his death, Sir Mortimer Dogsbody was invited by the BBC to give the Reith Lecture. The following is an extract from his submitted script, which was, in fact, rejected:

The exact connection between the Romans and the Saxon Dogg-bodies (or, as some believe, the Eggbodies) has never been satisfactorily established. These were very Dark Ages. A great deal is now revealed, however, by a long fragment of early Anglo-Saxon poetry, which speaks of a King Baldwulf, living in the time after most of the Romans had gone home. This king had three sons, Everwith, Never-with, and Cidd, and one daughter, Doggbilda.

Doggbilda (or, as some say, Eggbilda) entered the religious life at an early age, in the great Celtic convent at Wulfhampton, whose nuns

CAIUS IMPRUDENTIUS DOGGBODY (early 5th century)   *Born C. I. Corpuscanis. Married the nun Dogg-bilda (or, as some say, Eggbilda) and changed name to Doggbody. Father of Weord the Wulfing (WEORD DOGGBODY).*

led a mendicant life (a note in the margin of the ms. calls them 'the Wulfhampton Wanderers').

Doggbilda, in the course of her travels, seems to have come across a villa where lived one Caius Imprudentius Caniscorpus, a late descend-ant of the great Roman family, who had for twenty years been on the verge of answering the call of Rome, but owing to a bladder affliction had never seemed to get around to it. The young nun was persuaded to renounce her vows, but insisted that C. Imprudentius should be Saxonized. We meet for the first time the composite name Doggbody (Dr A. L. Growse, tiresome as ever, reads Eggbody throughout).

WEORD DOGGBODY (late 5th century)   *Son of above. Great Anglo-Saxon fighter, known, for some reason, as 'the Wulfing'.*

The ms. revealing this is in the form of a riddling saga, almost totally incomprehensible and very long, even in fragment. The follow-ing translation gives the flavour:

> I am the brand of Eorful the Hnit, woeful in war,
> lordly in the lays of the Island-Gleoms and
> Toofingas. Griselhur gave me to Weord the
> Wulfing, son of Doggbody. His faith it is to fight,
> being valiant in victory, burning in battle his
> breast, deadly in daring his doings. Eggbilda was
> his mother, mourned of minstrels in the mead hall,
> sister of Cidd the Harflung, supple of sinew,
> scourge of the Mucfliccas, of Worthmanric the
> Toedbera, and Saeon and Saeferth . . .

... and, indeed, so on and so forth, at about that pace. It almost reconciles one to television.

PAUL GRIFFIN

*c.*A.D. 800
King Lear

SIR MAX DOGSBODY (1865–1923)   *Son of Jasper and brother of Tancred*. Littérateur, bon viveur, *collector of ephemera and expert on Chaucer, he cultivated a wide acquaintanceship in artistic and literary circles*.

SIR MAX DOGSBODY has made available the letter from his cousin Nancy, enclosing the following item:

Darling Max,

This is a very rough translation of that old document we found in the attic at Rannoch Castle. All in Middle English – frightfully FOF!*

Love,
Nancy

Ancient British documents are virtually non-existent, so it is exciting to find that the Hon. Nancy Dogsbody must have possessed one. A translation in her inimitable style is all that survives.

* For Old Fogeys.

HON. NANCY DOGSBODY (1900–1960) *Daughter of Lord Dogsbody of Rannoch, of whom she wrote a biography. Fashionable novelist and essayist. Originator of classification of male humanity into SIC (Safe In Cabs) and NADGE (Not A Dinner Guest Ever).*

With Farve, it was a question of life-style. I suppose we girls were lucky to be brought up in those luxurious surroundings. Ginny even used to say it was better than a formal education to hear the old chap carrying on like an articulate brontosaurus about what used to happen when he was a boy. Sometimes he was jolly funny; but after Muv died he got a bit repetitive, and the fun went out of it.

Farve's brilliant idea for retirement filled us with foreboding.

'He'll never *do* it!' wailed Ginny. 'Catch him living a quiet life. The moment we want to do anything new, he'll raise the roof.'

'*I* think he's an old dear,' said Delia. 'I don't really care what he does, as long as he's happy. And,' she added, 'as long as he doesn't involve me.'

It was all right for her; she was engaged to this rich Frenchman; and sure enough, when the balloon went up, she married him and went off to some château in the wine country, in an atmosphere of immense righteousness, leaving us tied to our dull British upper-crust husbands, and coping with Farve.

I see what was in Farve's mind. He was obsessed with keeping the Treasury's paws off his estates; but it was all muddled in his mind with a long-standing need for affection. We three girls were supposed to sit up and beg before there could be any capital transfer. Delia couldn't be bothered, and bolted with Monsieur le Duc. Some of the staff put in a word for her, but at the end of it all there was Ginny in one half of the ancestral property and us in the other half, with Farve plus old retainers paying indefinite visits, and muttering that he didn't know he really didn't. He started with Ginny. It took me no time at all to work out that my turn came next.

I know it sounds rotten to say it, but he had never really added up to twelve pence in the shilling. Certainly, at this stage, he was a candidate for one of those wildly expensive nursing homes; but who was going to tell him that? Sooner reason with a sabre-toothed tiger. In-law problems are bad enough without doubling the tempers and troubles.

Inevitably, he stormed out of Ginny's home, leaving one or two sore heads among the domestics, and headed for us. The moment we heard the news, we lit out and went to meet him, running him to earth with one of his old cronies. A terrible scene followed, in the middle of which Ginny turned up. Really, at that point, Farve went berserk.

The next thing we knew, he had wandered off into the countryside muttering fire and slaughter, on the filthiest night you could imagine.

That, believe it or not, was the day war broke out!

Honestly, you could have turned it into rather a depressing play.

PAUL GRIFFIN

*c.*A.D. 850
The Vikings

Ethelfrida the Unravished

THE FOLLOWING fragments are all that now remain of a journal or diary of Ethelfrida Doggsbodie, who lived in the small village of Athelney Marsh, near the coast of Lincolnshire. They are undated, but are thought to have been written towards the end of the ninth century.

Wodensdaie: The Vikings have been here, burninge, steilinge the caittel, ande ravishinge wymen befor theye dragg them tae ye grate long botes. Twice theye cam to ur hutte, an the first tyme theyr ledere luke atte me an jeste larght. The seconde he seeze me by ye haire and dragg me into ur strete an it wor hisen fellowes whu larght an pointed to mine facen. I knoe I am noe butie, ande my Adelbrane saie my countenants ys homelie, butte I dyd notte thinke an vikinge wolde turne uppe hisen nose atte me the whiles alle ye village wymen were hevinge itte in ye strete or onne ye beche . . .

Freida's Daie: Lif ys harde. Ye Vikynges ar departen ande tuken moste wymen of ur village, butte sum fourtie menne an boyes ar lefte. Soe itte ys me whu hase tu cuke ye fude an tende ther wundes. Methinken ov ye sexie helmes ov ye Vikynges . . .

Sunsdaie: My Adelbrane wente huntynge fer dere. Ny alle ur cattel wor stoll bye Vykynges. He wolde be awaie three daies, sae there us a tappe at ye dor ov ye hutte. Ther wor a lotte of menne whu wayte to have itte wythe me. Maybe I wor luckie atte laste . . .

E. O. PARROTT

ETHELFRIDA DOGGSBODIE (842–*c.*888) *Born in Athelney Marsh, where she was also brought up. Knew her way round the swamp, unlike her husbands Athelbald and Adelbrane, both of whom fell irretrievably into the bog. She died in about 888, and her recipes were passed on by word of mouth until collected by Alan of Monmouth (cousin to Geoffrey) in the twelfth century. Not a widely travelled woman, Ethelfrida is said once to have visited Glastonbury.*

*c.*A.D. 878
King Alfred

TRANSCRIPTION BY Nancy Dogsbody of a very tattered twelfth-century recipe which purports to be a copy of a much earlier one, passed down from Ethelfrida Doggsbodie of Athelney Marsh:

Black Scones

A recipe I have always found cheap but tasty and unusual is as follows. Take flour, butter, some soured cream, and beat very firmly together until a doughy substance is produced. Make balls of this dough, and coat them in strong, thick black mud, before heating them over a fire. The mud acts as a miniature oven. However, black scones will keep for reasons other than culinary. No one will eat or steal a black scone, because they think it's burnt. I had some prince or whatnot come by one day, who dropped off while I was cooking some. I boxed his ears, I can tell you! I said he'd scorched my cakes. Later I heard he'd seen the Danes off. That's black scones for you.

BILL GREENWELL

1002
The Monastic Life

F R. TATWINE (born Titus Doggsbody) (930–1003) *Under-abbot of Exeter. Devised* The Exeter Book *as a weekly exercise for the monks, presumably as a means of spiritual cleansing, or catharsis. Only the best offerings went into the book.*

> God backs me up: I guard Hell,
> Snapping three heads at once.
> I walk four-square, have a rising star,
> My days are hot: in heat my earthly part
> Lusts, names shops, rusts not.
> Rots in the earth, a shell's shell.
> Is all, is nothing: a right cracker.

A riddle by Fr. Tatwine from *The Exeter Book*, an anthology of riddles and other humorous writings by the monks of Exeter. Translated by Auberon Dogsbody.

The first bishop of Exeter, the historian Leofric, recounts of Tatwine:

Hee weare constante inne hys riddling, maken alway of hys riddles into scrolle. To cheere the leene monthes didde hee on occasyon putte in gunne-powdre into ye scripted scrolle, the which when pullen craked and crakled, even flammed, a-frighting men from devotions.

For thysse he were y-clepped of the monks Crakers, for he were aye craken his japes inne the library and atte festes with hollye and ale.

The disastrous fire of 1003, after the great Christmas festival, destroyed most of Tatwine Doggsbody's riddles, and only this unsolved fragment remains.

D. A. PRINCE

1040
Canute and a Love of the Sea

IN 1947, Willoughby Dogsbody, then Honorary Chief Archivist, was invited by the British Council to undertake a lecture tour of Polynesia. He chose the unlikely subject of King Canute. Even by British Council standards the tour must be accounted a total disaster. This was a pity, since the lectures contained much new material unearthed by Willoughby himself.

The following is a reconstruction of part of Willoughby's talk from his notes:

King Canute was no mumbling geriatric sitting on a beach, the butt of jokes from his disdainful thanes. He was a scholar and a poet, and also a man of action, a great expert in all that pertains to the sea and its ways. A ruler, who might, if he had lived longer (he died at the age of forty), have become the all-conquering Alexander of northern Europe. The famous incident of his encounter with the waves was not the defeat for him which popular legend has always suggested. This is borne out not only by his own poems but also by the journal of Athelstan Dogesboddye, Saxon bondman to Canute and one of the army of scribes he employed in his scholarly work. It was the King's boast that as a result of his studies he could now accurately forecast the high- and low-water marks on any day along Britain's eastern sea-board. That, according to Athelstan, aroused the derision of the thanes. The scene on the beach is depicted in one of the few poems of Canute that has come down to us. No complete translation has ever been published owing to the great difficulty of the language. A certain Mr Eliot in the 1920s did in fact propose that Faber's should publish a translation of the poems, but the work was never completed. The following was taken from his preparatory notes for the projected volume, to which I was kindly allowed access by the Board of Directors.

> A cold evening we had of it
> Just at the worst time of the year
> For the tide foretelling,
> And the thanes scornful and unheeding,
> Here was I, a proud king,
> But alone in my understanding,
> And partly understanding
> Of the ways of waves.
> Of the moon and the sun and the stars
> Showing the mark in the sand
> Unmindful of the joking,
> For what they deemed my defeat was
> My victory.
> In my Ending was my victory's beginning.

Here Mr Eliot added a footnote: Canute, who had been secretly engaged for years in the compilation of the first-ever tide tables for northern Europe, clearly indicated the correct high-water mark, but losing temporarily his sense of direction, stood below it, thus getting his feet wet. The thanes obviously imagined Canute had got it wrong, but were soon forced to concede that he was completely right. According to Athelstan, Canute responded with the comment that since the sea had kissed his feet, the thanes could do no less.

Athelstan relates how, after this act of homage, he and his fellow scribes moved among the thanes selling copies of the new tide tables.

Nancy Dogsbody says she once asked Eliot why he had never completed his version of the poems.

'They are very difficult,' he said. 'They would require too many footnotes. I prefer to keep on with *The Waste Land*.'

E. O. PARROTT

1066
The Norman Conquest

ONE OF THE FIRST of the French Dogsbodies to arrive in this country was William le Corps de Chien of Bayeux (1040–1121), who had developed a potion which was, he claimed, efficacious in all cases of internal complaints. He had connections in the army of the Conqueror and managed to be among those who first landed in 1066. This enabled him to set up his stall on the beach and sell his potion to those who had suffered from sea-sickness. Many of these unfortunates were also persuaded to buy 'passports' without which, William insisted, it was illegal to enter the country. He can be seen in a little-known offcut of the Bayeux Tapestry. The scene was later excised from the main work and kept in the Dogsbody family for advertising purposes.

N. J. WARBURTON

BAYEUX TAPESTRY OFFCUT

1066
The Battle of Hastings

SHORTLY AFTER THE Norman Conquest, Odo, Bishop of Bayeux, commissioned a tapestry depicting the Battle of Hastings and the events leading to it.

In April 1067, Baron Guy le Corps de Chien, Clerk of Works for the project, submitted preliminary sketches of the tapestry for Odo's approval.

B ARON GUY LE CORPS DE CHIEN (1040–1121) *Born in Caen, Normandy. Sailed with Norman invasion fleet in 1066. Official war artist at Battle of Hastings.*

An extract from Odo's reply (discovered at the site of the Saxon School of Embroidery at Herne Bay in 1892) reveals that one of the best-known 'facts' of English history is untrue:

As to the mortal wounding of Harold, I accept that as you were present at the battle you can vouch that the arrow did pierce his scrotum. I do not think it seemly, however, that a thousand generations of children should delight in repeating that Harold copped it in the goolies. I beg to advise that the fatal arrow be shown entering his heart, or, since you were an eye-witness, let it strike him in the eye.

V. ERNEST COX

1086
The Domesday Book

THE FOLLOWING EXTRACT is vouched for as having been written down by Jankyn Doggesbody from the missing Norfolk copy of the Book:

In Itching Hundred,

From the Abbess of St Eadred, Maudde Hogge seemstresse, holds 1 hide with hutte, wherein she sewen scenes on shyrttes. Herre lewde stitcherye much takken up by soldiery, and y-stemed for her flaxen shyrttes with mottoes stitched, viz. *Ecce unum in oculo per Harold*, with pictures.

Value: post-1066 – 100*s*.; pre-1066 – 3*d*.

REMNANT OF 11TH-CENTURY SHIRT: One of many sold by Maudde Hogge, later Corps de Chien, to Norman troops. Her embroidered designs exerted a strong influence on the development of heraldry, and obviously led to the modern tee-shirt.

That there are no further records of her work in the vicinity of Itching suggests that Maudde removed from the area, perhaps as consort to one of the many French soldiers (*'les bestes de Bayeux'*) garrisoned near Itching from 1066 to 1070. Of her vigorous embroideries little trace remains, although much research remains to be completed on possible French connections.

D. A. PRINCE

1170
The Murder of Thomas à Becket

FROM JOHN OF DOGGESBODY to his kinsman Bertram:

Right well-beloved cousin, greetings and Goddes blessing. I have this month tydings of grete moment from the court, for Master à Becket is slayne at his own altar in Caunterbury. There is full grete grief and dole at the court, for though he was a right haughty and unconvenable man, yet when a high prelate cometh to swich an ende there is trouble for some onne sure. There wylle bee much chyding and reproche, and alle men here look to there backes. But the manner of Master à Becket's passynge makyth a pretty tale, truth to telle.

It semeth there was a grete banquet at the court where, Quene Eleanour not beynge of the companye, the talk at the King's table turned to overweenynge wyves, and of the Quene's mighty will in causing King Henry to doe whatsoever she pleaseth. At this the King saith (as a pleasantrie he now saith): 'Will noe man rid mee of the truculent piece?' This conceit, it semeth, was passed by mouth down the lower tables, and muche corrupted in the tellynge. My Lord de Bohun, hearing that the King wished an ende of 'this crapulent feast', departed for bedde forthwith. The Lord Bishop of St Albans, notynge that the King was displeased with 'this corpulent beast', sent worde to the kitchens to remove the roast pygge. It is lyttle wonder, then, that four knights at the lowest table heard that the King would be rid of 'this turbulent priest' and took horse straight for Caunterbury where they slaughtered Master à Becket.

Now cometh the jeste. The King, tho' innocent of Master à Becket, durst not owne to what his wordes were, lest the Quene should knowe of it. Soe hee goeth on penitent pilgrimage, choosing to wear the hair shirt in Caunterbury rather thanne in his owne palace.

As for mee, I wille to the countrie and keepe my head downe a-whyle.

Your lovynge cousin

J. D.

NOEL PETTY

JOHN OF DOGGESBODY (1142?–96) *Yeoman and pig-farmer of Tydde in Norfolk. Supplier of pork to the royal kitchens. A genial man by all accounts, he was a favourite among the royal servants, who would regale him with all the latest gossip on his frequent visits to London. Married 1170 Sukie Butte; one son, Jankyn, born 1175. Killed at Norwich when a pig fell on him.*

1174
The Tower of Pisa

EXCERPT FROM A REPORT by the rascally Clerk of Works at Pisa Cathedral, Guido Corcano, who gave the campanile project to his Irish cousins, Rory and Kevin O'Doaghsbhoade, while concealing this relationship from the cardinal and the duke. This is perhaps the most interesting of a bundle of documents relating to this construction, the others consisting mainly of accounts and progress reports.

I have at last obtained planning permission for the campanile (see enclosed expense sheet). I have interviewed many builders and my personal leaning is toward two Hibernian brothers I interviewed yesterday, Rory and Kevin. (Their family name is too complicated to spell out here.) Their tender is the most competitive and their method simplicity itself. Dispensing with sextants, protractors, compasses, spirit levels, plumb lines and all the cramping paraphernalia of mathematics, which they are inclined to dismiss as 'all a bit of an old cod to put the price up', they measure a circle on the earth and, very carefully, lay a ring of bricks on it. Then in the words of Rory (the elder brother), they 'just keep on building up and up till it's done', laying each circle of bricks on the one below. I must say I tend to be impressed by the simplicity of this notion. The brothers, whom I will send to see you if you list, are well accustomed to working together and are indeed complementary, one being right-handed, the other left-handed, which they say speeds things up. You may not at first like the look of them, they being somewhat ill-favoured. Both are broken-nosed – the result of an accident involving a wall – and each has a cast in the eye, Rory in the left, and Kevin in the right. I beg you to take my advice in this matter and employ these fellows. I am aware that you have been inclined to tilt at my suggestions in the past but I feel instinctively that what my cousins, that is to say our cousins from over the sea, will build, will last. And there should be no trouble in getting it classified as a listed building . . .

Another of the many items unearthed by Professor Philemon Dogsbody during the year he spent in Italy on research for his book, *Dogsbody's Renaissance*:

From: The Clerk of Works at the Pisa site
To: Caniscorpore-Forte e Figlio, Caterers

Gentlemen,

I am in receipt of yours of Friday 13th.

I must advise you that I am returning the entire consignment. I do not (repeat NOT) require fifty tons of variegated pizzas. Whoever informed you that I was making a tower of pizzas in the piazza was pulling your legs.

We are making a campanile or bell-tower here, but of marble and other conventional building materials. A tower made of pizzas would immediately tilt from one side or the other and shower the piazza with tomato purée, Parmesan cheese et cetera.

Thanking you for your interest,

Yours,
Guido Corcano
Clerk of Works

GERARD BENSON

1200
The Crusades

THESE TWO FRAGMENTS of letters are among many written by Bertram Doggsbody, armourer and locksmith of Havering in the County of Essex, to his cousin John at Tydde. A contemporary chronicler describes the sign outside his workshop, which read:

BERTRAM DOGGSBODY
Locksmith and General Ironwork
Supplier to the Nobility
of
Racks, Thumbscrews, Iron Maidens, Shackles, Fetters
and the Like
Chastytie Beltes a Specialytie

. . . Syr Gervase Fitzsimmons ys returned from ye Crusayde, verie fytt butte muche putte about fer he hath losten ye key to my Laydys chastytie belte, soe can I make hym anothere for he doth waxe marvellus randie. Sae I asume my grayvest countenynce, strok my chin, humm an haw, saieing thatte given tyme an wax enow thisen may be dun. I myght hav lette hym have one of ye golden ones my Ladye had me mek for her byrthdaie. I dyd have my owne, newlie cutte for the firsten hadde becum muche worne . . .

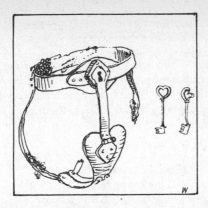

WROUGHT-IRON CHASTITY BELT (12th century): Made by Bertram Doggsbody, armourer, for the crusader Sir Gervase Fitzsimmons. Portions of the original miniver lining still adhere to the metal. The three hundred silver pennies paid to Bertram by the Sieur de Maldemer for a duplicate key laid the foundation of the Essex Doggsbodys' fortune.

. . . agenne I presse Syr Gervase fer ye settlememente of my bille. Dyd not my key give hym grete relief? Yt ys harde fer a man to be putte to hisen own thumbscrews, and them notte payde for . . .

E. O. PARROTT

1215
Magna Carta

HUGO DOGGSBODY (1182–1216) *Blacksmith of Havering, Essex. Son of Bertram. Was present at Runnymede, being listed in contemporary records as a member of the Earl of Essex's retinue. He is said to have 'disappeared' in mysterious circumstances when his smithy was seized by the Earl to form the site of a slurry pit.*

The Runnymede Song

The manuscript of this rare fourteenth-century song is thought to have been originally the property of Hugo Doggsbody, but it is not known whether he was the author of the first two verses, or of the third, which, scholars agree, was added to the original some time after its composition.

> Fredome ys icumen ynn
>   Lhude syng hura
> Kynge du sine, Baronnes wyn
> Magna Carta duth begyne
>   Syng hura hura.

> Sune shal cum democracie
>   Lhude syng hura
> Lette alle tirantes qwale an cowar
> We shal hav ye peeplys powre.
>   Hura, hura hura.

> Thynges be wurs than tymes afor
>   Softe syng goddam
> Pesants ar ye slawterd lam
> Magna Carta ys a sham
> Fer Baronnes ruin we crie goddam
>   Softe syng goddam.

In one corner of the ms., next to what could be a bloodstain, another hand has added: 'Butte not softe enuff.'

E. O. PARROTT

ILLUMINATED MUSIC MS. (13th century): This illuminated ms. of plain-song was discovered by Aloysius Dogsbody in a book-binding in 1928. It is an erotic love-lament to Héloïse, attributed to Abelard and set to this rousing tune by the crusading Knights Infirmerers of Beer-Sheba. Banned by the Church because of the indecent version sung by the common soldiery, the tune was lost for centuries until it amazingly resurfaced during the First World War.

1216
King John's Crossing of The Wash

ADONIJAH DOGSBODY (1509–80)   *Lawyer, bank-er, author, etc. Eldest son of Micah Dogsbody, lawyer, and Doll Fleecem. Walpurgis College, Cantab., and Rackett's Inn; 1531–40, secretary to Thos. Cromwell, M.P. Married 1536 Rose, daughter of Wakeham Earlie, fowler and bird-limer (two adopted sons, three daughters). 1540–57, lawyer and banker to divorced Queen Anne of Cleves; 1557–80, banker and usurer, Putney. Murdered by debtor. Publications:* De Gentibus Dogbodiis; Tudor Worthies: Life and Times, *etc., etc.*

THE COMPLETE *De Gentibus Dogsbodiis*, Adonijah Dogsbody's sixteenth-century family history, is now lost, but a few mouldering sections from it were found in the cellar of Anne of Cleves's Richmond house when it was demolished in the 1920s. These surviving portions contain tales of Dogsbody deeds either passed down by word of mouth or taken from earlier records:

Our thirteenth-century forebear Jankyn Doggesbody farmed ten virgates of good land at Tydde, in Norfolk, with rights of fish and fowl. He was a proud and prosperous yeoman who loved a jest, but resented a slight.

Upon a mid-October day of 1216, as he came from Nene Sands by Crosse Keyes with his cousin Fildyke the Reeve, they beheld a train of men, horses and wagons coming across the fen, and from thence a horseman spurring towards them. Now, these two Doggesbodies, having been a-fowling since before dawn, were laden with a dozen muddy mallard, a grey goose, and dripping fowling-nets, and were much bemired, wherefore when the richly caparisoned horseman reined in before them, he addressed them in very haughty and peremptory terms: 'Ho, there, fellow! Art come off the marsh?' To him Jankyn replied, doffing cap and assuming manner and speech of a

J ANKYN DOGGESBODY (1175–1238) *Farmer, fisherman, fowler and fenman of Tydde. Son of John of Dogges-body and Sukie née Butte. Misplaced sense of humour caused loss of King John's baggage (a handsome wench), and impedimenta, to his own considerable gain. Unmarried (eleven sons, fourteen daughters). Died, unshriven, of multiple stab-wounds inflicted by the four brothers Styward of Tydde-by-Nene, whose eleven daughters and three grand-daughters he had severally betrayed.*

rustic clown: 'Nay, me lord. Us be still on 'un.' The horseman called him 'Stinkard Clod', and asked testily if they had ever passed across the sands and marsh to Fosse Dyke on the Lincolnshire shore. 'Aye, good sir, a-many times,' answered Jankyn, humbly, whereupon the gentle-man demanded that the way be pointed out by which he might lead His Grace the King and his baggage across.

'Readily, my lord,' said Jankyn, and gave careful directions thus: 'Ten score paces beyond Sutton Mydde marker post yonder; then half right-handed till the edge of Gednye reedbed be gained by our old coy pond. Kepp then to left of the gibbet till you be opposite Holbeach church, and then turn straight towards Boston church as you wade o'er Welland estuary flats, and there be Fosse Dyke afore ye.' With no word of thanks, the officer threw down a half-farden, turned, and galloped back towards the baggage train, hallooing and waving so that the leaders wheeled in his direction.

F ILDYKE DOGGESBODY (1179–1226) *Reeve and wainwright of Tydde-nexte-Sea, cousin and toady to the above. Son of Ulfe and Alys Doggesbody. Married 1201 Hope Cheste (five sons, six daughters). Died of bloudie fluxe in 1226.*

Jankyn and Fildyke stood watching as horsemen escorting a mule-litter, followed by sumpter animals and wagons, straggled past them and out on the sands and reedbeds; then they continued homewards. 'Cousin Jankyn,' said the Reeve, presently, 'thee didstn't tell royal baggage-master as how yon way across to Fosse Dyke be only possible at ebb-tide and slack water; and tide be a-making already.'

scorium Reg·Joh: ex palude eripiunt

KING JOHN'S BAGGAGE (13th century): Border decoration from Holbeach Abbey illuminated *Historia de Parudibus*, depicting Jankyn and Fildyke Doggesbodie and Ughtred Arblaster recovering Nan Shortshift from the Wash.

'Why, so I didn't, old jocky,' said Jankyn, 'but then yon buttock-brained bagger as can't tell a freeholder from a felon never asked, now did he?'

How they did laugh. And at low water on the morrow and for days thereafter they and many another fenman had rich pickings from what they ever afterwards called King John's Boggage.

W. F. N. WATSON

Que riche yenglion
ist Custan
ce . O . le Cu
n . e . uostr

PAGE FROM THE GESTA LAURENTII (13th century, Dogsbodleian Museum): Nancy Dogsbody has demonstrated that this is a part of the very improper medieval French history of the illicit love of Constance Doggesboddie, Dame du Château Lys, for Malheures, her Lord's *garde-chasse*. The descendants of their union were legitimized in the name of Corpsdechienne, and became hereditary Masters of the Royal Hunt.

1305
King Bruce and the Spider

FROM THE JOURNAL of Bridget O'Daoghsbhoade, housemaid, Seaview Hotel, Isle of Rathlin, 1305:

. . . Sure an I'll be havin' no more of it. Did I not go round the rooms this mornin' as usual, but when I goes into Room 23 an' starts to ply me feather-duster, does not the Scotchman Mr Bruce say to desist, because he wouldn't have the spiders disturbed in their webs because they are a great inspiration to him. Well sez I they're no inspiration to me an' I'm here to do a job, an' I'll be havin' no webs in my rooms collectin' dust so that's it.

Well he calls Mrs O'Shaughnessy an' she tells me the customer knows best so he does, and to stop with me duster.

In that case sez I ye can choose between me an' the spiders, for there's no room in this place for the both of us.

An' gave in me notice.

W. S. BROWNLIE

1315
Bruce and de Doggesbodie

SIR PONCEFOTE DOGGESBODIE (1298–1340) *Knight, of Ashenputtel, Hampshire. Son of Anchient Agarick Doggesbodie and Lucette née Panky); kinsman and esquire to the above. Married 1322 Joleta, natural daughter of Gismond Hautbois, Abbot of Badberry (two sons, one daughter). Killed by Greek fire at Battle of Sluys.*

THIS ACCOUNT by Poncefote Doggesbodie esquier, recorded in Anno 1315 by my forebeare Friar Pennefether Doggesbodie of Crewkesdyke Minster, was among the fewe poor pages of ye famose Crewkesdyke Chronicle saved from destruction by me, Cornet Resurrectioun Day Dogsbody, in 1648 when my Companie of Godly Dragones burned down the Minster.

Now, whan that Ser Buerke de Doggesbodie saw how ye Scotts Kynge Robert, wel y-cleped Robert ye Bruise, did caitiffly slay gude Lord de Bohun, not lance-pointe to lance-pointe, but drawynge asyde and smiting hym wanchance with battel-axe up-on hys sconce, thenne was Ser Doggesbodie full wrothe.

SER BUERKE DE DOGGESBODIE (1278–1315) *Knight-Banneret of Fugglestane Episkopi in Wiltshire. Son of Count Rogier de Doggesbodie and Fiammetta née Lapoitrine. Married 1293 Bernice Critchett (sans issue). Slain at Bannockburn 1315.*

'Now shaltow right spedilly be revenged, Ser Bohun,' quod he, and couchynge lance and setting spores to hys grey destrier highte Dappel Domplynge he charged furiousely to-wards ye Bruise tavenge forthwyth the unknichtely deede, followed by hys faithful esquier and kinsman Poncefote Doggesbodie. Alack, per malaventour, diverted by sighte of Ser Bohun's riderless steede cavortynge and vertynge doune and uppe betwene the armyes, Ser Buerke's warhorse tourned somdeel fro hys strechte career. Despyte all hys maistres woundy cursynge and pull-divel-pull-baker on ye reines, he carryed hym yerdes a-wide of Kynge Bruise.

The ungentil Scotis knichtes, borsting of theyr armor-buckles a-laughing basely atte hys sorry plyghte, openned theyr rankes and lat ye misfortunat champioun bolte ful-galoph throghe to the verray reare of theyr battel lines. Ther, amonge tentes and pavillons, th'onrewely beeste tript oer a tenterope and fel crupper over testrière, right amungste blacke smythes, farrieres and armoureurs bisy a-forgeing horseshoon and spyked caltrips. Thereto, whan Ser Doggesbodie cam a-somersett erse oer heede, by most ill hap twas ful upon an anvill whereon two grete Scots smythes were hameringe a rede-hote iron bar, on-to the which the gode knighte pitched astryde, setting of hys culliones grievously a-roste to hys grete disconfort. Eftsoons, ere he could offspringen, the two smythes, continuing of theyr strokes, smoote hym murily with theyr sleedge-hameres so that he was flatened aldermoste lyk pannecaik, at sighte of which hys povre yonge esquier fell a-swoonding fro his palfrey and was made captif.

Ye Englysshe knichtes, sore dismayd at the unseemely fate of theyr champioun, were rondely put to rout in the battel, to which the trionfant Kyng Bruise gave therfor the name Ballocke-Burne. Allsoe he sett up a tombe and on it in scorne of ye tombe of owr Kynge Edward I, y-clept Hamer of ye Scots, he made carve 'Here lyes Ser Doggesbuidy, ANVIL OF YE SCOTS'.

FOOTNOTE TO the above, dated 1605, by Master Walsinghame Dogsbody, Scrivener to the Lords Temporal of Great Britain:

When our two Realmes were made one under our Soveriegn Lord Kyng James Sixt and First, twas agreed that to end all fleering ribaldry and scorneful jeeres, this Scotish victory should henceforth be known as Bannock-Burne, after ye Scots border-raideres saying 'To Burne ones Bannockes', that is to say, to determine to conquer or starve; and in retourne, the English victory of 1513, called by them Floggedem, should be renamed Flodden.

W. F. N. WATSON

1350
The Stonemason of Tydde

IN THE COURSE OF my research at the old farmhouse at Tydde in Norfolk I came across the following copy of a most unusual epitaph. Diligent search revealed Martin Dogsbodie's much-neglected grave in the nearby churchyard, although the original inscription is quite illegible.

Willoughby Dogsbody

MARTIN DOGSBODIE 1309–1350

HERE LIETH MARTIN DOGSBODIE, MASON — SET UPON AND DONE TO DEATH BY DIVERS PARISHIONERS OF TYDDE IN THIS COUNTY OF NORFOLK.

THIS KNAVE DID, BY EMPLOYING CUNNING FLATTERY AND BY PRAISING THE COMELINESS OF THEIR FEATURES, PERSUADE MANY UPRIGHT AND VIRTUOUS CITIZENS OF THIS TOWN TO SUFFER HIM TO DRAW THEIR LIKENESSES, ASSURING THEM THAT THESE PORTRAITS WOULD BE SET IN HIGH EXALTED PLACES TO HELP IN THE LORD'S WORK.

THE TREACHEROUS VARLET DID THEN FASHION THEIR IMAGES IN STONE, BUT IN THE MANNER OF FOUL DEMONS AND CREATURES OF LOATHSOME AND HORRIBLE VISAGE, WHICH HE DID THEN SET ATOP SUNDRY CHURCHES IN THIS PARISH AND THE COUNTRYSIDE ABOUT, TO SERVE AS GARGOYLES OR RAIN SPOUTS FOR THE DISCHARGE OF RAIN WATER FROM THE GUTTERING OF THESE EMINENCES.

FURTHERMORE THE FACES OF THESE EFFIGIES BEING OF SATANIC AND MALEVOLENT UGLINESS INCITED SUCH MOCKERY THAT THOSE UNFORTUNATES IN WHOSE IMAGE THEY WERE

SHAPED WERE MUCH HUMILIATED AND SCORNED BY
THEIR FELLOWS.

FINALLY TO ADD TO THIS SCANDALOUS BLASPHEMY,
NOT ONLY DID DOGSBODIE DESIGN HIS
ABOMINATIONS TO SHED WATER FROM THEIR
HIDEOUSLY GAPING MOUTHS BUT ALSO FROM
OTHER ORIFICES FOR MORE UNSEEMLY AND
INDELICATE PURPOSES.

THIS GRIEVOUS SINNER WAS DESPATCHED WITH
THE VERY MALLETS, MAUL, HAMMERS AND OTHER
IMPLEMENTS OF HIS TRADE WHICH ARE INTERRED
WITH HIM.

PHILIP A. NICHOLSON

1350
The Black Death

THE EXACT NAME of the member of the Dogsbody family who
donated this ancient handbill to the archives is unknown. It is merely
annotated: 'Too late. B. D. Cheapside, 13 October 1350'.

DON'T DIE OF IGNORANCE.

The Black Death *can* be beaten; but only if you behave
sensibly. Remember, you can't tell who's got it, so

KEEP AWAY FROM PEOPLE.

Don't trust confident apothecaries, unlicensed witches'
remedies, casual astrological predictions. You can't catch it
from your dog; otherwise, you're best on your own.

AVOID YOUR WIFE AND FAMILY.

(Gov't warning)

PAUL GRIFFIN

1381
The Peasants' Revolt

DOCUMENTARY EVIDENCE of the bolshie mood among the peasants of the late fourteenth century has always been scarce. Here at last we have it, from a peasant for whom the last straw was clearly being asked to decorate the local church for Christmas. Did I say 'asked'? Found by me among the pages of the Parish Register at Tydde. – Willoughby Dogsbody

> Ye hollye and ye ivye
>   And ye Christmas tree so faire
> Are a mekill peyne to a poore villein
>   Who hath litel tyme to spare;
> > *O ye scrubbynge of ye lecterne*
> > *And ye deckynge of ye tree*
> > *And ye blowynge of ye murie organ:*
> > *Must they alle be done by mee?*

> Ye hollye beareth prickle
>   As sharp as any spike;
> Ye may stick a briar in our gracious squire
>   Atte anie tyme ye lyke;
> > *O ye lightynge of ye candles*
> > *And ye polysshynge ye brasse!*
> > *Yf this be ye Feudal Systeme,*
> > *Rolle on, ye Myddel Classe!*

(The ms. offers an alternative version of the last line, which it seemed better to ignore.)

PAUL GRIFFIN

1387
Chaucer: *The Canterbury Tales*

FROM THE COLLECTION of Sir Max Dogsbody.

One of the most remarkable documents in the Dogsbody archives is what is, almost certainly, the final passage which Chaucer wrote for his masterpiece *The Canterbury Tales* and which unaccountably remained unpublished. The portrayal of Dogsbody seems to be taken from life. Whether he was indeed a guide at the Cathedral, or whether Chaucer encountered this difficult fellow elsewhere, is not known.

These wordes above the massie doore were writ:
HEERE BEE THE SHRINE; and also nigh to it:
NO HOUNDËS NOR EXPECTORACIOUN
ON PAINE OF EXCUMMUNICACIOUN.
'Folwe mee now!' than cryede our Host; 'perdee!
Wo be to anyone that leseth me,
I urgëd have your need to hym who stonds
Hard by the doore, and gresëd have his hondes
For twenty-nine, namoore, and not oon lesse;
Nay, thank me nat for any bounteousnesse,
For this included is within the prys
I quoted you for this our enterprise.
Now lat ye enter in the blessed shrine
Ful joyously; your pleasure shal be myne.'
Alas for man! Alas and wellaway
For all the hope he setteth on one daie!
This doorman eke – Dogsbodie was his name –
Upon the martyr's shrine had made his claim,
That hee, and hee alone, of it should speke;
Hee talkëde on until wee alle were seke.
'Lat be!' cryede Harry Bailly; 'holde thy honde,
Good Dogsbodie! In all of Engëlond
Neer heard I oon who ratted on so longe.
Spare these good folke, and stente thy endless songe!'
But all the moore hee spake, right angrilie

Ayenst our Host, urging his dignitee
And how hee was a member of a Guilde
Till all of us with werinesse were filde
And beggëd wee our frend, the gentil Knighte,
To use his swerde, and putte the man to flighte.
'Nay,' cryëde he; 'come all, and lat hym byde,
And out of Caunterbury lat us ryde.
Oon martyr is enow, as mote I thee;
To Thomas lat us nat add Dogsbodie.
We cam to finde a Saint, and found a sinner;
What more to seye?'
　　And so we went to dinner.

PAUL GRIFFIN

1400
Chaucer: *The Abdication of Richard II*

CHAUCER DIED, 'in bedde' as he had hoped, in 1400, not very long after Henry IV usurped the throne of England, so this piece can well be claimed as his last work. Though originally allegorical in conception, it turns into recognizable if somewhat metaphorical history and we should note that, though during John of Gaunt's lifetime Chaucer enjoyed his patronage (they were related by marriage), he seems here to distrust John's son and obviously had no intention of *publishing* this 'tale'. Sir Max Dogsbody, in whose possession the manuscript now is (he vouches for its authenticity, but refuses to say how he acquired it), assumes it was written, like the *Treatise on the Astrolabe*, for Chaucer's son Lewis – a plausible theory.

A povré widwé, that Britania highte,
Was whilom wedded to a gentil knyghte.
This Edward wex ful godli in his lyf
And seven noble sonnes he yaf his wyf,

Of whom the eldrest Deeth untymely hente
Afor his fader to his faderès wente.
This sonne, yclept The Blak, hadde eke a sonne,
Richard, who now his grandsyres feeldès wonne;
At thilkè tyme, as I have understonde,
The heyrè took the lady with the londe.
This yongè spriggè royalliche ybore
His lordschippe, tho hys eldres tryed hym soore;
Certes, Wat Tyler and his meynee hot
He tamed, and showed hem allè what was what.
But pryde and powre bismoterèd his name;
His moder, grandmoder, and eke his dame,
Britania, triply neerè to his herte,
He leased aroundè, as a pymp his terte.
Whan uncle John his nephew rapped, and dyde,
His londès Richard seyzed, and more bisyde.
But Fortune yaf her wheel a privie shove
And undernethe he slydes that was above.
So cousyn Henri, bannysshèd erewhile,
Returned in armes to claym his faderes pile.
Lykning his passage to a boyling brooke,
Britania's servauntz soon theyr lord forsooke,
Folwèd from coign and creyk the risynge tyde
Which swypèd Richard fro Britanias syde.
Now Henri, erst but sonne to John-a-Gaunte,
Hath wedde at ones his granie and his aunte.
What nedeth wordes mo? who rules, ywis,
Sholde pleasaunce han on erthe and hevenes blis;
Discrecioun his houshold wel besemeth,
Lest freend as foo too redily he demeth;
And sith the moldiwarp his feeldes hath dugge
And in hys arras lyrkes the curious bugge,
And sith that I be somdel stape in age,
Behooveth mee to myndè my langage,
Lest to an hastie jugement I ben ledde:
I woldè lyve in pees and dye in bedde.
Let ootheres now youre ytchyng eeris bende,
I kan namoore, my tale is at an ende.

MARY HOLTBY

1403
The Battle of Shrewsbury

ARMY FORM 242

Charge: against 14403657 L/Cpl Dogsbody C. under Section 40 of
the Army Act.

Conduct to the prejudice of good order and military discipline in that
he, while serving as batman to Henry Percy Hotspur on 20 July 1403,
did fail to pack his officer's kit correctly, so that on the day following
his officer was at the Battle of Shrewsbury while his sword was at
Berwick.

W. S. BROWNLIE

1415
The Battle of Agincourt

THOUGH CENSORED, this letter is believed to be from Piers
Dogsbody to his mother:

Somewhere in
██████████
St Crispin's Day, 1415

Dear and Honoured Mother,

Should this letter reach you, I feare it wille bee mightie strange
reading; for our lord hath decreed a securitie blacke-oute, so that alle
letters are to bee censored. Suffice it to saye that an uncomfortable
time wee have hadde of it. We landed atte ██████████ and took the
towne with a prettie sharpe siege, but since then what littel victualls

---

PIERS DOGSBODY (1399–1462) *Ran away from home under the impression that he was joining a band of itinerant tumblers, which turned out to be a recruiting band for Henry V's expedition to France.*

---

we have hadde have given us great gripings and incontinence. It is true what people say that the ▮▮▮▮▮ flyes are worse thanne the Englyshe.

After a long wearie march trying to finde a place to crosse the River ▮▮▮▮▮ alle wee want is to gette backe to ▮▮▮▮▮. Wee are now camped before a place they calle ▮▮▮▮▮▮. Oure corporal, Master Nym, saith we are like to have a skirmyshe here todaye. The ▮▮▮▮▮▮ are great in numbere and have a fine ▮▮▮▮▮ but I doute not that our ▮▮▮▮▮▮▮ wille scatter them with their ▮▮▮▮▮ if they have strength to ▮▮▮▮ their ▮▮▮▮.

Nowe I must goe, as a fine fair-spoken lord hath drawn uppe to address us; some saith it be King ▮▮▮▮▮ himself.

Yr loving sonne

▮▮▮▮▮▮

NOEL PETTY

1457
Yorick's Joke Book

EXTRACT FROM the Joke Book of Henry V's court jester:

LAMBERT: What was that Ladle I saw you with last night?
YORICK: That was no Ladle that was my Knife.

LAMBERT: Why did ye Elk cross ye Roade?
YORICK: Because it was ye Chicken's night off.

YORICK: I quoth, I quoth, I quoth. I just shot my Elk Hound.
LAMBERT: Was he Madde?
YORICK: He was furiousse.

LAMBERT: Ho, Varlet! There's a Fly in my Pottage!!
YORICK: Hush, my Lord, or they'll all want one.

LAMBERT: Who crept up on Sir Mortimer?
YORICK: Sir Prise, of course.

LAMBERT: Whyche Kinge is Schizophrenicke?
YORICK: Henry ye Fourth – parte twoe.

LAMBERT: Whoe has a leane ande Hungrye Looke?
YORICK: Whye, Johnne of Gaunte.

LAMBERT: Why is an Amourouse Knighte lyk unto a welle-fortifyed Castel?
YORICK: Because he Keeps a Stronghold on ye Breast works.

'WHY IS AN AMOUROUSE KNIGHTE LYK UNTO A WELLE-FORTIFYED CASTEL?': This illustration in *Yorick's Joke Book* (1457), un-doubtedly filched from the 12th-century Tydde Testament, in fact depicts part of the story of David and Bathsheba. The entire page is missing from the copy which Henry V presented to his father-in-law the King of France.

YORICK DOGSBODY (1357–1436)   *Usually worked with Lambert de Fool, his straight knave. Played Number One Castle Circuit for many years; also did coronations and pageants.*

LAMBERT: I quoth, I quoth, I quoth. Why has ye Duke of Norfolke gotte a bandage on his Noble Browe?

YORICK: Forsooth he was putting somme Toilette Water behind his eares and ye seate felle on his Heade.

LAMBERT: Who is ye best Cooke in ye Castle?
YORICK: Warwicke, ye Chicken à la King-Maker.

LAMBERT: How couldst thou telle thatte thou wast eating of Venisonne?
YORICK: I just hadde a Haunche.

LAMBERT: Was Sir Cedric upsette when he putte on his new armour upside downe?
YORICK: Yeah Verily, his heart was full of Greve.

LAMBERT: And was Sir Cedric also nonneplussed when this happened?
YORICK: Odds Bodkins, he knew not whether he was on his Cuirass or his Crossbow.

JULIAN JOY-CHAGRIN

1469
Richard III

ACCOUNT FOUND in 1750 among the Parish Records of Stillebourne in Dorset, and included in the Canon Oswald Dogsbody's *Natural History and Antiquities of Stillebourne* (unpublished), to explain the origin of the name Codd's Wallop given to a local coppice,

CANON OSWALD DOGSBODY, M.A. (1731–1805) *Much sought-after society preacher and respected amateur botanist. Cousin of Matthew. A confirmed bachelor, he kept a house in St George's Square near his cousin, and a country retreat at Faringdon, where he botanized and wrote his great treatise,* Silicious Particle Patterns in the British Horsetail. *Kicked by his horse when on a field expedition, he died instantly.*

the more unusual in that the Wallops (Over, Middle, Nether, etc.) are above thirty miles away in the next county. The said account written by his forebear Isaac Dogsbody, Parish Clerk 1450–90:

Concerning Codd's Wallop, a coppice ½ furlong West of Chetterwode Farm:– In the Yeare of Oure Lord 1469 Richard, Earle of Gloster, ye Kinges broder, and himself future King Richard III, coming alone from hunting in Cranebourne Chace, passed through this parish of Stillebourne. Here he encontred Cecilie Doggesbodie, a very comely, well-grown and virtuous mayde, scarce sixteen yeare, doghter to my cousin Matthew Doggesbody, farmer of Chetterwode,

CECILIE BRAZIER-HORSECOLLAR née DOGSBODY (1454–1525) *Elder daughter of Matthew Dogsbody, farmer, of Chetterwode. Famed for encounter with future Richard III, which the latter never forgot. Married (i) 1470 Thomas Horsecollar, steward (died 1524, five sons, four daughters); (ii) 1525 Eli Brazier, woodsman (died of apoplexy during wedding night, aged 65).*

she going a-milking of her faders cowes. This Prince besoghte to companie her a-milking for to have a drinke, for his great thirst. She, kindely disposed, gave him leave, whereat he tied hys Courser and walkt besyde her. But entering a bosky dell, he sought to kisse and toye; she sayde Nay; he rewdely snacht away her Kerchief, and inflamed at disclosure of her bosome wolde have rafte her maydenheed. Alas for him. My cousin her fader was ever a grete wrastler and so too the Maydenes seven broders with whom she had a-many times wrastled in childhood, and wotted wel the art. So whan this younge royall lecher made seisin upon her, the lusty wench threwe him bravely with a trewe Dorsetshire Cross-buttock, and as he lay a-sprawle much pained of his bakkbone, she fetcht him a shrewd buffet of her oaken milking-stool ful upon hys coddpiece, and another acrost hys shouldere which shattred that too, so that he never again stood square or walked unhalting. Thus to all Dorset he was called Crutchebroke which decency later changed first to Crouchbacke, and then Crookbacke; while the glade where Mistress Cecilie so wel defended her virtue has ever since been known as Codds Wallop.

W. F. N. WATSON

1470
The Invention of Printing

PRINTED HANDBILL from the Max Dogsbody Collection of Ephemera:

THE MACHINE THAT THINKS!

English brains and technology now bring you the indispensable machine for recalling vital information – the most powerful adjunct to the thinking man since the abacus – something you can chain to your desk and refer to in moments of difficulty. Everything you need can be at your fingertips in –

THE PRINTED BOOK.

For details and prices, contact William Caxton, Box 207.

PAUL GRIFFIN

1478
The Death of the Duke of Clarence

Extra Speciall

Limytted Stocks onlie
MALMSEY WINE
botelled from
ye VERY CASKE
whereinn
H[ys] Grace of Clarence
met hys Sadde Ende

HANDBILL (1478): To advertise a special bottled Malmsey: a full-flavoured wine with plenty of body.

DOGSBODY & DOGSBODY
Wine Shippers
London
March 1478

Memorandum from Mr Dogsbody to Mr Dogsbody:

Ye death of ye Duke of Clarence, while regrettable from the point of view of his Grace, presenteth us with a rare opportunitie to promote Perkins & Perdhuelho's fine Malmsey. Alle the talk here is that ye Duke was drowned in a butt of Malmsey; if wee bringe alle our stock to the market quicklie, bearing a label stucke on which saith: 'Duke of Clarence Special', ye Lancastrians will drinke it to celebrate hys down-falle, and ye Yorkists will drinke it to revere hys memorie. And wee wille cleane uppe. I have ordered ten thousand labels.

Do you thinke there could be any thinge in a five-starre label which purporteth the contents to bee the verie butt in which hys Grace perished? Or would this be over-trickie?

D.D.

NOEL PETTY

1480
The Renaissance

THE RENAISSANCE in Italy is famous for the flowering of creativity in the arts. Less well known, however, is the story of commercial art at that time. A brief extract from the autobiography of the sculptor Da Cani: The problem was that his clients required a faster turnover of work than he was able to provide. They also found it difficult and expensive to mail the sculptures which represented their products. As with many of his projects, Da Cani's autobiography was abandoned at an early stage:

One of my first commissions was for a new type of vest which made use of a revolutionary approach to knitting. The idea was that the fabric would enable wearers to skip about in snow without feeling the

1. Warm vest. 2. No ball. 3. Boundary: 4 runs. 4. One short

5. Bye. 6. Out. 7. Wide.

Preliminary sketches by Leonardo da Cani for his first two commercial projects. From the archives of the Museo nel Gabinetto Fuori, Florence.

cold. I had doubts about its success but set about the work with enthusiasm. My first attempt showed a man in raptures on first trying the amazing vest (see Fig. 1). I thought this turned out rather well but

LEONARDO DA CANI (1456–1520)   *Of obscure origins, he worked for various established carvers before getting tired of doing drapery, toes and the bits round the side, and setting up his own studio in 1479. He was employed for a brief spell by the Doge of Venice. His attempts to use his skills in the market-place were not successful, and he achieved only vicarious fame through copies of his work made by other artists.*

my employers said the man looked uncomfortable. I put aside my disappointment and threw myself into the next project: designs for a coaching manual based on a new game. To me the game seemed rather pointless and tedious. One player had to lob a ball for another to hit. The second player then had to run up and down between two sets of sticks. I was not surprised when the game did not catch on. Most people considered that it was ill-suited to sunny and warm countries such as ours. All the same, my designs were much admired. Figures 2 to 7 illustrate signals made by the supervising officials of the game. They are as follows:

Fig. 2 – 'no ball'
Fig. 3 – 'boundary – four runs'
Fig. 4 – 'one short'
Fig. 5 – 'bye'
Fig. 6 – 'out'
Fig. 7 – 'wide ball'

I didn't fully understand all this but I'm only the artist . . .

N. J. WARBURTON

1483
The Princes in the Tower

FROM *De Gentibus Dogsbodiis* by Adonijah Dogsbody:

Dame Ermelyne Doggesboddie became a widowe at sixteene yeare of age when her goodman Lewis Doggesboddie fell at ye Siege of Orleans in Anno 1429, a twelvemonthe after her brydalls. This vaillant man-at-arms, befor being slayn by the satanic weapons of the French harlott Jehane Dark, wounded that vile witch, so that her hell-bought courage bigan to wane thereafter, whereby within a yeare the Burgundyans tooke her captif at Compieygne.

In recognitioun of this service by Ser Lewis, the widowed Dame Ermelyne was given a place at court as one of Queen Margarete Danjou's ladies, and gouvernante to Prince Edward her son; and thereafter lykewise to Queen Elizabeth Wodevile and her boys.

Upon Kyng Edward IV's deeth in Anno 1483, the times being daungerous, these two royall boys were, for their greater safety, given lodging in the Tower by their good uncle Duke Gloucester, the Protectour. The faythfull Dame Ermelyne, now somdeal advaunced in age, accompanyed them, being strictly enjoyned by His Grace that she should guard them well, and with all kindnesse mother them as though they were her own. To this she solemnly swoor.

The nexte night, the worthie Protectour rode from White Halle to the Tower for t'assure himselfe of his dear Nephews' wel-being and confort, and to his royall rage and greefe, found the poor yonge things starke dead a-bed.

'Harrowe and allas!' he cryed, and summoning Dame Ermelyne, wrathfully demaunded: 'How now, thou faythlesse Hagg, didst not sweere to be close guardienne of my sweete nephewes, and with every fondnesse mother them? How comes it, Beldame, that I find they be lifeless corses?'

'God-a-mercy, Lord Richard,' cryed the poore deaf old crone Dame Doggesboddie, falling upon her knees a-weeping, 'I do vow I thought thou saydst "smother them".'

W. F. N. WATSON

'THE GODE DUKE GLOUCESTER REBUKETH DAME ERMELYNE':
Woodcut from the 15th-century Basebourne Chronicle, showing the discovery of the corpses of the young King Edward V and his brother the Duke of York, inadvertently slain by Dame Ermelyne Dogsbody.

1485
Richard III at the Battle of Bosworth

A. Dogsbody & Sons
Liveriemen
Leycester

To: ye Execufours of RKHᵈ of YORK
late Kyng of England

Quantity	Ytem	Deliverie Date	Deliverie Poynte
1	Chestnutt Hors (entyr)	22 Aug 1485	Bosworthe Field

To deliverin sayd Ytem agenst
Urgent Ordure: to retreeving
same and retourning to Stor, Clyente
a-bein onabull to tak deliverie.
£2:3s:0d
Termes Strictlie Nette

NOEL PETTY

1508
The Painting of the Sistine Chapel

COPY OF A PAGE FROM a letter shown by Michelangelo to his friend Leonardo da Cani, whose newly invented paint-sprayer he had been trying out:

To His Holiness Pope Julius II
The Vatican
Rome   15 April 1508

   . . . so I wondered if your Holiness would like to consider changing your mind regarding the ceiling, and settle for a nice cerulean blue. It is a holy-looking colour and very popular for church ceilings. You can't go wrong.

Your humble and obedient servant,
Michelangelo Buonarroti

E. O. PARROTT

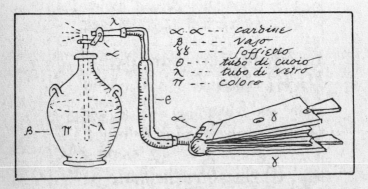

PAINT SPRAY (15th-century): From the notebooks of Leonardo da Cani. A comment written under the drawing seems to suggest that a prototype had in fact been constructed, and lent to Michelangelo. Reproduced by kind permission of the Museo nel Gabinetto Fuori, Florence.

1522
The Loss of the Mary Rose

THIS DOCUMENT appears to have been painstakingly pieced together from fragments found in the Admiralty waste-bin by Edmund Dogsbody, who was employed there as a clerk. It seems to have been subjected to an early form of shredding, the technology of which was not perfected for some centuries.

Memorandum

From: Clerke of the Shippes
To: Lieutenant of the Admiralty   Deptford, July 1522

My Lord,

The learned fellow from Cambrigge you sent to us last monthe hath carryed out hys businesse and gone. He claimeth to have founde a wondrous new theorie of shippes whereby he useth the Mathematicks to tell, before a shippe be built, how it wille stand in the water, using onlie drawings, measurements, models or the like.

Such a theorie would commend itselfe to your Lordships. However that may bee, when we tryed out the method on a model of the *Mary Rose* full laden, it saith that the shippe would topple over like a full-armed man struck from hys horse, nor right itselfe. Since the said shippe is on the sea and well founde, I took liberty to sende the fellow back to hys bookes at Cambrigge to trye again. These dustie fellows are noe good for practickal matteres.

Yr respectful servant,
Thos. Scroggin

NOEL PETTY

1536
The Dissolution of the Monasteries

THE SECRET DIARY of Friar Francis Dogsbody, an illuminated manuscript writer at Puppisham Abbey in Suffolk, is a significant find. It is in surprisingly good condition, considering that it was discovered by workmen who were removing the paper from a privy wall in Ipswich. We take a typical year:

1536

Januaris primus: Resolved to accelerate. Worked for 12 hours on letter G. Completed outline. Prayers. Apples. Cold in bed. *Solus sum.*

Jan. 2: Abbot admired G.

Jan. 14: Letter G going very well. Tinted – *Gules.*

Feb. 8: Colouring of letter G finished. Begin decoration tomorrow.

Feb. 9: Visit by Bishop. Prayer all day. *Gloria.*

Feb. 10: Prayer all day. Rain.

Feb. 11: More prayer. *Taedius est.*

Feb. 12: Drew a pattern of leaves round letter G.

Feb. 13: Began to mix a green pigment for leaves.

Feb. 14: Pigment too dark. Visit of abbot's sister. Surprisingly young. A saucy wench.

Feb. 15: Diluted green pigment. Herring and split pease. Bro. Geoffrey broke wind during Compline. *Brutus est.*

Feb. 16: Pigment over-diluted. Rain.

Mar. 8: Perfect *vert* for leaves. It is worth taking trouble *ad Gloriam Dei.*

Mar. 9: Coloured two leaves. Bro. William praised design.

Mar. 10: Pigment spilt. Bro. William is a clumsy churl. His breath smells like a military privy.

Mar. 11: Penance for evil thoughts toward brother monk. Walk barefoot to Colchester in shift.

Friar Francis Dogsbody the Illuminator left Puppisham Abbey on the Dissolution, taking his unfinished initial G (of *Gratia*). The ms. containing his last finished initial, a D, was preserved for posterity by his kinsman Adonijah, Thomas Cromwell's henchman. Clearly Friar Francis's mind was not entirely purged of ideas inspired by the Abbot's sister's secular songs, which he mentioned in his Diary. A sketch made by Dora Dogsbody of this very fragile manuscript, during a visit to the Dogsbodleian Museum.

Mar. 19: Footsore. Began to mix new *vert*.

Mar. 29: Vert ready. Began third leaf. Rain.

Mar. 30: Two more leaves.

Mar. 31: Getting into stride. Two and a half leaves. Forgave Brother Bill. Lampreys – the gift of the abbot.

Apr. 1: Painted leaf. Pigment was blue. Brother William grinned *et 'Stultus Avrilis' dixit*. The idiot cannot even decline simple Latin.

Apr. 2: Began to erase blue on leaf.

Apr. 8: Leaf erased. Rain.

Apr. 9: Prepared neutral base for spoilt leaf. Abbot's sister visited and sang secular songs during evening meal. She will receive as penance a light scourging from the abbot himself.

Apr. 12: Spoilt leaf now painted *vert*. It is difficult to tell the difference.

Apr. 14: The abbot's nephew, Brother Gavin, an artistic lad, apprenticed to me. I show him how to shape a brush.

Apr. 15: Look at tools with Bro. Gavin. Taken ill after eating mutton.

Apr. 20: Begin to recover.

Apr. 21: Much better.

Apr. 29: I walk about my cell.

May 4: Back to letter G. I colour most of a leaf. Bro. Gavin has been mixing colours and has discovered a lovely pale azure.

May 18: Leaves completed. I offer ten *Aves*.

May 19: I begin to draw beasts, round leaves. Brother Gavin begins to gold leaf outline of letter G. *Bonus puer est*.

May 26: Made 2 gallons ink. King's envoy, fellow named Tom Cramwell or Cromwell visited – a boon. We had fresh pork. More of these royal visits would be a good thing. We might fatten up a little.

June 4: Beasts going well. Abbot much happier. His sister has taken up residence. Brother Will smiling a lot. But he should beware. He spends less time at private devotions.

June 5: Bro. Gavin troubled with the flesh. Helped him. Set him to painting beasts. Wonderful detail. Rain.

June 7: Gilded lion's mane.

June 10: Beasts progressing.

June 18: Beasts completed. Brotherly kiss *inter Bro. Gavinus et meum*.

June 20: A few touches and G will be finished. Alleluja. Br. Gavin has moved into my cell – so as to expedite illumination.

June 21: Gold all day.

June 22: Gold . . .

June 23: Gold. Should finish page within a week.

June 26: Monastery dissolved. *O Dies Infortunata.* My G must remain forever incomplete. Rain.

Aug. 9: Started firm of signwriters in Ipswich: Francis & Gavin – Brothers of the Brush. *Tempera mutantur.*

Aug. 12: Gave incomplete G to Gavin – not sacrilege, Father Cecil assures me, since not finished.

Aug. 14: Our first job: a sign for lawyer, Master Mac Locklin.

Aug. 17: Re-paint sign for lawyer, name McLaughlin.

Aug. 20: Business very slow.

Aug. 28: Still very slow.

Aug. 30: Gavin has changed his name to KEVIN. Thinks it sounds nicer. Wants a K.

Sept. 15: Business very slow indeed . . .

GERARD BENSON

1540
Anne of Cleves

EXTRACT FROM *De Gentibus Dogsbodiis* by Adonijah Dogsbody:

Of ye nexte materes, alle whereof I was not myself witnesse, was told to me by those directly concerned.

My Father having rendered some Legal service to Master Hans Holbein when first he came to England in 1526, that great paynter tooke as apprentice and pupill my brother Amyas, then fourteen and skilld with his pencill. He remayned with Master Holbein above a dozen yeares, of which during severall in Germany and Switzerland he masterd the German tongue, to his future gaine, and in alle grewe so practist and trustworthie as to become nighe indispensable. Much of the Paynteres worke was done by him, save, in portrayts, the final likenesse of features, which must have the Master's touch.

A MYAS DOGSBODY (1513–59)   *Painter, steward, etc.*
*Youngest brother of Adonijah. Pupil and assistant of Hans
Holbein the Younger 1526–40, in England, Augsburg, Basel, Italy,
etc., including period when Holbein was Court Painter to Henry
VIII. 1540–57, steward, chamberlain, etc., etc., to former Queen
Anne of Cleves (two sons, three daughters, natural). Died of melan-
cholia (unmarried, sans legitimate issue).*

When therefore in 1539 my Master, Lord Grete Chamberlayne
Thomas Cromwell, soughte as successor to Queen Jane a Royall Bride
to binde ye Protestant Cause in alliance agaynst France and the
Emperour, he proposed the sister of Duke William of Cleves, leader of
the German Lutherans, and desired Master Holbein to paynt her
portrayt for the King. My brother Amyas being accordingly that
summer dispatched ahead to Cleves with the Envoys, to make alle
ready for the portrayt, writ to me on this wyse: 'This Castle of Düren,
Brother, is a verie Camp and Arsenall wherein everie man goeth armed
in haqueton and gambeson. Alle talke is of noghte but Stratagemes,
Sieges and Ambuscadoes, and of those Enginns hight Chevaux de
Frise, made of tree-trunkes or wooden beames furnisht all about with
sharpe spykes and blades, which the Besieged place in Breaches or
narrowe approaches, that the formost attaquers, prest by those
behinde, be impaled thereon.
Over this Spartan and Martiall domayne, and amid such tales, the
debonnaire fresshe yonge Edelfräulein Anne destyned to be owre
Liege Lady, ruleth bravely as Chastelayne. Thoghe no grete Beautie,
yet is she, methinks, well enow. ''Tis sayd she hath no Dowrie: certes
she hath but little Boke-learning nor speketh no tongue but German.
Being raysed in narrowe retirement, meseemeth she lacketh fyne
wayes and courtlie accompleshments, yet hath wondrous Art with her
needle, and alle huswyfly skilles besyde. Withall, she is the meriest
Lady, of sweete and simple demenoure; hath a fayre rose-hewe
complexioun alle unscarrd of ye smale-poxe, yellowe hayre, soft
voyce, a shape wondersly wel y-tourned, and allwayes neately thoghe
not richely drest. Of her breath and persoun she smelleth ever sweete
and wholsom as newe-bakt cakes.'
Thus my brother Amyas had wrote, wherefor when I companyed
Master Cromwell attending upon the Kinges Majestie to Rochester

on Newe Yeares Daye of 1540 to meete this Duchesse Anne, greate was my astoniement to see a misshapen womman of grosse forme, ill-ordered dress, one legg seemingly shorter than thother, at tymes crosse-eyen, and withall, so my Master sayd, of the foulest breath and rankest persoun ever he encontred. Myn owne eares hered the King saye: 'They have sent me a Flanders Mare,' and he after berated Master Cromwell that the Duchesse was no-wyse as Master Holbein's portrayt shewed her. Six dayes later, on the Wedding Morrowe, he angrilie declared his invincible repugnance towardes her; and swearing the marriage had not been and could not be consummated, he demanded a divorce. Thus in July the marriage was declared Nul and Voide, the rejected Queene being graunted, for her aquiescence, a handsome income, saving only she remayne in England. My Master went to the block, and I lost both employment and favoure.

For long I heared noughte of my brother, we both being much busied, he with Master Holbein's important workes during a great part of that summer, and myselfe with my disordered affayres, but in November Amyas sent to me to bringe my wyf to Richmond. To owre surprise he presented us to a fyne fayre Dame, as being Her Grace of Cleves, to whome he was, he sayd, Steward. Thereafter, while the Ladies conversed in broken Englisshe and mangled German, my brother, taking me asyde, confyded alle. Briefly, this admirable gentlewoman, being of the Sanguine Humoure and kept from marriage longer than she liked, was at first verie desirous to wed King Henry. But, hearing from a serving-wench the Royall Envoyes' report of the King's age, then fifty-one to her twenty-three, and of his casting off his faythful Queene after above twenty yeares and cruelly beheading her yonge successour, owre Duchesse Anne now awayted her Bridalls with loathing. Moreover, being much with my brother during his worke on the portrayt untill Master Holbein should come to finish it, she began to finde Amyas greatly to her lyking, as a proper yonge fellowe but two yeares her seniour. Then Lyking became Lovyng, and she sadly sayd: 'Deare Love, know this: a dowreless mayd hath but two thinges to give to her Trewe-Love. One is alle her Hearte, and allready thou hast mine. The other, if I give it not to thee, shall never be given to that cruell King, nor to no man. Rather will I die, and this I sweare.'

Thereafter, Master Holbein being come, the portrayt finisht and much to His Majesty's taste, and the Marriage Treaty signed in the Autumn, in December this yonge loving Duchesse set forth for

PORTRAIT OF ANNE OF CLEVES (15th century): A light-hearted sketch done by Amyas Dogsbody, and initialled by him, showing Anne of Cleves as she presented herself to Henry VIII, and as she really was. The inscription '*La masque et la vérité*' appears on the reverse. Preserved by Adonijah Dogsbody after his brother's death in 1559.

England with a small, trustie entourage. For dayes aforehand, and throughoute the journey, she partook of nought but garlick, leekes, oniones, highely-spyced meates and strong ales. Allsoe, she stuffed her kirtle and stomacher with pyllowes, wore a great olde-fasiouned cap, and studied to appeare as odious as she might.

But in the five dayes after meeting the King in this gyse, despight all such devices, discourtesyes, hoydenish wayes and endlesse shrille complaynings in German, natheless for verie shame His Grace held to his purpose, lest Cleves should go over to the Emperour. So, on the Nuptiall night, though she wept, argued and struggled, still he woulde not be denyed, therfore must she have resorte to the last tourne she might make and still live. Thus all we attending in the antechamber heared, of a sodeyn, great bellowes of rage and payne from His Grace, who stumbelled forth from the Bridebed furiously cursing and swearing, nor ever retourned. For, remembring of the strategeme of besieged defenders, this gentil lady first feigned to surrender and yield up the Pass, then at ye proper moment, did set righte in the path of the King's now trionphant advaunce, a *Cheval de Frise*, to wit a Horse-brushe having long stiffe bristells of split whaleboone, upon which the Vanguard of the Royall Assaulte was instantly transformed to a Forloorne Hope; and the Bride, albeit with blackened eye and bloudie nose, kept her Promise and her Mayden state.

Little remaines to tell. The faithfull Lady, awarded a fine house at Richmond and another at Bletchingley, soone left the Court. She sent to Amyas to be her Steward and Chamberlayn, which offices also he fulfilled to her great Satisfactioun.

Myself became her Man of Lawe and Banker, and oure brother Ralfe, her Physician (for such he was). The two sons and three daughters born of this joyous union were delivered in secret by Ralfe and given out as being his wyf's or mine, so never scandall arose to mar her happinesse in the seventeen yeares until her deth in 1557.

They two had oft playd at Chesse together, and sat somtymes longer thereat than the fond Dame was minded to, as I gesse from these Verses which I found among Amyas's papers long after, writ in her hand in 1545.

It sheweth her pretty Wit, and eke how trewe 'tis that Love is the best Teacher, since in five yeares, Love had taughte her so great mastery of the English tongue:

Cleve to thy Cleves, not thy Chesse

How often, Amyas, deare Lord,
I've held in Check my fond desire,
While I sate mumm by thy Chesse bord,
Nor bade thee from the Game retire:
I care not that my Knighte be thine,
Thy hand stretch'd forth to take my Pawne,
The Night the sooner shall be mine,
And thy hand to my Brestes be drawne.
Come, how much longer must I fast
Till I Love's Opening Gambit make,
That, when thou Matest me at last,
My Castle shall thy Bishopp take:
In Love, not Chesse, then Queene Ile prove
Thy Mistresse in Love's everie Move.

W. F. N. WATSON

1542
Ned's Joke Book

EXTRACT FROM THE Joke Book of Henry VIII's last jester, Ned Dogsbody:

Q What do your wives and lovers have in common?
A They usually end up under a sod.

Q How do you commit a cardinal sin with an axe?
A Chop Wolsey's head off.

Q Why are you a good alchemist even though you can't make gold?
A You dissolved the monasteries.

Q How do we know Anne Boleyn enjoyed animal sports?
A She made you wear the horns.

Q Why did you marry your elder brother's widow?
A There was nothing else of his you could fit into.

Q Why is Sir Thomas twice dead?
A He's no More and no more.

Q Why are you suspicious of Roman graves?
A You don't like Popish plots.

Q When were you the enemy within?
A When you sported with Ann of Cleves.

Q How do you get rid of dirty habits?
A Burn the monasteries.

Q If your mother was a Yorkist, what does that make you?
A A prick from a rose bush.

TIM HOPKINS

NED DOGSBODY (1510–90) *Last jester to Henry VIII. Came of a long line of jesters, including the famous Yorick, whose Joke Book he inherited and added to. His sister Meg was employed in the royal laundries.*

1547
Thomas Cranmer

THE LETTER BELOW is from Archbishop Cranmer to his wife, and from the internal evidence was apparently written in about the year 1547. It came into the Dogsbody collection in a most curious way. The Rev. Comenius Dogsbody (1740–86) had in his library a rare copy of the *Ars Amatoria* of Ovid. Anxious to keep the volume, but to conceal its nature from his parishioners, he decided to have it re-bound as *Collected Sermons* of Bishop Mottershead. In the re-binding, the Cranmer letter was revealed in the old binding.

My owne hearte,

Please do not | chide . me with | neglect; for I have been | mightie | busie | latelie.

The King, yea, even King Henry, hath made | manie de | mands; and I have not known | whether . I was | coming or going.

For he hath been going through queens like a | dose of | salts; and taxeth my brain to thinke of new ex | cuses | every | time. But it will alle be | different | now; because the King is | dead . and we | have a | new one.

I might be able to get one of those Six | Arti | cles repealed; I mean the one that decrees exe | cution . for | married | priests. I'm still kicking myself about letting | that one | through; but still, you'd better stay out of | sight a | wee bit | longer.

There's a nasty rumour going round that I keep you in a cabin trunk | in my | baggage . train; some people will say anything, but never despair, we'll be to | gether | any . year | now.

Sorry this letter is rather short, but I'm up to my ears in an | other new | prayer book; and I | can't . get it | out of . my | mind.

Yr loving husband

† *Cantuar*

NOEL PETTY

1553–8
The Persecution of the Protestants

IT IS BELIEVED that 300 Protestants were put to death in the last three years of Queen Mary's reign. Inevitably, a Dogsbody was involved, as we now know from this story told by Edwin Dogsbody, a Catholic torturer, to his uncle, old Ned, the jester:

Stonewall could not stay Wynkyn, God have mercy on his soul, from merry jests. We torturers are used to keep sad countenances, but Wynkyn, even in the midst of his work, was the merriest torturer alive. He would laugh so that his victims could not forbear to laugh also, even as they descended into the pit of Hell. Nay, Wynkyn would, in a manner, torture his fellows, Wat and myself, and even the good Father Pecock. God rest the Father's soul, for he did no hurt but once, and himself, by the decree of fortune, suffered torture and death.

It fell on this wise. Wynkyn twice told Father Pecock he had seen a varlet robbing his house, on which the good priest ran off to catch the fellow, leaving his work untended, a heretic unassoiled, and Wynkyn laughing abundantly. Twice the mild Father found his house unbroached, and returned doubting what were truth and what were lies. But a third time it happened, and thus began his bale.

Mild Father, do I say? Surely, but even a priest may come to cry: 'Enough!' Next day, when Wat and I laboured over the boiling oil, a Protestant blubbering at our elbows, in runs Wynkyn and cries to the priest: 'Father, Father, thy house burns down!'

'Why, so!' says Father Pecock of a sudden; 'if my house burns down, so may thee, thou turbulent wretch! Discomfort thee thus!' And he seizes Wynkyn by the collar and casts him into the grisly vat. 'Oh, my God!' he cries instantly, rending his breast, 'what do I? Alas, for my venomous temper!' But it is too late. Wynkyn is dead, and thenceforth our work is the less gladsome.

Father Pecock is taken by the officers before the Bishop's court. As he is borne away, all besprent with tears and bitings of conscience, he passes his house. He lifts his head, and lo, what sees he? Red ashes, and smoke as black as Hell.

I tell you, at that moment, the good Father Pecock began to laugh, and stinted not laughing until he joined Wynkyn in the vat; but this was not the laughter of Wynkyn. It was not such laughter as a man may enjoy to hear.

PAUL GRIFFIN

1554
Elizabeth in the Tower

From *De Gentibus Dogsbodiis* by Adonijah Dogsbody:

Dick (or 'Saul') Dogsbody, being Assistant Quartermaster at ye Tower of London, his dutye was to receive high-born Prisonours at the southern entrance. A Cholerick Fanatick, he customarily signifyed to such Prisonours his loyall abhorrence of Treasoun by instantly giving each a hearty kycke to the codpiece.

Thus, theyr painfull halting progress thence to the Bloudie Tower became knowne as Traytours' Gait.

The future Queene Elizabeth, imprisouned by her sister Bloudie Mary in 1554, and by reasoun of Sexe and Farthingale not so kycked, shewed disapprobatioun of Dick Dogsbody's cruell custome by allwayes addressing hym as 'Saul-Saul', in learned allusioun to Owre Lord's reproach to Saul upon the road to Damascus.*

The kycking being forbade, and the trewe significatioun of Traytours' Gait forgot, the name Traytours' Gate has took its place.

W. F. N. WATSON

1558
The Death of Queen Mary I

Acquired by Meg Dogsbody, a laundress with the Royal Household, and given to her brother Ned:

* Acts IX:4.5 ... Saul, Saul ... it is hard for thee to kick against the pricks.

Report by the Physician to the Royal Household

The autopsy was duly performed in the usual manner.

As formally instructed by the executors, special investigation was undertaken to determine whether there was or was not any cardiac abnormality.

There was detected a slight constriction of the left ventricle, not so marked as to have had significant symptoms.

Contrary to expectations reportedly expressed by the deceased while yet extant, no inscription of a geographical nature was discovered upon or within the organ in question.

(Sgd.) Hubert Philtre (Dr)

W. S. BROWNLIE

M EG DOGSBODY (1520–72) *Laundress and amateur sleuth. Sister of Ned. Was adept at acquiring documents such as the above. She eventually amassed enough money, by various means, to buy a property in Drury Lane, where in 1562 she opened a lodging-house which gained a certain reputation. Died following a fall from an upper window while berating a client.*

1558
The Vicar of Bray

BEFORE THE FOLLOWING prayer could be first delivered, altered circumstances dictated its sudden revision. It and the amended version were preserved by the churchwarden of the Parish, Ephraim Dogsbody (1500–1592).

1 God bless and save Our Sovereign Mistress Mary. Look kindly upon her, Lord, with the light of Thy countenance in that she has extricated the nation from the snare of the abominable protestant heresy and returned it safely to the fold of the True Faith. May she and her ministers continue to cut down and commit to the flames those mildewed branches fit for the burning by dint of foul apostasy. Protect and succour all those who do God's will as made manifest to us by the Holy Father and this his most dutiful daughter . . .

2 God bless and save Our Sovereign Mistress Elizabeth. Look kindly upon her, Lord, with the light of Thy countenance in that she has extricated the nation from the snare of the idolatrous popish abomination and returned it safely to the fold of the True Reformed Faith. May she and her ministers continue to root out and deliver over unto death those renegate and apostate priests who would most foully and traitorously bind thy true servants to the whim of the Scarlet Woman, that great Whore of Babylon seated in Rome. Number among Thy Saints, O Lord, all those cruelly martyred in the lamentable reign lately and mercifully concluded. May Thy will continue to be made manifest to us by the scrutiny of Thy Holy Writ . . .

The deft re-drafter of this edifying orison, Simon Aleyn, remained Vicar of Bray in Berkshire until his much-mourned death many years later.

MARTIN FAGG

1567
Sir Walter Raleigh's Cloak

FROM THE Account Book of Jermyn Doggesbodye, clothier, 1567:

Dydde this daye tak in toe be
restord from Capten Ralegh
One goode new Cloke much staynd
as thuogh having bin trode up-on
in a Plashie Plaice.
Charges askt and agried is to be :-
To Dry ye Cloke .... 1 pence
to scrap Hores ja dung offen sam.. 2 pence
to dº Dogges dº dº dº... 4 pence
to throughlye brusshe .... 1 pence
to Ayrand sent with Roes pettles,
Voilet assense and Lavandor .... 2 pence
⸻⸻⸻⸻
Totell   10 pence

W. S. BROWNLIE

1567
Mary Stuart – The Short Casket Letter

THE FOLLOWING IS thought to be one of the missing Casket Letters attributed to Mary Queen of Scots. The originals of these letters disappeared in the sixteenth century, but transcriptions were used to implicate Mary in the murder of her husband Darnley. This letter, known as the Short Casket Letter, casts new light on Mary's innocence. It mysteriously disappeared after the trial and was found among the effects of Solomon McDogsboddie, Court Usher at Edinburgh, after his death in 1579.

Ye will not beleve how colde it is heare. An I hadde bene Quene of Spain it wold at leste have bene warme, but I ges it is Scotland for lyf for me nowe.

All thynges are grimme and gray heare, and littel mirthe. There is a long-face fellow callit Knox quha lecturis me by the houre on salvation and like matteris. He is nat muche for the ladyis.

My husbande Darnley snoreth like a verie pigge in bed, and I have nat sleepit this twelvemonth, but ane of my ladyis tellit me to speik with the Erle of Bothwell, quhich I have done, and he hath promisit to cure my husbandis snoring for good, but I am nat to knowe how. He saith the cure is verie certain.

Praye God it happen soone.

Marie R.

NOEL PETTY

BROADSHEET ON THE MURDER OF DARNLEY: Circulated by the enemies of Mary Queen of Scots. From the Max Dogsbody Collection of Ephemera.

1584
Origins of Dogberry

MOST OF THE documents in the archive relating to Shakespeare are concerned with his theatrical experiences in London. But one, at least, gives a clear indication that he utilized much material from his Stratford days later on in his plays. The following article, which is based on a lecture given to the Stratford-on-Avon Literary Circle in 1906 by Nicholas Dogsbody, a local antiquary, reveals that there are amazing parallels between local archives and certain works of the bard:

Who said: 'Comparisons are odorous'? Most people would probably say: 'Mrs Malaprop.' Not *you*, of course, who know that it was Dogberry, the comic constable in *Much Ado About Nothing* – precursor of Mrs Malaprop by nearly 200 years.

Shakespeare probably based the character of Dogberry on Nicholas Dogsbodie, the village constable at Stratford-on-Avon. Proceedings at Stratford Assizes, recently disinterred, record the following gems from his lips.

I caught Master Shakespeare and Mistress Hathaway in the long grass in the very act of capitulating.

Evidence must always be treated with circumcision.

He was perspicuous by his absence.

When I curmudgeoned the prisoner, who came from some black African diatribe, he became very obstetrical.

A mean and parsimonial fellow.

The priest was teaching the boy his cataclysm.

I told him the very idea was prepostiferous.

I would not submit to his prettyfrogging and toadying dispensations.

She is a whore for whom life is nothing but men, men, men: she is, in a word, mendacious.

STANLEY J. SHARPLESS

N ICHOLAS DOGSBODIE (1533–1610) *Constable at Stratford-on-Avon. Married Jemima Foote, cook to Mistress Anne Shakespeare at New Place.*

1588
The Spanish Armada

LETTER TO HIS mother and father from 308074 Pte Dogsbody:

> Tilbury
> 8 August 1588

Dear Mum and Dad,

. . . we was got up this morning a bit earlier than usual, and we got all togged up and lined up and was inspected with me getting a bollocking because the officer said he couldn't see his face not that he was missing much in my belt buckle which was not surprising as I only got issued with it the other day and haven't buffed it down yet it takes time.

We was then marched a long way ending up in a field where we was stood easy in a long line but no smoking even if you've got any for bloody hours. What for I don't know nobody tells you nothing in this army.

Anyway along comes a woman on a horse and as she goes by she says she has the body of a weak and feeble woman though she looked healthy enough to me and disappears.

We was then marched all the way back to camp the way we had come and by the time we was fell out the NAAFI was shut. I don't know what I joined for honest I don't.

> Your affectionate son,
> *Walter*

W. S. BROWNLIE

W ALTER DOGSBODY (1569–1651) *Son of Gervaise.*
Invalided out of army after shooting himself in the knee
during exercises; returned home and carried on his father's business.

1588
Queen Elizabeth's Notes for her Tilbury Speech

THE FOLLOWING ARE Queen Elizabeth I's notes for her famous speech at Tilbury. Pte Walter Dogsbody, whose platoon was detailed to clear up after the occasion, picked up the discarded notes:

~~Ladies and Gentlemen~~ (*no – not true*)

~~Unaccustomed as I am~~ (*no*)

My loving people (*much better. But with conviction – remember, if you don't believe it, they won't*)

We have been persuaded by some that are careful for our safety to take heed how we commit ourselves to armed multitudes, for fear of treachery (*unwise to give them ideas. Press on fast*) but I assure you, I do not desire to live to distrust my faithful and loving people. (*Long pause. Dudley says he'll get the cheering going from the back*)

I have always so behaved myself that, under God (*cast eyes upward*) I have placed my chiefest strength in the LOYAL HEARTS and GOOD WILL of my subjects (*lay it on here*) not for my recreation and disport, but being resolved, in the midst and heat of battle, to live and die amongst you all, and to lay down for my God (*eyes up*) and for my Kingdom (*sweep of hand*) and for my people (*outstretched hands*) my honour and my blood, even in the dust (*not part of the plan, but it certainly has a fine ring to it*).

I know I have the body of a weak and feeble woman (*the things you have to say in this job*) but I have the heart and stomach of a King, and a King of England, too (*with luck they should have forgotten about father by now*) and think foul scorn that Parma (*will they know about this? Where is it anyway? Isn't it the place we get those fantastic hams?*) or Spain or any prince of Europe should dare to invade my realm (*if comic relief needed here could tell them the one about the lady-in-waiting and the Spanish onions*) to which, rather than dishonour shall grow by me, I myself will take up arms, I myself will be your general, judge and rewarder of every one of your virtues in the field (*Drake didn't seem too keen on the general bit, but will leave it in*).

I know already for your forwardness you deserve rewards and crowns; and we do assure you in the word of a prince, they shall be duly paid you (*Burghley says we can't afford it, but he's a fool. Tax them to pay for the war then give them some back, and they'll be all over you. Besides, if we lay on free sack on victory night they won't remember a thing*).

NOEL PETTY

1588
Drake on Plymouth Hoe

From: The Secretary of the Plymouth Bowls Club Disciplinary Committee
To: Sir Francis Drake   Copy to: Gervaise Dogsbody.

Sir, ye are required to appear before the committee so that answer may be given on the following charges:

1 That thou didst attempt to undermine the confidence of thine opponent (Gervaise Dogsbody, Mayor of Crippelstile St Agnes in the County of Devon, county bowler and Hon. Sec. of the P.B.C. (Discipline)) by the employment of such phrases as 'ye Spanish are coming' and 'murdered in ye beds' as thine opponent was about to bowl.

2 That thou didst employ a certain low person of the town to run across the green calling in a loud voice: 'Sire, Sire, the Spanish fleet has been sighted!' and strike his foot against thine opponent's wood as it was about to nestle against the jack.

3 That thou didst wilfully cause panic and much mirth to arise in spectators by declaring on several occasions: 'There is time to finish

this game and beat the Spanish fleet', knowing that the sweaty palms this caused would be to thine advantage.

4 That thou didst leave the match in haste, declining to partake of the traditional bread and cucumber fare provided by thine hosts.

We hold that such behaviour bringeth the game of bowls into disrepute and doth damage to the spirit which maketh this realm glorious and P.B.C. great.

Jethro Marshall
(Hon. Sec.):

N. J. WARBURTON

GERVAISE DOGSBODY (1551–1603) *Glovemaker, Plymouth. Rose to some prominence in that town but failed to become Mayor owing to a personal dispute with Sir Francis Drake, whom he pursued with complaints. On one occasion Gervaise found himself off the coast of South America before he was able to deliver a strongly worded letter to the well-known sea-dog. Eventually became Mayor of Cripplestile St Agnes. One son, Walter.*

1593
Shakespeare and Marlowe

THOMAS DOGSBODY (1555–1625) *Small-part actor and failed playwright. Brother of Doll. A close associate of William Shakespeare, he spent the whole of his working life at the Globe Theatre.*

SOME OF THE MOST CRUCIAL documents in the archive are concerned with those hitherto unsolved literary mysteries, the death of Christopher Marlowe and the actual authorship of the so-called Shakespeare plays. The following items were among the many collected by Thomas Dogsbody during his years at the Globe.

Unto My Lord of Burghley, in ye Strand
Atte Cecil House, from William Shakesperes hand.

My Lord, Pursuant to your wish I came On Maye the thirtyeth to
Deptforde where Within the Horse and Trumpetts taverne I Ask'd for
your envoy Marlowe as you bade. They sayde that he had for an howre
there been And so hadd met your God-child, go-between And doxie
Doll Doggsbodie, who because She'd privy matteres from yourself to
tell, Above stayres went with him, twice in the houre.

Thenne came Sir Thomas Walsinghame's henchman, One Yngram
Frizer; Robt. Poley too, And Nichol Skeres, to dine and sup with Kit,
Who comming downe with doublett all unlac'd, And Doll with cap
awrye whom they did greet: 'Odso the Whoreson Strumpett 'tis,
herself!' Thenn call'd for wine a-plenty for them alle.

Meantyme, saith Marlowe: 'Here's ye five Playes, Will; of Henry
Sixt I have rewrit the whole; Likewise Andronicus and eke The
Shrewe; Of Richard Third reshap'd actes III to V; This, Comedie of
Errors I renam'd' – For you should know, my Lord, Kit was by waye
Of journeyman to me, this many a day.

So, whiles we wroughte, the other four carous'd Till Mistrisse Doll
now somedeal in her cups, Vowing she hath more matters to impart
That she before forgot, pray'd Marlowe mount Upstaires agayne to
hear those greate affaires Still all untold, still lock'd within her breste.
Unwilling, he writ there and thenn a verse, And mirthful show'd me;
of which more anon; Then sighing 'comp'ney'd her, as she did sue,
Above once more, till strook of halfe past two.

Then downe agen, when Doll perchance doth find The verse that
Kit had whilom wrote, and read It out, not pleas'd, my Lord,
methought; of which, Though, more anon. Then all for dinner call.

Now though it was the merie month of Maye We had a fire, for
'twas a dismal daye, And for the nonce, a-waiting for ye roste, Dol's
fancie was a slice of bread to toste, Whereto, when breade was
brought she begg'd the loan Of Frizer's poniard for a tosting forke.
Meanwhyle the rest, a-reading Marlowe's verse, Did rallye hym for
laggardrie in love; And Skeres did quote from Ovid's *Amorés* In Kit's
translation such lines as: '*My force Is spent and done*': and

> '. . . *Like one dead it lay,*
> *Drooping more thann a rose pull'd yesterdaye*'.

Then jesting wordes betimes to horseplaye pass'd Thoghe in good part, a push here, there a shoove, Till Marlowe, losing ballance, by ill-hap, Fell back on Mistress Doll, plump on her lapp.

Doll shreek'd with laughying; Kit with agonie, That had sat squaire upon ye poniard hot Which neither he nor any had espied, And so pierc'd to his vitals, poor Kit died.

All was confusion. 'Twas, Doll loudlie swore, No faulte of hers, and if to Justis broghte, She'll bruit all the secretes she has borne 'Twixt Marlow and yr Lordship, and before, Untoe the late Sir Francis Walsinghame; And name the Envoys you and he employ'd.

So all agreed, Frizer wolde take the Blame On plea of Quarrell and of Selfe Defense, Which all will sweere to, if Your Lordshipp's grace Will pardon, and grant all safe 'liverance.

They being gone away, to fetch the Watch And a Chirurgeone, I pickt up the Verse, Which same I for Your Worshipp now indite – The last poor tunefull Marlowe e'er did write.

> And soe, my Lord no more there doth appear
> From Your most humble Servant,

> > > Will. Shakspere

P.S. My Lord, excuse my wordy flight –
  Save in Iambics, I nor think nor write.

The last Verses writ by Christopher Marlowe, entitled:

To his Too Importunate Mistress

> Wait, lovely Laïs; loose thine eager arms;
> Restrain the warmth of those too ardent charms:
> I know that Youth's a stuff will not endure,
> But it will last a few more hours, 'tis sure.
> O Mistress mine, what art thou at? O fie!
> Time's wingèd chariot is not all that nigh!
> True, his fell hand thy beauty may deface,
> But what's the haste? Thou still hast years of grace;
> Certes, we'll gather rosebuds while we may –
> But – must we gather all of them today?

> > > > W. F. N. WATSON

DOROTHEA (DOLL) DOGSBODY (1576–1667) *Shakespeare's 'Doll Tearsheet'. Third daughter of Thomas (1535–95, steward to the Cecil family) and sister of Thomas, the actor. Godchild of Robert Cecil, whose mistress (or light-o'-love) she became; used by Walsingham and Cecil (Lord Burghley) as go-between and secret emissary. Accidentally killed her lover Marlowe during tavern knees-up; induced Frizer, by her favours, to plead guilty; and Shakespeare and others similarly, to confirm. Becoming notorious, was shipped to Virginia in 1614.*

In memorie of
my right welebelovyd friende
CHRISTOPHER MARLOWE
who died in a
Tragic Accident
at Deptford
30 May 1593

Alas, my Kit, how treacherous the fate
That by some blacke mischance cut short thy breath,
Thy lease of life hadde all too short a date,
From vaulting triumph to untimely death.
Not thirtie summers hadde passed o'er thy head
Before that fatal steele pierc'd through thy guts,
And now we mourn, as, valedictions said,
The cold grave's marble jaw upon thee shuts.
Thou fount of friendship and my source of playes,
Sweet Kit, thou wert my writing-kitte indeed,
Thine was the fecund pen that earned me praise,
I reaped the harvest, but thou sowed the seed.
And now, poor ghost, where'er thou mayest bee,
Thou ne'er wilt ghost another playe for mee.

Will Shakespeare

STANLEY J. SHARPLESS

1594–1616
Extracts from *Anne Dogsbody's Diary*

A NNE DOGSBODY (1578–1655) *Only daughter of Sir Walter Dogsbody, minor diplomat; sister of Robert and Chidiock. Anne achieved a certain notoriety in her youth for a series of ill-considered and ill-concealed sexual liaisons. In later life, ironically, she became a fanatical puritan, reputedly a friend and confidante of Cromwell himself. She attempted – not surprisingly – to destroy the candid diaries she kept during her youth. Happily, though, a few fragments were pieced together painstakingly by the great family archivist Hugo Dogsbody in the 1870s, and these illustrate, if nothing else, her rare ability to attract literary talent.*

2 May 1594: I have of late formed a sentimental attachment with Master William Shakespere of the Globe Theatre, a very pretty fellow who weareth an ear ring. Lawks, how he doth prattle! I swear he hath more words than the Lexicon. He loveth me, I do believe, as I love him, but alack we must needs keep our love hid, for 'twould never do to broadcast my affection for a low actor; besides, there is the small matter of a wife he hath away in deepest Warwickshire.

23 August 1594: My friendship with Master S. continues apace, and so that we may go abroad together I have taken to covering all my visible parts with singed cork, and affect to be the veriest blackamoor! Strange to relate, when I am in this guise my Will doth my will (a merry jest, is't not?) with more than customary vigour, which pleaseth me well enow, for I confess (this being my most priviest journal) to being uncommon lickerish.

8 October 1594: W.S. tells me he hath written some very pretty sonnets about his mysterious 'blackamoor'. Though I fear he will have no more success with these than with his precious play-writing (I have perused some scenes and i'faith it is sorry stuff), yet I shall will my Will to do what he will well (Lord, I am merry tonight!).

13 February 1595: Alas, my Swan of Avon (for thus he braggadochio'd posterity would dub him, though I preferred the Swaggering Turkeycock of Southwark) is flown! He hath formed an intimate friendship with Mr W.H. and I doubt not that each hath had his paw in t' other's doublet. For a certainty Master S. hath not shaken his spear in my direction for a month or more, whether I played the merry blackamoor or no! At Christmas-tide he express'd an interest in red-hot pokers but, though my tastes (unlike, I thank the Good Lord, my religion!) are catholick, I gainsayed the proposal as unnatural i' th' extreme. Well, we parted on good terms, and I leave God to judge him and all lisping bum-boys when the time cometh.

9 June 1598: Forsooth, the poeticall tribe must have something about 'em, for I am lately attached (as often as possible, i' faith!) to Master John Donne, courtier, poet and philosopher of metaphysick. At first the poor fish was circumspect, believing his papish background (now, I thank God, thoroughly renounced) would cause my father to wax cholerick and forbid our liaison. In truth, the dear old gentleman is growing desperate to marry me off and, regarding a young man about court as a certain improvement upon a play-writing pederast, throws us together with monstrous winks and leers.

24 April 1600: Master Donne continues to visit my bed, though he talks precious little of marriage. Well, he suits me well enow, though he doth compare our love with some mightily strange things: here nauticall instruments, there the terrestriall globe itself, and even a blood-gorged flea! Faugh – my own gorge rises! God preserve us from these brain-sick intellectualls. But, he is a worthy successor to Master Shakeshanks in that, when we have swyved our fill, I amuse myself with such merry jests as: 'Hast thou done, Master Donne?' and 'Tonight my John Donne is a veritable Don John!' He likes my quips and swears he will work 'em into his verses, though I doubt I shall get any of the credit.

3 February 1602: Alas, I am undone! My second poeticall lover has left me, like the first, for the arms of another (one Ann More) and e'en now they are married. Doubtless she hath a sweeter pair of bubs than mine, and doubtless too he shall ere long be comparing 'em with some out-landish Tropickall fruit or the like. My only solace is that I hear his father-in-law (seemingly a deal more fastidious than my own dear papa) is set on procuring his imprisonment for this clandestine marriage. May he languish long in a cold cell, and dream of the sweet body he hath so cruelly spurned!

16 January 1616: Post-scriptum on the affair of Master John Donne. I have lately heard on the grape-vine that my one-time lover, sated at last with lechery, has thrown himself into the arms of a chaster bride, namely Mother Church! E'en now this monstrous hypocrite preacheth in Lincoln's Inn upon the perills of fornication! But I have this Doctor Donne over a barrel, for I shall choose my moment to publish abroad the following lines, written and dedicated to me in his own fair hand:

The Farte

Humbly dedicated to Mistress Anne Doggesbodie, whose bodily lineaments do so sweetly belie her name

Get thee behind mee, most unrulie farte!
Or rather, since from my behind thou came,
Get thee before! That cur shall take the blame
Which doth, by dint of subtill canine art,
Distract her from my amorous intent.
Yet wait! For may not devious logick prove
Thee, stynking farte, an emblem of my love,
Her bedchamber's most fytting ornament?
Thou'rt aerie, insubstantiall, yet hast pow'r,
Like love, to move both beggar-man and king!
Thus may the vilest emanation bring
Love's fragrance to this everywhere, her bow'r.

PETER NORMAN

1600
John Donne

THIS MS. WAS found, together with a gold locket containing a faded lock of hair, in the secret drawer of a bureau belonging to Lady Anne Paramount, formerly Anne Dogsbody. The projected elopement never took place; a rumour survives that the eloquent lover actually *did* contract a secret marriage, but with his employer's daughter, confessing in his later, more sober years as a dignitary of the Church of England that his behaviour as a young man had been regrettably wild, particularly with regard to the fair sex. In this connection it may be of interest to note an entry in Lady Paramount's diary of 1626: 'All throng to Paules this Lent to heare the Deane preaching on the *Penitentiall Psalmes*. I trust *he* hath repented who preaches of penitence to others. A fine thing when Youth is pass'd to weare a gowne and speake sorrowfullie of sinne . . .'

> Come, my Caninia, come; soft, lest we rouse
> The kennell'd Guardians of thy prison-house,
> Thy growling Father, whose imperious Paw
> May strike our Loves with threat'ning of the Law,
> Thy whining Dam, who dreams her precious Pup
> By some devouring Wolf snatch'd fiercely up.
> Come, let me loose thy Leash, and draw thee hence;
> A stronger power claims thy Obedience.
> Nor to thy customary Collar cling;
> Leather must yield to Gold, and that's my Ring.
> See where mute Sirius sheds his chearful light;
> Fear not those beames which bless our nuptial Night,
> Nor torrid Season men the Dog-days name,
> Scorch'd with the imprint of a purer Flame.
> Come, from thy perfum'd sheets so softly steale
> That none shall hear the Houndling at my Heel,
> Nor dog our pilgrim footsteps, as we track
> Love's right true end, which knows no turning back.

MARY HOLTBY

1600
A Madrigal

THE FOLLOWING fragment, which appears to have been written in emulation of the work of the English madrigalist Thomas Morley (1557–1603), is presumed to be by Chidiock Dogsbody (1580–1645):

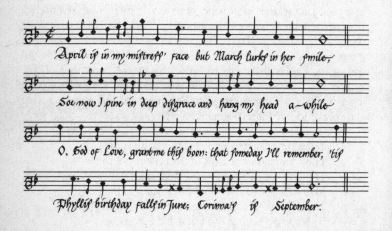

April is in my mistress' face but March lurks in her smile,

So now I pine in deep disgrace and hang my head a-while

O, God of Love, grant me this boon: that someday I'll remember, 'tis

Phyllis' birthday falls in June; Corinna's is September.

NOEL PETTY

1601
Sonnet Composed by *The Earl of Essex on the Eve of his Execution*

FOUND AMONG HIS effects by Robert Dogsbody, and smuggled out of the Tower by him:

R OBERT (later SIR ROBERT) DOGSBODY (1568– 1602) *Son of Sir Walter, and brother of Anne and Chidiock, the composer. Eventually accused of complicity with Essex and executed for treason. Two sons, Rupert and William.*

All lovers lose their heads: once dispossest
By Fancy, Reason needs must flee the court
That once her sceptre sway'd – her sage behest
Unheeded now, her sovereign rede unsought.
But of their frenzy lovers ne'er complain:
So dire the draught that Fancy doth dispense,
To all who drain her potion it is plain
Such madness is the sweetest sort of sense.
    But every spell, albeit strong, must fail
    Some time: the lover sees with eyes made keen
    Again that she he did as Venus hail
    Is nothing but a false bedizen'd quean.
    But sense regain'd, alas, is branded treason:
    I lose my head by having found my reason.

MARTIN FAGG

1605
The Gunpowder Plot

WE CAN NOW be reasonably sure that one of the Dogsbody family was implicated in the Gunpowder Plot. Whoever he was, he cannot have enjoyed this Satire; several hundred copies were discovered by Nancy Dogsbody in the attic of the family home, having presumably been bought up to prevent their being circulated.

    Go to, I will not name thee, for to break
  Thy secret is myself to love the stake;
  But this I say, and may he grasp who thinks,
  That DOGS have BODIES, and their bodies stinks

Which other beasts avoid or do desire
According to their nature. So, when fire
Runs in the blood, as sure in yours doth run,
No salamander can resist the fun.
Ask Fawkes, and Catesby of the noisome breath
What drew them to your side, brought them to death?
From that foul kennel where they found your name,
Who set them snuffling for the stink of flame?
Agog to live in fire, they sniffed from thee
Their burning passion for incendiary,
And cast to set the frame of things alight,
Fanning the cosmos into red and white.

That Parliament needs fire, I'll not gainsay,
But single elements may not hold sway,
Save in their realm; the place of fire is Hell,
As these conspirators by now know well.
Thou DOG! thy BODY in the upper air
Yet burns to join its odious fellows there!

PAUL GRIFFIN

1606
The Scottish Play:
The Birth of a Legend

ANOTHER ITEM FROM Thomas Dogsbody's collection:

Excerpts from Richard Burbage's Diary:

Mondaye: We beginn rehearsing Will's latest tomorrow to openne newe seeson: *Macbethe*. Fine part for me. Murder, battles and a good death. Pavey plays my wife, which is fine by me. Dogsbody plays my servant, Seyton. He will be dreadful, but at least I shall get a chance to kick him. I shall make one, if not several.

Tuesdaye: Will has clearly taken leave of his senses. Instead of starting on the new play, he said he wanted a newe style of acting, whatte he called 'a method approach'. I asked whatte was wrong with our olde method of learning his lines and thenne speaking theme gude and loude soe thatte the groundlings could heare everie worde. But he wolde have nonne of this, soe we spent the whole daye improvising scenes from Lady Macbethe's mother's childehood and pretending to be trees. I said I was a sycamore as that was howe I felt. Will Kempe was the onlie one who laughed.

Wednesdaye: We hadde to improvise being witches and thenne col-oures, and thenne items at a banquet. Here I gotte fedd uppe and said I felt like a stoup of ale and whatte was more, I was going to gette one at the Mermaide. Onlie a weeke to our first performance ande we have donne not one line of *Macbethe*. Took Pavey home with me and we did two houres hard laboure as Macbethe and his spouse. He is a talented boye and verie versatile. After this, we even worked on the scripte for a while.

Fridaye: We start doing the playe, but Will says we muste use our owne words. 'You are using mine, Richarde,' he cries. I telle him they are whatte I have learnte and I know no others. We alle beginne to hate the verie name Macbethe and instead calle it the Scottishe playe. Home with Pavey, but didde no rehearsing. We coulde not beare to.

Tuesdaye: The first performance of . . . that Scottish playe was a disaster. No one seemed to knowe their lines. We were booed offe the stage. Soe muche for our trye to please the Scottishe kynge. 'Lette me never heare a line of this playe,' cried Mastere Heminge, but Will began to saye that it was because we had notte had the time. He talked of startinge rehearsals with a monthe or two of discussion. 'Aye, Will,' says Kempe, 'butte howe will we eate and drinke until thenne? Shalle we notte learn your lines and roar them out to the groundlings till we have gotte it right?' And he didde wink his eye at me . . .

E. O. PARROTT

1614
Raleigh in the Tower

From the diary of Jeeves Doggesbodye, brother of Jermyn and trusted manservant to Sir Walter Raleigh:

These I founde, while I dyd diligentlie searche on *Sir W. Ralegh's* behalfe through certayn papers, hee beeing fast in the Towre for resons of State. The said Sir W.R. bade mee sette in ordre the said papers, that his gratious Maiestie's servants myght not be misled in the matter of Sir W.R.'s loyaltie to *England's Solomon*. This I have endevored to performe, albeit with much toile, but seeing that Kinges are lykewise iealous for the honour of theyr Predecessors as for theyr owne, sith they are as it were an *Union* of *Gods Anoynted* (U.G.A.), I made bolde to convey otherwhere certayn verses, *item*, lines writ on an occasyon well-remembred from the raigne of our gratious Soverain Queene *Elizabeth* of blessed memorie, somethyng unheroique in tenour and peradventure to the lewd, smacking of dis-loyaltie to the said Princess, and *item*, verses which our Poet dyd himselfe cast asyde, being his first replie to *Master Marlowe's* prettie conceit of the *passionate Shepherd*, later and wyslier mended in the dittie 'If all the Worlde and Love were yong . . .'. As to this Dyscard, the witte is curious, but sith our *Rex Pacificus* waxeth contrariwyse *Bellicosus* when the *Divils Smoak* is lauded, it semed beste to mee to remove these verses together with the former, lest his Maiestie become yet further ynflamd towards Sir W.R. rather than assur'd of his loyaltie to his Maiesties Royal Person.

> Give me that trollop on the quiet
>   Who took my cloak to walk upon . . .
> I had to scrape and save to buy it,
>   And what'll put its bloom back on?
> My frowns of fury, groans of rage,
> Must perish on this private page.

Mud you'd think would hardly harm her –
    Some other aid *could* have been given –
She can't resist creating drama,
    But what a way of getting even!
    On to the satin bouncing,
    Over the flounces flouncing,
    Into the mess
    Goes Bloody Bess,
    And dunks – infernal gall! –
    Pearls, rubies, lace and all.
My cloak was *great* (and dry) before,
But I can't wear it any more.

Raleigh's Reply to Marlowe's Passionate Shepherd

My withers totally unwrung,
I hear these rustic pleasures sung,
Since others rank so far above
Such simple briberies of love.

Better to plough the pastoral field
And teach its barren womb to yield
The grateful tuber's shapely form,
In summer sweet, in winter warm.

Forget the fading charms of roses;
I've other scents to tempt the noses
Of girls, who'll shun the rural scene
To taste the joys of nicotine.

O'er sparkling eyes to pull the wool
What need, if plate and pouch be full?
A surer lure, ye hopeful studs,
Are fuming fags and steaming spuds.

Time tames a timid lust for health –
Come, virgins, try Virginia's wealth,
And shepherds, learn to draw the nub-
Ile nymph with tuber and with tube.

False swain, whose smooth and lying lips
Would cheat the fair, you've had your chips;
Forbear – be sorry that you spoke
When all your hopes go up in smoke.

MARY HOLTBY

1616
The Death of Shakespeare

How grave my Will, who now a grave doth fill,
Until he had his wanton will with me.
I willed it thus: a willy-nilly Will
Was not the Will I willed my Will to be.
Now Will hath left, yet leaving, leaves a will –
Which will remains, altho' my Will be gone.
These leaves he leaves embody all his will:
His disembodied will I look upon.
  The guerdon for my wifely faith? A *bed*
  (The *second*-best) – for which I firstly paid:
  The bed whereon he took my maidenhead –
  And then essayed and laid (the jade!) my maid,
  And many another strumpet, trull and harlot –
  Until my toadstool stew despatched the varlet!

JEMIMA DOGSBODY née Foote (1553–1632) *Wife of
Nicholas. Became cook to the Shakespeares at New Place, Stratford-on-Avon, in 1613, three years before Will's sudden death from a
mysterious intestinal disorder. She continued in Mistress
Shakespeare's household for the first years of her widowhood, enjoying,
it is said, unusual privileges for a servant; and eventually retired to
her native Redditch with what was – by the standards of the time – an
enormous pension.*

NOTE: This ms. was added to the Dogsbody archive by Jemima Dogsbody. The poem has been declared authentic by no less an authority than Dr A. L. Growse – by his own confession the greatest scholar of all time, and a ruthless demolisher of the megalomaniac pretensions of others. Certainly, the elephantine tedium of its word-play lends extra motive to Shakespeare's evident desire to spend as little time as possible in the company of a woman capable of perpetrating such a literary atrocity.

MARTIN FAGG

1620
The Voyage of the Mayflower

ELIHU DOGSBODY to his aunt, Lady Anne Paramount, in England:

> First Street
> Plimouth
> New England
> Christmas, 1620

Madam,

We are at last safe arrived in this place after great tribulation on the seas. Our ship the *Mayflower* was tossed like a very mayflower in a thunderstorm, and very shortly made us more mindful of a sewer than a flower. After five weeks at sea, Master Godbehere declared that the King was head of the Church after all, and demanded to be returned home to Scrooby. A week later he came out for the pope of Rome. The Master was for committing him to the deep, but Mr Bradford had him close confined, in which state he still lies, Mr Bradford daily calling on the devil to come out of him. Master Godbehere speaks no more sedition, but mutters in a low voice that he wants to go home.

I must say that tho' Mr Bradford is a fine leader, I cannot but feel that to arrive on these shores in such a season as this was an ill-timed piece of planning. Words cannot describe how cold it is, and the general bleakness and barrenness of the land do not at all accord with the prospectus we were offered in London. Also, there are reports of wild, painted men lurking near our settlement. There is talk that we are come to landfall in the wrong place, but Mr Bradford says firmly that we are where the Lord would have us be.

It has been decided by town meeting that my name is not fitting for a servant of the Lord, and I am henceforth to be known as Master Godsbody. I mention this in case my name should chance to be writ in any legal document you may be drawing up.

Your affectionate nephew,

Elihu

Post scriptum. If you or the other charitable ladies should raise a scheme to send food parcels to this benighted land, they would be a great relief, our stock of weevilly biscuits being very low.

NOEL PETTY

1640
Nick's Joke Book

DIVERS SHEETS FROM Ye Collected Jestes, Japes, Riddels and Contes of Nick Dogsboddy:

Questioun: What is ye difference twixte a Hawke and a Handsawe?
Answeir: A Hawke flyeth o'er ye wood; a Handsawe maketh a short cut through it.

Rede me this Riddel:

> Ye Lances gleamed, ye Armour shone;
> Kyng Crookeback cryed: 'On, Stanley, on!'
> Were I in noble Stanley's place,
> 'Twould bring a Teare to everie face.

Answeir: ONION (on-I-on).

NICK DOGSBODDY (1613–43)   *Court Fool, etc. (Son of Diggory Dogsboddy, lutenist and strolling player, and Honour Backe, goose-girl. 1623–8, child player; 1628, assistant, drudge and butt to Archie Armstrong, Court Fool to James I and Charles I. Retained by Charles after Armstrong's dismissal for insolence to Archbishop Laud. In 1643 made an untimely jest belittling Prince Rupert's victory at Roundway Down as 'Runaway Down'; Rupert riposted by setting his poodle 'Boy' at him in jest. Boy, lacking a sense of humour, tore his throat so that, with a last quip that 'Dog it seems doth at times eat Dog's body', he expired, mourned by several.*

Questioun: When is a Portcullis not a Portcullis?
Answeir: When 'tis a-loft.

Questioun: Prithee, what's o'clock, goode Master?
Answeir: Verily, sirrah, ye round thing on yon Church tower.

The Seneschall sayd to me, he sayd: 'Haste and tell Kyng Hal a fayr mayden waits withoute', so, quicke as Flasshe from Gunne, I sayd: 'Bring her in forthwith, Master Seneschall. I warrant she'll not be withoute for long.'

Questioun: Wottest thou on what Queene Anne Bulleyn broke her faste, upon Maye ye fifteenth of 1536?
Answeir: Nay, I wot not on what she break-fasted, but certes she had a brace of chops right soone thereafter.

Furthermore, one evening Queene Katharine Parr sayd unto old King Harry: 'My deare Lord, prithee drinke no more Wine this nighte. Remember what happened yesternight.' Thereto His Majestie, much displeasd, made reply: 'Go to, Kate, thou shrewe; nothing happened yesternight', whereupon the Queene sayd sharpely: 'Verie trewe, my Lord. And therein lieth my compleynt.'

W. F. N. WATSON

1642
The Closing of the Theatres

SIR RUPERT DOGSBODY (1600–1645)   *Elder son of Sir Robert Dogsbody. Loyal servant of Charles I. Enthusiastic but unskilled cavalryman; killed at Naseby.*

MANY PEOPLE WOULD say that the closing of the theatres in 1642 was not so much a triumph for Puritanism as a triumph for art and good taste. Interestingly, we now know that this view was held in some Cavalier circles at the time. The younger brother of the Cavalier Sir Rupert Dogsbody (1600–1645) was a playwright, William Dogsbody (1602–1645). We have a letter from Rupert to the Speaker of the House of Commons, enclosing the plot of a play by William and desperately urging a multilateral approach to the matter.

'I beg you, good Sir,' he writes, 'to heed the sufferings of such as ourselves and to put an end to the torture to which we are nightly subjected. Brotherly love urges me to plead for a merciful sentence on him with whom I spun tops and played Nine Men's Morris. A whipping will serve for him and his like, so only that the playhouses be rased to the ground, and all fined who attend unlicensed performances.'

Reading the plot, one can well understand why Parliament did exactly as requested:

WILLIAM DOGSBODY (1602–45)   *Caroline poet and playwright. Younger brother of above. Best known for short poems: 'Up, and to't, my pretty bird', 'Smothered in thy fragrant breast', and 'Fallen, we who fight for Love'. Author of fifty-seven plays, of which three survive:* 'Tis Mercy She's a Pimp, The Whore's Supper, *and* The City Innocent. *Enlisted in the Cavalier army after the closing of the theatres. Shot by an indignant farmer before Naseby.*

'Tis Mercy She's a Pimp

by W. Dogsbody

Count Scorccia of Gerona is in love with his virtuous twin sister Mercy ('Tumbl'd wee not i'th'wombe? Wherefore bee coy?').

She in desperation disguises herself as a pimp and hires a feigned astrologer 'to cast the Count's horoscope' – in fact to put him surgically beyond reach of temptation. The astrologer turns out to be a decayed English gentleman called Wearwell, so disguised in order to persuade two Geronese worthies, Orelio and Notrelio, to marry his daughters, who have, as he thinks, been seduced by Count Scorccia. In fact, these girls are leading lights in Mistress Mattress's brothel, owned by one Spurio and the disguised Mercy.

Spurio is really Mercy's long-lost swain, Apollo the shepherd-boy, formerly Prince Vagrante, who long ago left his father's kingdom to woo the beautiful young Countess in pastoral guise, hoping thereby to provide some excuse for masques, shepherds' merrymaking, and rustic clowns. Awake now to the realities of Caroline drama, he nervously waits for his true love to be served up *fricassée*, or for himself to be immersed in a bath of acid.

Wearwell, discovering the truth about his daughters, persuades Orelio and Notrelio to challenge Spurio and Mercy to a duel, or, to be precise, a quartel. Spurio kills Orelio, but Mercy, terrified, takes one of those well-known pills, reveals her identity, and falls senseless. Spurio, believing Mercy to be dead, chases Notrelio off and drags Mercy's body to Count Scorccia's charnel-house, where a procession of ghosts foretell some pretty nasty things. Spurio is on the point of stabbing himself with a poisoned dagger when the Count runs in and reveals that he has recovered from his operation, has been converted from his evil ways, and has become the Abbot of Gerona. Mistress Mattress and Wearwell's daughters come in and reveal that they have become holy nuns. Wearwell then arrives and reveals that he is Prince Vagrante's father, the King of Olbutsia.

There is now a touching scene in which Mercy awakes and believes she is in Heaven (song: 'Joy, O Joy, this dream unending'), before tearing her hair and rushing from the stage, hopelessly mad. There follows a terrible scream, and Notrelio returns in an agony of remorse, holding Mercy's bleeding head.

All sing: 'Away ye baits of world and pleasure', and pass round the poisoned dagger.

The subtitle of the play is *All in a Day's Work*.

PAUL GRIFFIN

1645–9
The Roundhead's Bible

THE PRAYER, inscribed inside his Bible, of Ezekiel Lay-Thy-Rod-Of-Affliction-Upon-Mine-Enemies-And-In-Thy-Great-Mercy-Grind-Their-Bones-To-Very-Powder Dogsbody, on the eve of the Battle of Naseby:

O Lord, in Thy Loving Kindness, cast down that Man of Blood, Charles Stuart, and all who consort with him in the oppression of Thine Elect; and by Thy Tender Providence, pitch them into the nethermost pit of fire, there to dwell in torment through eternity.

Lift up, O Lord, Thy Godly Vessel, Oliver, and let him be numbered at the last among the congregation of Thy Saints; for, verily, he hath smote the wicked hip and thigh and hath troubled the Abominable One in the privy lair of his infernal heart.

And do not, O Lord, on the morrow, altogether neglect Thy humble servant Ezekiel. Let him be cleansed in the Wash-Pot of Thy Grace and winnowed by the Holy Fan of Thy testing; and if it shall please Thee that he should survive this trial, let him continue steadfastly thereafter as a Living Tabernacle of Thy Praise. But if it shall please Thee that he should, in the defence of Thy Sacred Ark, succumb to the wrath of the unrighteous, let him sleep serenely in the soil of England until Thy Day of Judgement, and then come soon to Paradise.

Rebellion is as the Sin of Witchcraft.

The Damn'd Diſsenting Mar-Texte pitcht Head-first to Eternity by a bungling Fellowe-Rebel.

WOODCUT FROM A ROYALIST BROADSHEET (1645): A satirical representation of the accidental death of the fanatical Leveller preacher–soldier, Ezekiel Dogsbody.

NOTE: The pious wish of this doughty Puritan, a stalwart of the New Model Army, was speedily granted. While partaking of his breakfast the following morning, before the battle had even begun, he was slain outright by the accidental discharge of a comrade's musket and went, we presume, straightway up to glory.

MARTIN FAGG

*

It appears that this Bible was inherited by Ezekiel's younger brother, who outlived him to become a prominent member of Cromwell's government, since the manuscript of the following poem with its dedication was found tucked into its pages:

To my good friend,
Nehemiah Resurrection Day Dogsbody,
I present this poem, writ on the very day on which
Charles Stuart was compell'd to meet his Maker,
like so many better men before him.
Let God arise and let his enemies be scatter'd.
Vengeance is mine, saith the Lord.

John Milton. High Holborn. January 1649

On the Execution of Charles Stuart

Hence, vain deluded Prince!
    Who feeds on folly bites a bitterer bread:
Thou to the full hast fed,
    Thy boasted Genius fled from thee long since.
Men curse thy idle reign,
    When Fancy fooled thee that thou didst possess
A Nation's soul, no less.
    See where the man who self as God esteems,
Forced from those frantic dreams,
    His blasphemy beholds at last writ plain.

Farewell, thou King of debts and taxes!
Hell's edge is keener than the axe's.

'Tis vain the hero's part to play:
Think on thy second Judgement Day.
What posture then shall do thee good,
Arraigned 'Charles Stuart, Man of Blood'?
No struggle for reluctant votes
God needs, to cast thee with the goats.
Yet can I hear the coming age
Praise thy performance on this Stage:
A Martyr crowned above the scrimmage,
Fit to become a graven image.
Should men so soon forget the past,
Myself would turn *Eikonoklast*,
None raise the shattered Idol, nor
Such Shards to Royalty restore.

The head is off! and hark! the crowd,
To greet his passing, groan aloud:
Let others give their frenzy vent:
My mind is calm, my passion spent.

MARY HOLTBY

1666
Pepys's Diary: Before the Fire

AN UNPUBLISHED ENTRY in the Diary of Samuel Pepys. One of
three items discovered by Max Dogsbody in the course of his research
into the family history during this period:

1 September: Up betimes. To the office and anon by coach to Sir W.
Batten's, with my great cold still upon me and hoarseness. There
were some good ribbs of beef, and an eele pye, and stewed prunes.
There was a great deal of fine discourse, sitting after dinner. I drank
no wine, but metheglin, which did please me mightily. Mrs Pierce
was there, as fine as possible, having cut away a lace handkerchief

sewed about her neck down to her breasts almost, out of a belief
that it is the fashion.

In the company was a sober, civil man, Mr Lemuel Dogsbody,
who had been a Victualling Officer to the fleete, now with the Fire
and General Insurance Coy. He spoke with fine persuasion, explaining that so great had been the progress of house building and
of what the French call the Pompiers, that the possibilities of
conflagration were as naught, especially in our great city. So it was
that establishments such as his own were passing rich, being
forever with an intake of money yet with hardly an outlay from one
month's end to another. He spoke so much to my satisfaction that I
was resolved to place some funds with him in the expectation of
profit, and pressed upon him a bill of £300, which he accepted with
demur.

There was more merry talking, and singing by Mrs Clerke, a very
witty, fine lady, though a little conceited and proud.

Thence by water home late, put myself to bed in great content,
and so to sleep.

2 September (Lord's Day): Some of our mayds sitting up late last night
to get things ready against our feast today, Jane called us up about
three in the morning to tell us of a great fire they saw in the City. So
I rose . . .

NOTE: The entry for 2 September was in fact published, so that there
is no need to repeat it here.

W. S. BROWNLIE

LEMUEL DOGSBODY (1626–66) *Insurance broker
and business associate of Samuel Pepys. Perished while attempting to put out the Fire of London with one bucket.*

Mr. Secy. Pepys difcufsing wth Miftrefs Bagwell a place for her hufband Wm Bagwell as Shipps Carpenter -

SKETCH BY APPRENTICE NAVY OFFICE DRAUGHTSMAN OLIVER DOGSBODY: Inscribed 'Mr. Secy. Pepys difcufsing with Miftrefs Bagwell a place for her hufband Wm. Bagwell as Shipps Carpenter'. Initialled 'OD', it is dated 23 Jan. 1665.

1666
The Great Fire of London

FILE REPORT IN Royal Armouries, 3 September 1666:

To Master, the Royal Armouries.

On Friday last, on your bidding, to meeting in City to discuss Armes Trayde with D—tch men over theyre excellente ginn. These pesky warres, where oure shippes doe lyttle butt be laughing stocks, need calle for much discretion in meeting 'foes'. (I in disguise as travelling pox doctor.) Herr Hooch, theyre spokesmann, much in his cuppes, did offer to display theyre Flaming Rockett, which he did before the astonished co. A fearsome sighte, vanishing by Pudding Lane (a close alleye of cookes and such) with much sparkes and crackling. It would fright the Fr—nch when next we fight, as we doe every few yeares.

Herr Hooch most affable, his high spirits not quenched. He promises ready partes once oure warre with them ended. Thence to a bawdy house where Mr S—'s sister did accommodate us alle and merry too, and nexte morning (with vile head) to my cousin in Plymouth.

What news?

Parkin Dogsbody

D. A. PRINCE

PARKIN ('FIREBRAND') DOGSBODY (1622–73) *Elder son of Sally and Parkin Dogsbody, Senr., of Pudding Lane, London (both died 1666) and brother of Lemuel. Entered Royal Armouries as clerk, 1639; employed as arms-dealer during Dutch wars. Retired in 1667 after insurance settlement on parents' bakery. After brief association with Nell Gwynne, died of syphilis December 1673.*

1667
From Mrs Pepys's Diary

IT IS NOT WIDELY known that Mrs Pepys also kept a secret diary, much of which was destroyed by the puritanical niece who inherited the volume. However, Max unearthed some fragments:

January 1712: The joynt being a little burnt at dinner today, Samuel took occasion to complain of the maids and of the Sluttery of women in general, whereupon we had very high words, and so fell out. *Mais mon Dieu!* What is a little blackness of the meat compared to the Fire of London? Was not a man – and he a baker – the cause of that? It pleased me mightily to remind him that it was an English King that once burnt some cakes.

But now I am somewhat cooler I recollect that Samuel, *le pauvre*, is mighty troubled with the monies for the victualing of His Majesty's Navy, and the discovery of old mismanagements. *Ces hommes Anglais!* What do they know of housekeeping? Will they never have the wit to let a woman manage their affairs? *Ce jour-là, on le verra bien!*

JOYCE JOHNSON

1675
St Paul's Cathedral

PERCIVAL DOGSBODY made plans for a West Gate to St Paul's Cathedral which, he said, could be 'tacked on to' Sir Christopher Wren's larger and more flowery designs. He spent several months making sketches, writing notes and carrying out market research before submitting his ideas. Little remains of his toils, but painstaking labour with computer design programs has enabled us to reconstruct his plans. Dogsbody's diary reveals that Wren was 'most interested in the notions for St Paul's' but ultimately rejected them on the insubstantial grounds that they did not, in fact, provide access to the main building. 'On this petty oversight,' he continued, 'my architectural fortunes stumbled, never to recover.'

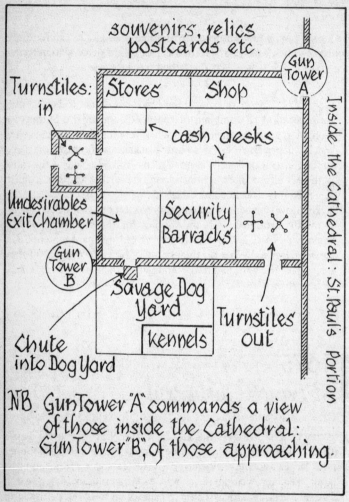

ST PAUL'S WEST GATE: Designed by Percival Dogsbody.

N. J. WARBURTON

1720
The South Sea Bubble

IN ANSWER TO his enquiry regarding the purchase of shares in the British South Sea Company, Horatio Dogsbody received this reply:

Dear Enquirer,

As you probably know, the Government is planning to offer shares in British South Sea for sale to the public this November. This is in line with the policy of creating a share-owning democracy, and it is widely expected to be the largest and most successful share offer ever mounted.

You will be sent a prospectus in due course. Meantime, here are answers to some questions that you may have:

Q What are the activities of British South Sea?
A These are many, varied and imaginative. Here are some examples:
  1. For making oil from poppies.
  2. For transmuting quicksilver into malleable and fine metal.
  3. For a wheel for perpetual motion.
  4. For making salt water fresh.
  5. For fattening of hogs.
  6. For eliminating the National Debt.

Q How much money do I need?
A As little as £2. There is no upward limit.

Q What financial benefit will I receive?
A There are two main benefits that can come from investing in shares: dividend income and growth in the value of the shares.

Q What about the level of dividends?
A The prospectus is likely to contain a forecast of the first dividend and indicate when it will be paid. You should note that a company is not bound to declare a dividend.

Q What about growth in the value of my shares?
A The British South Sea share price will be affected by many factors

including the view investors take of the company's performance and prospects. Obviously the value of shares can fall as well as rise.

Q Will I have to pay tax on my shares?
A No. Income Tax and Capital Gains Tax have not yet been invented.

Q Can I sell my shares?
A Yes, you will be able to sell your British South Sea shares to anyone who will buy them. The amount you will receive will be based on the market price of the shares when you sell.

Q Are there any special incentives for investors?
A Yes. Individuals who purchase British South Sea shares at the time of offer and retain them will receive vouchers entitling them to poppy-oil, fine metal, perpetual motion, fresh water, fat hogs, etc. Full details will be published in due course.

Being personally involved in the offer, I am, of course, not in a position to make a recommendation to buy shares. However, over the next few months there will be extensive publicity about the offer which should help you to make your decision.

> Yours sincerely,
> *Mandible Shark* (Bart.), J.P.
> (Chairman)

(This letter should be read in conjunction with the accompanying coloured brochure.)

W. S. BROWNLIE

Dogsbody's interest in these financial goings-on was considerable. Other letters to him survive in the Archive:

From: Messrs Perkiss and Grimes, Stockjobbers
       Benskin's Coffee House
       Exchange Alley
  To: Horatio Dogsbody, Esq.   5 August 1720

You must know, Sir, from the public prints, of the great advancement which has attended the purchasers of our recent offer of South

Sea stock. Great fortunes have been got by many of our clients; low fellows are become gentlemen, and gentlemen become great land-owners. We are sure you will not want the *Dogsbody* family to miss such opportunities in the future.

We believe South Sea will continue to flourish. However, numerous other projectors have brought to our attention schemes of merit whose great rise is yet to come, viz.:

For extracting silver from lead.

For importing Spanish jackasses from Spain to improve British mules.

For carrying on an undertaking of great advantage, but no one to know what it is.

Books will be open'd this day se'nnight at Benskin's Coffee House, and we will be pleas'd to enter you for 5000 *l* sterling in any or all of these remarkable offers on receiving your draft.

Think, Sir, how fine a fellow you will feel when *Mistress Dogsbody* is riding in her coach and six. We await your pleasure.

> Your servants,
> *Perkiss & Grimes*

N.B. We are constrained to advise you that it is theoretically possible for stocks to fall as well as rise; but we are mighty firm for the rise.

From: Winstanley & Smith, Solicitors
        Exchange Alley
  To: Horatio Dogsbody, Esq.   20 September 1720

We regret to inform you that Messrs Perkiss & Grimes are in no way to be found; but all is vexation here and many great families ruin'd.

Our account is enclosed.

> Yours etc.
> *Winstanley & Smith*

NOEL PETTY

HORATIO DOGSBODY (1660–1723) *Lawyer and staunch Tory. Brother of Percival, Wren's apprentice. An enthusiastic if rash player of the stock market. Against the advice of friends, invested heavily in the British South Sea Co. Took a walk on Westminster Bridge in November 1723 and was not seen again.*

1720
The Bubble Bursts

THESE LINES, ascribed by Horatio to Alexander Pope, are copied in a shaky hand on the reverse side of a letter from Horatio's banker. He gives the source as 'a magazine', but extensive research has failed to reveal which one. Pope did not include the poem in his collected works.

The Perils of Speculation

> 'Twould need a Sophocles and all his art
> The Terror and the Pity to impart –
> Sheer Penury defeats the poet's pen –
> Of what the South Sea Bubble did to men
> By bursting suddenly, when fill'd with hope
> Delusive as the Indian trickster's rope
> That seems to rise, in spite of rhyme and reason,
> And fools the gullible for a short season.
> One moment Greed and Avarice rejoic'd,
> Impervious to Caution's warnings, voic'd
> But disregarded by those mad for gain;
> Next moment, Ruin cried aloud in pain.
> The Whigs were all aghast: the King was caught,
> And e'en his mistresses – for all had bought
> The worthless stock – in the great web of lies,
> And England's monarch reign'd King of the Flies.

It could not be: the wily Walpole saw
His opportunity and from the maw
Of the monster Loss he snatch'd pale Gain
And sav'd the day by lessening her pain.
'Screenmaster General' by some he's known –
He cut Investigation to the bone;
Now for his efforts he's rewarded by
Being the First Lord of the Treasury:
Lucky 'twas for him he had no hand
In fashioning the scheme – I understand
'Twas luck not judgement – now supreme he reigns
And keeps the King and Cabinet in chains!

MARGARET ROGERS

1723
The Death of Sir Christopher Wren

HORATIO DOGSBODY clearly had an interest in poetry, since he also copied this item by Isaac Watts, presumably from the same unknown literary magazine:

Lines on the Death of Sir Christopher Wren

Upwards toward the skies his soul retires,
Rising above his earthly city's spires,
Fifty or so they must approximate,
To Saints and Martyrs all commemorate.
These now await to greet him as their own,
While animated cherubs, freed from stone,
And angels, lively wing'd, attend his flight.
What architecture now must meet his sight!
With what approving eye will he now scan
Th'eternal and celestial city plan!

> Bidding farewell to what he built before,
> He steps at last upon the crystal floor
> To take up residence in heav'nly halls,
> Vastly superior to his St Paul's.

JOYCE JOHNSON

1739
The War of Jenkins's Ear

CHARLES DOGSBODY (1695–1762) *Born 1695 into the bottling and pickling business of his father; specialized in the use of chemicals to keep meat fresh and glossy. Married Martha Worsfold 1725, and supervised laying-out of her body after her death in childbirth in 1727. After his death it was acknowledged that undertakers owed him a great debt, but they never paid it, so he was buried a pauper.*

EXTRACT FROM THE diary of Charles Dogsbody, bottler and wine importer:

This morn, a Capt. Jenkins came in, I sayd, What do you want, he sayd, an Ear. I sayd, I am listning, What do you want? What, he sayd, as the aristocrasy say, quit frequent, usually with a Ho, viz. What Ho (or Ho What). I repeted, What do you WANT? He sayd, come round this side, What. He sayd, I have bene to Spane, oh Very Nice, I sayd. On a bote, he sayd. Thus I past an hour or two whyle he talkd off his bote, I sayd at last, Do you want a bote in a botle, this being my skill. What, he sayd, what? Sir, I sayd, I have listned to your story, you have bene abroad, how can I help you? He sayd, see my Ear. I lokd, it was curvd, Verry nice, I sayd. Are you def, he sayd. Are you def, he sayd. Yes, I sayd, definitly. Definitly, my jok. Then he sayd, It is givn out I hav lossd an ear, tho I have not. Oh, I sayd. He sayd, And Mr Wallpoll wants to loke into my Ear. Is he an Ear fetisht, I sayd, bcoming bord by now.

He bcam angry. No, he sayd, Wallpoll thinks I have only one Ear. One what, I sayd. One ear, one mising one, one not mising, he sayd, the mising one being what the Spanyards cut of, the other ear stil in place. But I have two Ears, so I need an Ear. Where, I sayd, would you put it? Whereat, he sudenly produised an Ear, out of his poket. Capt. Jenkins, I sayd, That is an Ear. Yes, he sayd, and Wallpoll wants it. Why, I sayd, has he gon def, too? South Sea Buble burst in his lug-holl? No, he sayd, it is to mak the Hous of Parlement sit up and listn, when they see my Ear.

I bcam confussd. I mak you a happy new ear? I sayd. Its not yet Christmas, he sayd, No, I want you to put this spar Ear in a botle, he sayd, for an Ear can wax lyrical. At this, we fel aboute. And I brot out my solucion, and put his spar ear in it, he toke it. And payd for it. Two days later, he cam bak, saying, they have startd a war, bcause of my Ear!! But you stil have two, I sayd. I know that, he sayd, but it workd bcause *I had an earwig*. I let this pas. Why do you not, I sayd, cut of your Nose to spit your Face? War of Jenkins's Nostrill, he sayd, I will definitly think about that, Dogsbodie. We both rord, it was a Grat Historical Momment!

BILL GREENWELL

1743
The Methodist Revival

FROM THE JOURNAL of Enoch Dogsbody, Keeper of the King's Arms at Wednesbury in the County of Staffordshire:

16th May 1743

A black day.

At the hour before noon did arrive by horse that confounded itinerate Methodist preacher, John Wesley. He addressed a mighty crowd from a mounting-block in the market place and told them that salvation would be denied to those who drank strong liquor. All my customers left to mock and scorn the fellow but in a little while were singing hymns with him.

In all the remaining day I dispensed but two quarts of ale and a measure of gin which I swallowed myself to forget my ruin.

Then, I'll be damned, having quieted the mob and sent them on their way in prayer, the infernal Wesley comes knocking at the door beseeching me for the use of my privvy.

I did tell him to piss off.

V. ERNEST COX

1745
Lord Chesterfield

LORD CHESTERFIELD'S LETTERS to his son are well known. The following is one of the replies, a much rarer item. Philip Stanhope, the recipient of Lord Chesterfield's letters, was thirteen years old at the time of this letter, and attending Westminster School. It is surmised that he gave the letter to his fellow pupil Matthew Dogsbody to post. The boy forgot.

Westminster School, May 1745

Dear Father,

Thank you for the several letters which have reached me from you recently. It is very good of you to be at such pains to instil in me every detail of all the correct modes of thought and behaviour. I look forward to your letters with keen anticipation, and frequently read the passages of instruction to my schoolfellows, who envy me such a distinguished, wise, solicitous and learned parent. In their view, as in mine, you should be the King's first minister at least.

I am a little short of funds at present due to excessive expenditure on copies of Plato, Aristotle, etc. Could you forward me some more, as I am anxious not to fall behind your expectations of me?

I will terminate this letter now, as I am eager to return to my Demosthenes, which has reached a particularly exciting stage.

> Your respectful son,
> *Philip Stanhope*

NOEL PETTY

1745
A Lost Handel Opera

ORPHEUS DOGSBODY (1700–1787) *Fourth assistant percussionist at the Theatre Royal, Drury Lane. Married 1729 Harmonia Decibell, harpist in the same band; one son, Peregrine, born 1730.*

THIS SONG, THE only surviving extract from a lost opera by Handel, was presented by Orpheus Dogsbody. The work enjoyed a brief *succès de scandale* on account of the sensational Bordello Scene in Act II; for the Praetorians' Farewell Chorus, and because the opera was said to strike obliquely at the unfortunate Sophia Dorothea of Zell, George II's erring and banished mother. The Praetorians' Farewell is thought to have inspired Haydn's Symphony No. 45 ('The Farewell').

The Duty Cohort's Chorus
or Praetorians' Farewell, from *Messalina*

We are the Duty Cohort, set to keep
Safe watch and ward o'er Messalina's sleep:
Praetorians, in honour bound, decreed,
To serve our Empress at her lightest need.

Brutus is gone; be ready, Sextus, thou
Art next. Now, Tullius Longus to the plough!
Next Xanthus; then Nearchus; Balbo, 'shun!
Brace up, there, Fundus; she won't eat you, son!

Haste, Hortus! Leucon! Celsus – be not late!
Varens, away! Fallus, don't make her wait!
Now last, I, their Centurion so bold,
Advance; until past dawn the Pass to hold,

And prove that *Amor vincit omnia*,
(Including Messaline's insomnia).

W. F. N. WATSON

STAINED-GLASS WINDOW (*c.* 1750): Known as the Dogsbody Light, this window in the Lady Chapel of Tydde Parish Church is in memory of the Blessed Sapphira Dogsbody, who for almost four hours in 1745 selflessly detained a half-platoon of Barrell's Foot searching for Monsignor Donal Clanrackett, a senior Jacobite chaplain, who was thus able to escape. Her richly deserved canonization was withheld partly because she failed to achieve martyrdom by her ordeal, and partly because it was alleged that her utterances at the time were indicative of delight rather than despair.

1750
Gray's Elegy

SCRIBBLED IN THE journal of Anthony Dogsbody, gravedigger and rustic poet:

> The curfew toll'd the time to rise and work,
> The clumsy cows were ambling o'er the lea.
> Old John the ploughman gave a little smirk,
> And turned into the ale-house for his tea.
>
> Now evening drew apace as I embarked,
> My shovel snug inside my callous'd hand.
> I park'd it where my shovel's always park'd,
> And look'd the plot out, as the rector plann'd.
>
> The light was dim, and in the elm-tree's gloom,
> It hardly seemed to rate a second look.
> But some old fogey, feet up on a tomb,
> Was sat there, scribbling in a little book.
>
> His face was glum, his forehead in a scowl,
> And what he wrote was full of crossings-out:
> I hid, and gave a hooting like an owl.
> He raised his hangdog head and looked about.
>
> I did my swallow next, and then the cock,
> But this, it seem'd, could only set him off.
> He threw down words till nearly nine o'clock,
> Until, in fact, I gave a little cough.
>
> To dig a grave is not a noble art;
> There's few that rate it as a noble task.
> But any digger'll tell you from the heart –
> You need some peace. Was that too much to ask?

He heard the cough, and shudder'd like a fish
That's lately landed on some secret coast.
'What's that?' he cried. 'What is it that you wish?'
'Oh, sir,' I answered slowly, 'I'm a ghost.'

He backed against a headstone, turning pale;
He barked his shins upon my waiting spade.
I ducked beneath the nodding beech to wail –
By now the fellow really was afraid.

I hummed a tuneless, toneless sort of dirge.
'A hoary-headed swain, sir, I was born,'
I told him, as he teetered on the verge
And fell into a grave I'd dug that dawn.

'Oh, sire,' he call'd, 'my theme shall soon be chang'd –
The sentiments revers'd – the grave rever'd –
The lines shall be, and quickly, rearranged!'
At that he leapt up, ran, and disappear'd.

I lifted up some fresh and earthy sod,
And dug for fully quarter of the night.
I laughed. These fellows are so often odd
Who think a graveyard makes a sombre sight.

At length I finish'd, neaten'd up the edge
For where the coffin next day should be thrown;
I left my shovel standing 'neath a hedge
And took my son a baby finger-bone.

He put it with the knick-knacks by his bed,
The urn, the plaque, the finely polished skull.
And then I slept, to rest my weary head.
A digger's life is genuinely dull.

BILL GREENWELL

ANTHONY DOGSBODY (1720–79) *Born in Stoke Poges, Bucks., where he took up work as gravedigger in 1745 and continued to work at this trade until his death in 1779, which occasioned some difficulty, there being none to cut his sod. It later transpired that he was a versifier, and several bundles were recovered from his mother – he never married – after his demise, shortly before she used them to light a fire. He was the publishing sensation of the month of February 1780 in some areas of Clerkenwell.*

1751
Richard Trevithick and James Watt

LETTER DISCOVERED in an eighteenth-century 'Book of Good House-keeping' purchased in the year 1834 at the house clearance of the Trevithick family home, Redruth, Cornwall, following the demise of Richard Trevithick. This manuscript is now held amongst other archive material by Truro Museum, its chief curiosity being the technical drawings and mathematical notation which cover the reverse side of the domestic document. These notes are now recognized to be the writings of Richard Trevithick himself, mining engineer of that period and inventor of the steam locomotive.

From Miss Jean MacHuffie to her sister-in-law Mrs Ella MacHuffie née Dogsbody:

Greenock
October 1751

Dearest Ella,

Thank you my dear for your ever welcome letter. How time flies. It's five years to the day that the good Watt family took me in as their house-keeper. How feared I was that they should get to know that you and dear Flora were friends of mine, and of our part in sheltering dearest Flora and her maid. Good people though the Watts are, when they sing the praises of King George my heart still goes out to our Bonnie Prince pining away in France.

Ah me, but the years roll on! But I am for the most part content. Master James is a near grown man now but still much the same laddie, always asking questions, why this and why that? Only the other day he was watching me boil up the kettle for a nice cup of tea. 'Jeannie,' he says, 'why does that emerging hissing cloud flutter the lid like that?' These young lads, calling themselves men, but full of boyish questions! So I explained to him how when water boiled it gave off steam, vaporized water, that is. I told him how powerful it was, how it could lift the lid clean off an iron pot. 'Why,' I said, 'it's so powerful, if someone designed an engine big enough, built a fire fierce enough to boil a whole tank of water, why then it could pull wagon loads.'

He laughs, calls me a caution, then up and off to his room where he does all that drawing and writing. So I got on with my job. You just can't tell some folk! He'll make something of himself one day, I have no doubt.

Well, Ella my dear, enough of my prattle. You must pay me a visit soon and see Greenock before winter sets in.

Your ever-devoted friend,

Jean MacHuffie

CATHERINE BENSON

1759
The Capture of Quebec

JAMES WOLFE IS generally given the credit for the capture of Quebec; but it becomes clear from the personal account of his ADC, Captain Peregrine Dogsbody, that the responsibility rests somewhat differently:

'"The curfew tolls the knell of parting day",' began General Jim, his eyes glazing over as usual. The occupants of the Headquarters Mess looked at each other and groaned.

PEREGRINE DOGSBODY (1730–91) *Only son of Orpheus. Commissioned into the 37th Foot and served as a subaltern under General Wolfe, to whom he became ADC. Later transferred to Secret Service. Died of pox contracted in Paris during the Terror, when he was known as the Scarlet Pimp.*

'Here we go. Yet again. Give him another brandy,' ordered the Chief-of-Staff. 'Your duty tonight, Peregrine.'

They all tiptoed out, leaving me to listen to the General until the poem ended, the spirits had overtaken him, and he had laid his head on the table, muttering: 'The bosom of his Father and his God.' His voice was like a sick corncrake.

I motioned to the Mess Sergeant to carry him off, but it was too soon. He lifted his head and said: 'Battle tomorrow, Perry! We'll capture Quebec.'

My heart sank. We had no more chance of capturing Quebec than on any of the previous efforts.

'Don't worry, Perry. I'll read the men the Poem. That'll do the trick.'

He was crazy, and most of all about Gray's Elegy.

Next night, we rowed up the river in pitch darkness, towards the obvious landing place. The Heights towered black above us.

'Get the boats together,' ordered General Jim. 'I'm going to start the Poem.'

'Better not, sir,' I said. 'It'll warn the enemy sentries.'

But there was no stopping him. We listened for the hundredth time to the whole rigmarole. His voice was like a slate pencil, squeaking out of the darkness.

'Right, sir,' I said when he had finished. 'Now we must move on.'

'No,' he said. 'I'm going to go through it again.'

'Look, sir,' I whispered to the Chief-of-Staff, 'I can't stand this. Let's go ashore and get up that sheer cliff. Anything rather than "The boast of Heraldry, the pomp of Power"!'

'Good man!' he said.

Believe it or not, the General came with us, intoning. In a desperate effort to get out of earshot, we went up that cliff like monkeys. As I reached the top, I could hear 'For who, to dumb Forgetfulness a prey' coming up behind me; and so could the French sentries.

'*Non!*' they cried. '*Non! Pas l'Elégie! Ce n'est pas la guerre!*'

A shot rang out just as the General joined me. It dropped him at once, but didn't stop him immediately. Then, at last, there was silence.

'They run,' I said.

'Who run?'

'The enemy run. And I know why,' I added under my breath.

But he was dead, with the twenty-fifth stanza unfinished.

He never knew who it was who fired the shot.

PAUL GRIFFIN

1772
The Voyages of Captain Cook and the Discovery of Australia

THE FOLLOWING passage should have formed part of James Boswell's *The Life of Dr Johnson*. It would seem that this page of the manuscript was sent to Alexander Dogsbody for his approval and, through an oversight, never returned to the author.

Aetat. 63

Soon after the return of the voyage of Captain Cook to the South Seas which he had accompanied, Mr Alexander Dogsbody came to call on me, and as I was on the point of dining at the *Mitre*, I took the liberty of inviting him to join the company. He was much questioned on what he had observed, but to questions of climate, cultivation and manners, he could answer little, his mind being taken up with the *minutiae* of his botanical studies. After several hours of this, when there was a pause, with an air of self-complacency he turned to Johnson and said: 'Were not such sights worth three years of discomfort on board ship, Sir?' JOHNSON: 'Sir, you could have walked to Blenheim Park on naked feet and counted the petals of flowers and the veins in foliage with equal discomfort, and with as much information to entertain a company. Sir, I delight to hear of men, not plants.'

DOGSBODY: 'The savages, Sir, were of little interest. Some fled, others poked their tongues out at us.' JOHNSON: 'Sir, so would you, or any man, if a crowd of strangers came and began to make a close inventory of all your goods. Sir, a visit from bailiffs implies that a seizure of possessions will presently follow, especially, Sir, if you pocketed some in your collecting boxes.' DOGSBODY (not at all moved): 'The fauna there are most curious, Sir. The quadrupeds all have pouches in their skins, over the belly.' JOHNSON (rolling): 'Sir, a Scotchman will naturally discover animals with *sporrans*, since all of creation must be Scotch to him. We shall see a mass emigration of the Scotch nation to New Holland, in spite of its being called *New South Wales*.'

This brought a general laugh against Dogsbody, who was not at all mortified but stayed to be *crushed*, as Beauclerk said, with *vintage* patience.

A LEXANDER DOGSBODY (1745–1800) *Born in Duddingston, second son of David Dogsbody, Advocate, and Jean Buchanan. 1756–9, attended St Andrews University; studied divinity. 1760–67, secretary to Lord Lothian, with whom he com-piled* The Natural History of Haddingtonshire, *including the first description of the Bass Rock gannet* (Sula Bassana). *1768–71, secretary to Sir Joseph Banks. 1773–5, commissioned by the Royal Society to compile* The Flora and Fauna of Massachusetts. *Married 1775 Patience Goodenoughe, only daughter of Calvin Goodenoughe, Presbyterian Minister at Boston (seven sons, five daughters). 1779–1800, Presbyterian Minister at Charlestown. Died of scurvy at his house, 'Limeless'.*

1774   *Aetat.* 65

Dogsbody, who had just returned from America, told the company of the latest outrage at Boston performed by the American rebels. 'Sir,' (said Johnson), 'this is high dramatick stuff indeed. You tell us, Sir, of men throwing tea into a harbour, and when we are full of amazement, you replete us further by telling us they are disguised as American savages.' DOGSBODY: 'Sir, the fact was well attested by respectable witnesses.' JOHNSON: 'There can be no respectable witnesses in America.' BEAUCLERK: 'It seems redundant for American colonists to adopt a disguise of savages.' GIBBON: 'An ignoble savagery indeed.' JOHNSON: 'Sir, it is as if a lily *bleached* itself.' DOGSBODY: 'You are pleased to laugh, Sir, but we must consider the Colonists to be as much in earnest as the Parliamentarians in the English Civil War.' JOHNSON (puffing with anger, as he always did when hearing of that necessary, yet terrible rebellion): 'Nay, Sir, I do not argue the earnestness of Wilkes' rioters in their delight in breaking people's heads, nor of any riotous assembly in seeking destruction. I do not argue the earnestness but the *sense* of those who would lose an elegant commodity for an ill-considered principle.' BEAUCLERK: 'And who will drink cold tea made of sea-water?'

After Dogsbody had left the company someone observed that if Mr Fielding were alive he would write *Alexander Savage* as a companion volume to *Jonathan Wild*. JOHNSON: 'Sir, Dogsbody is too fond of the brutes. He will end on all fours.'

REM BEL

1773
The Boston Tea-Party

HENRY WADSWORTH DOGSBODY (1800– 1885) *Romantic poet, son of Alexander.*

HENRY WADSWORTH DOGSBODY looks back on the Boston Tea-Party:

Orange Pekoe

In the forests and the prairies
Round about the Big-Sea-Water
Lived a tribe of russet Indians,
All with names that fitted simply

Into one trochaic metre.
Oh! that I could write about them!
I would rather that than tackle
Jobs I really cannot cope with.
Still, here goes. I have to tell you
All the Indians I write of
Were Americans, and nothing,
Not a scrap, to do with real ones –
Indians like Mudjekeewis;
They were white men, in this get-up
So that nobody should know them,
Take their names, and have them punished.
They were there in Boston Harbour
('In' is speaking rather loosely)
To protest about the taxes
Levied by King George of England
On the tea they drank for breakfast,
Also for their tea and supper.

Loads of tea they seized and threw them
As a protest, in the harbour
('In' not loosely any longer),
In the harbour as a protest
Tea they threw, and having thrown it,
Went away to have their breakfast
And eventually supper;
Cocoa as a drink preferring,
All the circumstance considered.
Later this was well remembered
In the War of Independence.

So much for the great Tea-Party.
Now we leave the Orange Pekoe
Floating in the Big-Sea-Water
And return to Mudjekeewis
In the land of the Ojibways,
Where the beaver and flamingo
Make the task of writing trochees
So comparatively easy.

PAUL GRIFFIN

1778
Dr Johnson

DORINDA DOGSBODY (1762–1850) *Daughter of Matthew, and younger sister of Sarah. Both girls gained reputations as 'blue stockings', and both were 'pets' of the great Doctor. They remained unmarried, devoting their lives to the education of the poor and the sheltering of stray cats.*

A LETTER FROM Dorinda Dogsbody to her friend, Lucy Condiment:

> St George's Place
> London
> 2 March 1778

Dearest Lucy,

We were much complimented last Sunday. We were returning home from Church, where Canon Oswald Dogsbody, our cousin, had generously indulged us all with a two-hour homily on one of the Ten Commandments, which one, alas, I could not say if my life were to depend upon it, as I slept daintily throughout the entire sermon! Afterwards I was able to thank him truthfully for a most refreshing talk!

As it was a fine day, Father sent the carriage before and elected us to walk home. Who should be coming towards us but the famous Doctor Johnson! A burly man of stooping stature, his clothes food-stained and smelly, his face coruscated and crevassed and abounding in pock-marks, warts and other excrescences.

He greeted my Father most amiably and after some coughing and spluttering to clear his throat he expectorated a large quantity of phlegm on to the pastern of a passing horse.

Father introduced us to him.

'Aha! The Misses Dogsbody,' he said playfully in his hoarse voice. 'How de do?'

To which I returned cheekily: 'How de do what?', which reply delighted him hugely and, taking off his old half-wig, he laughingly mopped his greasy pate with a pair of bloomers drawn from a pocket of his greatcoat.

Upon my Father inviting him to our Sunday repast he pronounced himself delighted to accept and proud to be among such intellect (to my Father) and beauty (to us). Sarah giggled at this compliment rather more than was quite necessary and by this means engaged Doctor Johnson's sole attentions until we reached home.

The only memorable phrase I recall from the walk was his stopping suddenly to exclaim: 'Bugger! I've trod in some horse-shit.'

Upon arrival at our house and being ceremoniously shown into the drawing-room, the Great Man gladly accepted some Sack of which he drank huge drafts and then belched with great enthusiasm. My Father was pleased to take this as a compliment to the quality of our wine.

In his eternal quest for knowledge he declared himself eager to taste some of my Father's rarer wines, and to this effect imbibed, with much gusto and many eructatory indications of appreciation, a pint or two of old Madeira, some bottles of vintage Malmsey and a quart of pleasant mulled Sherry from the Canaries.

'Ah, stap me kidneys, that was good grapes. Ah Bacchus!!'

Which classical allusion brought us under the towering peaks of his giant intellect.

Dinner was served. The good Doctor was now sweating profusely; great drops pouring from his craggy brow down the red carbuncular nose from where they dripped noisily to his soup, which noise was soon drowned by the great din created by his huge lips slurping the scalding broth from the ladle.

Herewith some of his Table Talk:

'Hm, tasty drop of soup that – got any crackers? Ooh! I say, lobsters! Any man, sir, who hates a lobster is a fool – pass the mild beer. Gracious this mayonnaise is very good – burp!' (here the first of many complimentary belches, hiccups and eructations).

'Gad, this is a splendid fowl, may I trouble you for the spleen, Sir? Pass me some crackling, Miss – crunch – yum yum, any person, sir, who eschews Pork Fat is a cretin – please oblige me with some roasted 'taties, Ma'am . . . I declare that the potato is the fairest legume in creation, we have much to thank Sir Walter Raleigh for. An individual who cares not for Potatoes is a Tollwaddle. I'll gladly accept some Dumplings, Miss – berowp!!! Better out than in, as the poet says.'

'Aha, salad! Some asseverate that a mixed salad is for rabbits; any fellow who so avers is a numbskull and a bodysnatcher. Pass the Burgundy – glug, slurp, bola bola bola' (here Doctor Johnson's stomach took up the discourse). 'Pass the Fartichokes! Ha ha ha!' (a jesting allusion to that Vegetable's notorious propensity for creating wind).

'Begad, a fine pair of turbot. My compliments, Ma'am. The turbot is a noble fish – those that deny this fact are misguided galleymurphies and incorrigible rogues to boot. Pass the rough cider and oblige. Glagaaaaatch!'

With this he was sick over the Cinnamon Surprise.

'Phew! That's better – a good puke airs the guts.'

And after pissing in the umbrella stand the great man took his leave with much ceremony.

As ever,

Your friend,

Dorinda Dogsbody

JULIAN JOY-CHAGRIN

MATTHEW DOGSBODY (1730–1807) *Solicitor. Cousin of the more famous Oswald. Married 1758 Clarissa Faintly; one son, Jonas, two daughters, Sarah and Dorinda. Friend and benefactor to Dr Samuel Johnson whom he greatly admired and emulated, to the extent of touring the Highlands of Scotland in 1788, following in the great man's footsteps.*

1779
Dr Johnson

FOR DORINDA DOGSBODY (aged seventeen) from Samuel Johnson, for her birthday. It would seem that the Doctor kept no copy of his generous gift, for it has never been published before, so far as can be ascertained.

The Vanity of Feline Wishes

Thoughts on seeing a cat boarding a ship bound for America.
Dedicated to Dorinda and her cat, Spots.

Let all domestic cats adventurous
Be warned: better to be a pamper'd puss
Than, on a sudden feline whim, to stray
Far from home, exploring as you may
The vessels riding proudly in the port,
Wishful of engaging in the sport
Of rat-catching; know that these stately ships
Are not intended for mere pleasure trips;
And should a cat, intent on a wild chase,
Stay long, he soon may feel the waters race
Beneath him, as the tall ship slips away!
Too late then for repining, puss must stay
And share the sailors' fate: now tempest-tost,
Now sick to death, now given up for lost.
　But, should this feline voyager survive
The dread Atlantic, to disbark alive
Upon America's estrangèd strand,
What ills may he not meet on ev'ry hand?
A cat, accustom'd to a sceptred isle,
Must learn to love Rebellion's savage smile,
And get his living 'mongst the dogs of war:
For Independence was not gain'd by Law;
And, though George Washington's July decree
Claim'd Freedom for the erstwhile Colony,
Who knows what violence over there exists
Among the rebels and the anarchists?
　No, my feline friends, let not vain wishes
Tempt you from your tasty fireside dishes!
Travel's very well, but you should know
What you're going to, before you go:
Republicans may not want loy'list cats;
They may feel happier 'mongst home-grown rats.

MARGARET ROGERS

1780
The Gordon Riots

'BLEEDING' BASIL DOGSBODY ('The Sleeping Shrewmouse') (1699–1797) *Only son of Percival Dogsbody (1650–1793), architect. He was a bare-knuckle boxer, who lost more fights than any pugilist of his age. He was reputed to have been beaten by many blind contestants, elderly invalids, and even several ladies. His boxing academy, an advertisement for which appears below, was also unsuccessful, Dogsbody being regularly injured by his mildest pupils.*

FROM AN ADVERTISEMENT in the *Sporting Buck*, 1730:

> Basil Dogsbody will be pleased to meet gentlemen desirous of instruction in the scientific arts of defence and destruction at his Academy in Covent Garden, where the theory and demonstration of that robust and manly British tradition, with its comprehensive repertory of feinting, sliding, ducking, bobbing, weaving, gouging, biting, holding, hitting, and inflicting extraordinary pain, will be vouchsafed.
>
> Gentlemen of a particularly cowardly or delicate disposition will be accorded the most solicitous and tender treatment, to ensure that they do not suffer the inconvenience of burst noses, split lips, black eyes, fractured jaws, bleeding livers, ruptured spleens, punctured lungs, broken ribs, or other damage resulting in unacceptable distress.

Basil Dogsbody, however, was the confidant of men in high places, in particular William Brummell, father of the celebrated 'Beau'. William Brummell was Lord North's private secretary, and secretly engaged Dogsbody to infiltrate the Protestant Association with a number of his pugilists. The object of this was to dampen any excessive opposition to his master's Catholic Relief Act of 1778. On the one night (June 1780) that Dogsbody's private army was elsewhere (at a drunken gipsy coronation in Epsom), Lord George

Gordon summoned a rally in St George's Field. Fifty thousand demonstrators marched on Westminster, beating Members and destroying private property, including the Dogsbody Gymnasium.

William Brummell never really forgave Dogsbody, but many years later in 1794, when 'Beau' got his cornetcy, the young man visited the 95-year-old Dogsbody, now blind, who gave him this advice: 'Hit them Sir, when they're not looking; and when they are, run.'

RUSSELL LUCAS

1784
Robert Burns on Dr Johnson

MATTHEW DOGSBODY acquired the following manuscript from an Ayrshire innkeeper while en route for his tour of the Highlands in 1788. The document, which is somewhat obscured by whisky stains, had apparently been accepted reluctantly as payment for a round of drinks from a passing poet/singer who was temporarily out of funds. The hand is that of Robert Burns (1759–96).

Lines on the Death of Samuel Johnson, Esq.

Ye louns wha lust for mortal fame,
See how the Gods your heroes claim:
Great Samuel is gangin' hame
    Tae tak' his rest.
An' God help those wha bear that frame
    In oaken chest.

For tho' yon deep an' mightie mind
Was crammed wi' wisdom o' mankind,
His body too was sair inclin'd
    To lay up store.
An' Samuel's girth is weel enshrined
    In London lore.

Yon couthie Boswell oft he'd tease
An' nothing Scotch cuid e'er him please
Till, journeying tae the Hebrides,
   He seem'd tae thaw,
When plied wi' barley broth an' peas
   An' usquebaugh.

Ane service fine he did for Ayr:
This Boswell's mind he did ensnare,
Which did the young laird keep doon there
   In London's lap,
An' Auchinleck's braw lasses spare
   Fra' Jamie's clap.

An' as for me, I own my due.
When told yon Diction'ry had grew
To hold all words that poets knew
   In sober print,
I made a vow tae use a few
   That were nae in't.

NOEL PETTY

1788
The Vicar of Selborne

THE FAMOUS *Journals* of the Rev. Gilbert White of Selborne make mention of one Goody Hammond, his 'weeding woman'. After White's death in 1793, this same Goody Hammond was employed in a similar capacity by Canon Oswald Dogsbody in the neighbouring village of Faringdon. When he expressed interest in her former master, Goody gave him a journal she had kept in the course of the year 1788 while at Selborne. The entries are intermittent, but White's influence is clear.

30 January: Severe frost. Icicles. Parson stirs not.

17 March: Gentle thaw. Weak sun. Parson puts head out.

21 April: Much rain. Couch-grass starts. Parson eats two eggs at break-fast.

13 May: Ground much dried. Speedwell blossoms. Parson comes forth, marches about garden, rubs hands together.

6 June: Showers. Warm. Dandelions rampant. Cabbage moth appears. Parson busies himself with bean-sticks.

17 July: Burning sun. Bindweed rank. Thrips swarm. Parson shuns heat.

12 August: Great dew. Sultry. Daisies blow. Blackfly spreads. Parson very earnest for stray-berries.

16 September: Thunderstorm. Dock spreads. Moles erupt. Parson hides himself.

4 October: Hoar frost. Nettles die back. Parson eats little.

3 November: Thick mist. Swallows seen no more. Parson shuffles about; makes a hibernaculum in his study.

10 December: Heavy snow. Cold wind. Parson stirs not.

NOEL PETTY

1789
The Influence of the
French Revolution

FOLLOWING THE START of the French Revolution in 1789, a wave of republican sentiment swept through the United Kingdom and, on the express command of King George III himself, a new internal security force was set up in Whitehall. Young James Dogsbody, brother of Alfred, was among those recruited and his first assignment involved a journey to Scotland. There he was to maintain surveillance over the poet Robert Burns, who was notorious for his republican sympathies and whose verses, 'A Man's a Man for A' That', appeared to extol the virtues of the new and dangerous doctrine of universal brotherhood.

Dogsbody met Burns in Dumfries, where the poet was employed in the Excise, and it appears that the pair, having broadly similar interests, struck up a close friendship. They spent a number of convivial evenings together (see South-West Scotland Local Constabulary *Gazette*, vol. 893) and Dogsbody was, indeed, the person addressed in Burns's lost bacchanal, 'We're A' Fu' the Noo, Jimmy'.

Another poem, also addressed to Dogsbody, is printed here for the first time:

The Epistle to James Dogsbody
(A Young English Friend)

I lang hae thought, my English friend,
    Some good advice to proffer,
From wisdom that the ancients kenned –
    The best a Bard can offer.
'Twill help you thro' this Vale o' Woe,
    An' win Dame Fortune's smile,
An' bring bad tidings to your foe
    An' mak' him rin a mile.

'Twill gain you, if the truth be told,
    The favour o' the lasses,
An' fill your pouches fu' o' gold
    An' keep topped up your glasses.
'Twill mak' a guid man o' a bad,
    A scholar o' a dunce;
So pin your lugs back, Jimmy lad,
    I'll no' but say this once.

Gin aiblins clish-ma-clavers scrieve
    A daimen-icker thrave;
Gif oughtlins houghmagandie nieve
    Han'-wale it wi' the lave;
Tho' pickle, plackless pechans pyke
    An' a' gae tapsalteerie,
In orra duddies, on yer byke,
    Awa' an' ca' yer peerie.

The top secret papers relating to Burns's security classification were regrettably lost on Dogsbody's return journey, having been inadvertently left in a stage-coach somewhere near Burton-on-Trent.

T. L. MCCARTHY

1797
The Person from Porlock

ALFRED DOGSBODY (1773–1835)   *Publisher. Educated Lewisham College. Married Edith Catsup, poet, author of* From a Lewisham Window (1796) *and* Lakeland Scenes (1805) *under her maiden name.*

LETTERS TO Miss Edith Catsup of Lewisham from her fiancé, Alfred Dogsbody:

Bella Vista
1 May 1797

My dearest Edith,

It is with sadness that I have to tell you that Dr Muddle advises me that I must remain here at least another week until I am quite recovered. In my disappointment I sat at the parlour table here in 'Bella Vista' and wrote a small poem.

> Here Alfred sits, so sad and so alone,
> In exile from his love, Oh! hear him groan.
> Pity his plight who sadly sojourns here,
> All separated from his dearest dear.

This verse cannot of course bear comparison with your own lyrical effusions but it well expresses my thought.

I am sure you will be interested to learn of an incident that occurred on Friday last. Dr Muddle has encouraged me to be much in the air and on that day I walked a great way, almost twenty miles, through Dunster and Watchet to the small village of Nether Stowey, which the Country people call 'Stoy'. There I knocked at the door of a cottage to beg a glass of water and the door was opened to me, not by the expected cottager but by a gentleman in somewhat dishevelled dress whom I instantly recognized to be Mr Samuel Coleridge, the poet. I remembered him well from that unforgettable evening at Mrs D'Lally's soirée in Croydon only six blessed months ago when I was first introduced to your dear Papa. Mr C. professed to have no recollection of the occasion and my civil approach was brusquely rejected by him. He appeared to me to have just awoken from sleep but complained that he had been interrupted in the course of composition.

I was able to obtain the water I required at another cottage and so to return to Porlock in a bad humour and in a carrier's cart.

I must close now if I am to catch the post,

> Your ever affectionate
> *Alfred*

> Bella Vista
> 2 May 1797

My dearest Edith,

To my great surprise I received, only this morning, a note from Mr Coleridge in his own hand! I am invited to call once more at his cottage and he writes in the kindest terms about Mr Catsup – yet yesterday he professed no knowledge whatever of him or of Mrs D'Lally!

I shall take with me my copy of your own dearest book of verse – in case Mr C. is not acquainted with your poems. I cannot suppose he will be interested in my own writings but I think I will take a copy of the draft I prepared last week when I had heard the story of the old seafarer. You will remember that I wrote to you of the man's strange appearance and of the adventures to which he laid claim. His name is Albert Ross and he is well known to the people here and in Watchet, but he does not leave the coastal resorts and I do not think Mr C. will have heard of him. There is much that is truly poetical in his wild eyes and unkempt dress.

I will render you a faithful account of our meeting very soon; Dr

Muddle makes no doubt that I shall be able to return to Lewisham in the very near future.

(Some more personal matters are not copied from this letter.)

JOHN STANLEY SWEETMAN

1798
Lucy: The Truth

AN EXTRACT FROM the memoirs of Lucy Dogsbody:

I was an ordinery girl as livd in a cot, it was not far from Dove, where the springs is, hence the apple orgid that was still over yond hill, I was spining most of the time. this was a Nice life, also Pritty, there was flowrs and things, not much mony, but it was posibl to make ends meat. Until he come along, that is. I was just puting out my cloths to drie one day, it was clowdy & c. but no nead to worry, we never had much travelers in these parts, Evryone knowing it was untroden and such. Lucy, I says to my self, it is a Nice life out hear at, or at any rait near the springs, you know. well, I was suning myself, and suden I here a Sound, what is it, I bethought. WHO can it be, I had to dash, I was waring not a stitch.

anyHow I run rit into him, this gangly bloak, with a stuby litl pencil, he was not loking my direcsion so he didn't see me at first, then Halo, he says, what have we hear, nakid as Nature intended. No Point you rapping me, I said, I am only an inocent spining maid, and noone loves me, on acount it is Untroden Ways round hear. WHO are you, anyways, I said, runing inside my litl cot, ware we had an English fire blazzing, as in customery round this part. Tidles, I said to my cat, help. there is a strainge man, he is outside the door. help, help. Well, next thing, of corse he is in the cot door, and he says, only you and the cat, aha aha, funy lauf he had, aha aha, and then next, it was the usural rutine, you know, about him not having human feres, I was a rose, I was a vilet, it was a happy dell you hav here, my dere, and some coblers

·165

LUCY DOGSBODY (1778–1869)   *Born in the spa of Dove, or at least not far from it, Lucy was orphaned at an early age, but continued to live in her humble cottage and make what she could as a spinner. Destined never to marry, she took up writing late in life, and composed her memoirs between 1846 and 1849. Tending to the illiterate, these memoirs were briefly serialized in the* Cumberland Life *magazine after her death at the ripe old age of 90.*

about he was on a Nature Rambel, he was a Naturist, would I just be sportive as a faun againe, he was Nuty.

So he rapped me.

Now the rely funy bit, he finishes himself, wich took ages, he was gowing *out-in-out-in-out-in-out-in-out-in*, then a paus, then the same againe, only somtimes he went *in-out-out-in* at the start, or put an extrer *in* in, but basicly the same rithm, he finshes anyway, and Then he says Hows that for a Prellude. Blody long, I said, and he curld rit up. Whats your name, it was now. Lucy, I said, now go away, youve had your evil way. I tell you, I said, I've run rit out of motion, and also force, I'm nackerd, put it away. But no. He went over to the tabl, did some scribl, and then he says, your hips are like mountans, where I did feel the Joy of my disire. allways the same, these clevr dicks. He comes at me againe, says, I was borne in Cockamouth, I thought, oh dere No you do'nt, and wippd his thing into my spining weel. That coked his goose a bit, as it was by the fire, he scremd out lowd.

AnyHow he cloked me one, I was unconcous a bit. when I came round, he was siting at the tabl, puting down some more scribl. You've got an ichy quill, I said. No, my dere Lucy, he ansers, you are the one star in my sky, as I have just writen down. Yes, you guest, he was a rimer, and a pritty pore one, if you ask me. as you know, my own taste is for the pros side of things, with specal keeness for stremes-of-concousnes, and here I am, noked up by a New Rommantic, of all peepl. I've herd of you, I said, this may be Untroden Ways, but its a pound to a peny your that Mr Wordswith, who lives up at yond cot the other side of yond hill. You pratt, I said.

Tippicl. He smakd me rit round the head with his hand, and then cloked me againe with a bunch of pebls tied up in his hankicheif, whak, whak. I clapsd, and the cat ran off, so did he. I thought, Lucy, this is IT, youre a dead one, and past rit out on the flore.

After a bit, I came rownd againe, blody all over, but, namby that he was, proberly shagd out by his efort erlier, he had not killd me. He had gone, meanwile. I mopd myself up, and made myself a cup of hot coco, wich is what I allways do when I'm rapped round here, and was about to loke for the cat, when clakity-clak, I herd his horse comming. I new it was him, becaus he was speking to himself out lowd, he said Mersy, if Lucy should be dead! What did he expect, he was a nuter. Quikly, I hid in the shed, wile he went round and round, and then, I swere this, he startd diging a grave, pausing only to do more blody scribl. What was he doing, you ask. Well, it was dark, you see, what hed done was, hed found a bag of my wool on the flore, quit a hevy one, and, tippicl rimer, had gone all soft, they make usless murdrers these rimers, he was weping.

So he could'nt see, and he was Berrying MY WOOL! Berrying it!! Then he preforms a weard rite, he stiks in a hole lot of roks, stoans, bits of tree & c., and he lokd fertive in the extreem. Then he goes away, he thinks, I've killd her! It was enow to mak the cat lauf, in fact it did when it cam back, and I told it what had hapend. So if you are in Rydal Mount way, and you see the famus Lorreat, Will Wordswith, you have a lauf too. No wonder evryone thinks hes daffy.

BILL GREENWELL

1805
Ode on the Battle of Trafalgar

WRITTEN BY Joseph Dogsbody, later Vicar of Woddlestone, to be declaimed by himself at the village celebration of the famous victory over the French fleet:

> Now of England let us sing
> And of George the Third our King,
> But e'en as the church bells ring
> Let us weep;

For Lord Nelson is gone West
With a bullet in his chest
While consigning Boney's best
To the deep.

(An effective start, I think. Perhaps 'gone West' fails to reflect the dignified tone I wanted, but I will revise later)

In the sultry tropic heat

(Check this; is southern Spain hot in October? If not, 'sleet' will do)

Gathered Nelson's rare élite;
Never met so brave a fleet
As was his.
The *Leviathan* was there
And the *Mars* and *Téméraire*
And the *Agamemnon* fair
Off Cadiz.

(Thank goodness I saved Uncle's old Admiralty list. It may be out of date, but nobody will know)

Gallant sailors good and true
Never seek for much ado,
Just a modest prize or two
And some booty.
But they cheered from all the decks
When they saw Lord Nelson's text:
ENGLAND EVERY MAN EXPECTS
TO DO HIS DUTY.

(Splendid. I didn't see how I could get that in, but it goes rather well)

Then Lord Collingwood with verve
Closed with Admiral Villeneuve   *(Good!)*
And he sliced the French fleet's curve
Clear in two.

(At least, according to the Morning Post. *Actually, with details still coming in, I'll leave a few lines to fill in later with colourful details about marlinspikes and so on)*

. . . .
. . . .
. . . .
Hove in view.
Then, with victory hard nigh,
From the mizen top so high
Did a coward foe let fly
With his ball;
And the discharge from his musket
Fragile Nelson's tiny husk hit

(I'm having second thoughts about this triple-rhyme idea, but it's too late now. Tom Moore never seems to have this trouble)

Tum-ti tum-ti tum-ti tuskit
By his fall.
Soon that murd'rous enemy
Was shot down into the sea,
But the Joy of Victory
Greatly marred he.
For Lord Nelson, our great pride,
Lay below the decks and died,
As with final breath he sighed,
'Kismet, Hardy.'

(I believe the Last Words are a matter of contention, but I prefer this version, which is in any case less likely to be misunderstood by the locals)

So let's raise an English cheer
And an English glass of beer

(Here I hope the Squire will lead the way)

And remember sharp and clear
While alive.
Tho' our hero's breast was burst
Yet the Frenchies he reversed
On October twenty first
1805.

(Pronounced 'eighteen-five'. The Vicar has promised to lead the cheering, so that everyone will know I've finished)

The End.

NOEL PETTY

R EV. JOSEPH NEHEMIAH DOGSBODY (1786– 1880)   *Vicar of Woddlestone, Dorset, 1810 until his death. Married 1815 Amelia Bunney; one son, Richard, one daughter, Isabella. A great trencherman and amateur poet, he enjoyed robust health to the last.*

1805
Lord Nelson

FROM THE CATALOGUE of Dogsbody & Dogsbody, wine-sellers:

> BRANDY. Bottled straight from the Cask in which the body of Lord Nelson was brought back to London from his flagship *Victory* after the Battle of Trafalgar. 5 shillings a bottle.

JOYCE JOHNSON

1809
The Battle of Corunna

AN ITEM FROM the notebook* of an Irish clergyman, the Rev. Charles Wolfe, records his conversation with Corporal Arthur Dogsbody, an army veteran, whose testimony was later to emerge in a somewhat different form:

* There is no indication of how this notebook became a part of the Archive apart from the rubber stamp mark in the corner of the cover: 'The Property of the British Library'. Ed.

'What were it like?' said the old man. 'It were f— dark for a start, begging your pardon, padre. We buried him by dead of night. Had to put him in quick, see? No pickling in Spanish brandy this time. In he had to go. The Major said so. We had one foot on the boat, like.'

'But you had had a great victory, had you not?'

'Great victory f—, begging your pardon, padre. Fine sort of a victory that ends on a troopship, heading out into the Bay of Biscay in January. That weren't no victory. Cor, it were bitter cold, and, like I say, f— dark. Buried a few men in your time, I dare say, padre?'

'Indeed, yes.'

'Ever try a bearnet for digging? A f— bearnet? When you can't see a thing, and the ground's solid rock, and when the fog comes down the moment the moon gets up, and the lantern's not working proper?'

'Well, no. I don't actually recall . . .'

'Not with the R S M standing over you, with his hairs bristling, and the slightest noise makes you want to jump over the rampart?'

'No doubt the band, and the solemn prayers, buoyed you up.'

'Not a drum was heard. Not a funeral note. Weren't allowed to make a noise because of the Frog sentries. Course, we said a prayer, but it were the shortest prayer I ever heard, and it weren't for the General, lying there, well out of it, in his greatcoat. It were for us.'

'Even so, that great Scottish soldier lies in a grave dug by his loving men.'

'With f— bearnets? You're joking, padre. We hadn't hardly started when the bell went for off, and Froggy started shooting again. It were up sticks for us, and the devil take the hindmost.'

'Time perhaps for a simple epitaph?'

'Not a line. We dropped him and ran. It were a sod, padre, begging your pardon, a proper sod. You can quote me. Bearnets! F— bearnets!'

(I am doing my best to render this account by a simple soldier into verse.)

PAUL GRIFFIN

1812
The Luddites

JOSIAH DOGSBODY (1784–1842) *Carter, Brassington in Lancs. Fourth son of Gurney Dogsbody. Left the family home after many feuds to make his way in the North. Maintained an interest in all radical and revolutionary matters. Arrested and accused of spying for Napoleon but escaped to France, replaced in gaol by a wandering pie-seller who happened to be his double. Died of a rage on returning to England.*

JOSIAH DOGSBODY was noted for his fiery nature. The formation of a Luddite group in his village in Lancashire seemed to provide him with an excellent platform for his high ideals. The doings of the group, scrupulously recorded during its brief existence by an unknown secretary, have come down to us in pamphlet form. In this extract one of the group meetings is chronicled:

Jed. Rowbotham sent word that he could not attend and was sorry. Mistress Rowbotham had required him to remain at home to fix the butter churn which had gone wrong. Josiah Dogsbody sent word that he would be late and thus he missed the main item for discussion. Carter Wainwright declared that much time was being lost in writing out handbills announcing the intentions and the past deeds of the group. He had therefore managed to acquire a small press which would greatly speed the aims of the movement in our area. His words inspired us and we were all full of a keen determination when Josiah Dogsbody burst in and saw the press. 'Pray, let me be the first, masters,' he cried, his eyes shining. With that he drew a lump hammer from beneath his cloak and set to with a will . . .

N. J. WARBURTON

1815
The Battle of Waterloo

THOMAS HOOD'S 'The Battle of Waterloo' was never published and most of the verses have been lost, except for the last two, which came into the possession of Alfred Dogsbody:

> The one-time Corporal then knew
>   His Day of Doom had come,
> With piles of dead upon the field
>   And piles upon his bum.
>
> And everybody praised the Duke
>   That brave and booted gent,
> Who won the day and meted out
>   The Corporal punishment.

JOYCE JOHNSON

About one Dogsbody in the Napoleonic era we know little more than his name, Nestor, and that he was a 'dogsbody' – a publisher's dogsbody, or copy editor, employed to make sure that Jane Austen maintained her record of not mentioning great events in her novels. This appears to be a passage that Jane tried to slip into the second edition of *Mansfield Park*:

'The Emperor Napoleon,' announced Fanny, 'has been finally defeated in a great battle.'

'How unusual,' said Sir Thomas Bertram. 'Do you hear that, my dear?'

Lady Bertram sighed. 'Really,' she said, 'I cannot be expected to give my attention to such matters. I have promised to complete this embroidery for Mrs Jarvis in the village.'

Fanny persevered. 'There are to be prayers of thanksgiving for the victory on Sunday,' she said; 'and Dr Grant is to make a speech in the Square on Saturday afternoon.'

'How tiresome!' said Lady Bertram. 'He had promised to play bezique.'

'Come, my dear,' said Sir Thomas, 'we must shoulder our responsibilities. The servants will want the afternoon off. I must speak to someone.' He seemed unwilling to drink his tea. 'Some time,' he added.

'I am sure I do not know why *I* should do so,' complained Lady Bertram. 'My duties are onerous indeed, as are yours. Should not some other person be responsible?'

'My dear, I am not certain that this is our usual blend of tea. Was it not obtained from Humphries?'

'At Waterloo,' persisted Fanny; 'the Battle of Waterloo.'

Sir Thomas looked puzzled. 'The tea?' he enquired.

'The victory. It is to be called Waterloo.'

'Ah, yes. The tea, you see, has some other name. What is it, my dear?'

'Picquet,' said his wife. 'It was picquet, not bezique.'

Fanny, who had thought that contemporary history was passing unnoticed in the English countryside, was astonished at the consternation her announcement had caused.

PAUL GRIFFIN

Later, Nestor gave up Grub Street, took orders and was granted a living in Trimmer, the neighbouring parish to Chawton, Hampshire. He frequently visited his friend, and one day suggested she should write an historical romance, and when she demurred, saying that that would require more learning and poring over old books than she could possibly accomplish, he made the further suggestion that she deal with a very recent event. A week later he was presented with a tiny volume:

To Mr Dogsbody
The following short novel
is respectfully inscribed
by
His Obed't Humble Serv't
THE AUTHOR

Waterloo

Chapter 1

The Duke of Wellington was of a respectable family from Ireland which had risen in gentility and prosperity until he himself was now the Chief Commander of Europe, with several fine estates and £50,000 a year. Business took him to Vienna, where he enjoyed the intrigues of Ministers and Ballrooms. He had however only been thus engaged for about six weeks when news came that Mr Bonaparte, the former Emperor of the French, had arrived suddenly in France after his short stay on Elba.

Chapter 2

Tsar Alexander of Russia, a genteel young Emperor with pleasing manners and an air of melancholy, found the Duke looking not a little perturbed as he examined army lists.

'This is a great blow to us all, Sir,' said the Tsar. 'But is there not something a little amusing in all these quarrels over borders and secret treaties, now being so much wasted effort and business?'

'I was thinking of something very different,' said the Duke. 'We have no regulations of procedure for sentries when guarding abdicated Emperors.' He bowed civilly and went to write to his Quartermaster.

Chapter 3

Mr Bonaparte, the former Emperor, was of a respectable family in Corsica. An early success in his profession and general application had brought him and his family all of France and half the other countries of Europe. Those days were over, but he could not be content with a life of obscure retirement. He went off to Quatre Bras with

200,000 men, and having fought a battle there, then went to Waterloo, a fine flat battlefield between two hills.

Chapter 4

The engagement was as unsatisfactory as such meetings often are. Though only one side won, both thought they had the best right to victory, and some mistook right for fact. The Duke himself exclaimed that he was near to losing, and Mr Bonaparte is rumoured to be spending a good deal of his time on St Helena reporting his own success.

I abstain from dates, except to say that the battle was on June 15th. The Duke has now entered Parliament, though whether on half or double pay I cannot tell. True profit has been assured for the villagers living near the battle site, who make a good business selling mementoes to the curious. Eight respectable persons now possess the Emperor's hat and five the Duke's snuffbox.

THE END

REM BEL

1816
Jane Austen

THIS POEM WAS found in the collection of Alfred Dogsbody, but whether it was written by him or by his friend, William Wordsworth, is not known:

Jane

She dwelt among the untrodden ways
    That lie round Chawton, Hants,
And everyone who knows her says
    She lived without romance.

She told the children tales, she sewed,
    She waited for the gong,

And suffered, as was *à la mode*,
   Hours of inexpert song.

If ever she preferred a man
   Among the meals and chat,
Never a tremor of her fan
   Told anyone of that.

Thank God! for how are we to know
   If marriage tempers wit?
Emma is on our shelves; and oh,
   The difference to Eng. Lit.!

PAUL GRIFFIN

1819
Beethoven

FOUND AMONG THE effects of Hermann Hundekörper:

49 Singerstrasse
Vienna
17 November 1819

Good Sir,

I again submit to you my bill for repairs to your illustrious instrument, carried out on the 3rd, 4th and 5th day of August of this year.

I reply herewith to your communication which questions the amount owed. You ask, must it be? I reply, Sir: it must be! Indeed, sir, if it were simply a matter of tuning the instrument my price would surely have been too high. However, there cannot be many men of my profession who have to carry to their employer's house such tools of repair as I am needful of carrying to yours.

I do admit that I told you, through the medium of your notebook, which, as you say, is proof in writing, that my fees were the lowest in the trade, but at that stage I had not seen the piano in question. Your need was more, sir, for a master cabinet-maker than a simple piano-tuner.

I have much admired your Hammerklavier Sonata, for good music of an elevated kind is as food to me. However, your piano tells the sorry tale of your struggles in composition.

I am also, though a simple man, Sir, a man of dignity. I have few garments but those I possess I take pride in. The stains left after your outburst with the remains of your supper have proved impossible to remove and I have taken the liberty of adding the price of a new waistcoat and breeches to the bill for rebuilding and tuning the aforementioned instrument. For the libellous name-calling and insults hurled at me I make no charge. What price can be put upon a man's delicate feelings?

Finally, as to the cost of repairing your ear-trumpet, that is not a matter that can be laid at my door, Sir, since the bruising to my head and shoulders is proof enough of the reason for its now buckled condition.

I remain, Sir, in expectation of payment,

> Your humble servant,
> *Johann Hundekörper*
> (Piano-tuner)

CATHERINE BENSON

1819
John Keats's Diary

THAT JOHN KEATS kept a diary was unknown until this scrap turned up in the papers of Alfred Dogsbody:

. . . We were walking on Hampstead Heath in late evening, when some bird started chirping. It was a sparrow, as far as I knew, but Fanny stopped as if she'd been shot.

'The voice we hear this passing night,' she announced, 'was heard of old by emperor and clown.'

'It's cold,' I said.

'Imprison my soft hand,' she cried, 'and let me rave.'

'All right,' I said, 'but hurry up!'

'Darkling,' she went on, 'we listen . . .'

'You can darkle, Fanny love,' I said; 'but I'm freezing!'

'In a drear-nighted December, that would be true; but this is mid-May. Look – the coming musk rose, full of dewy wine. Oh, for a draught of vintage!' she said suddenly.

'The nearest pub's miles.'

'The Spaniards'll be open, up the hill. The day is gone, and all its sweets are gone. I want to burst Joy's grape against my palate fine.'

Joy the barmaid's a friend of hers.

It's a good job my memory's good. The sort of rubbish she talks comes in handy when I'm gravelled.

PAUL GRIFFIN

1830
The Rotten Borough Elections

SILAS DOGSBODY (1799–1874)   *A native of Rotenburgh. An opportunist by nature, he became agent to Sir Percival Crupper, MP for Rotenburgh, in 1824. After the Election of 1830 he offered his services to Sir Percival's successor, Horatio Fitzcrupper, and moved with him in 1832 to Staffordshire where he met and married Rachel Goodfarthing, a sturdy yeoman's daughter, who bore him thirteen children.*

1.   To Sir Percival Crupper, Bart.

Dear Sir Percival,

As your Agent, I have, I fear, some unpleasing intelligence it behoves me to impart. Since you first honoured Rotenburgh by becoming its Member in 1806, you have been consistently unopposed. This time, there is, alas, to be a contest. An inflammatory young Radical calling himself Horatio Fitzcrupper (on the strength of some alleged blood connection, albeit a *bar sinister* one) has proclaimed his intention to stand, animated, it seems, by intense aversion to your family. Do you know aught of the jackanapes's antecedents?

Yours most obsequiously,

Silas Dogsbody

2.   Beelzebub Club
                                                         Haymarket

Dear Dogsbody,

Damn the fellow's impudence! I know all too well who he must be – the scullion-spawn of a scheming little whore who had the effrontery to seduce my younger brother Peregrine (he is, as you know, now mouldering in New South Wales) when, as a boy of fifteen, he accidentally stumbled into her sleeping quarters after the Quim Hunt Ball. (I attribute all poor Perry's later frailties to this first blasting of his innocence.) When the housekeeper discovered the trollop to be in pup, she reported the matter to my saintly mother, who promptly slung the brazen little slut out into the snow. She died, very properly, in the poorhouse of a combination of typhus and puerperal fever. This bastard brat is patently the fruit of her low loins – he should have been stifled at birth!

That he should nurse a grievance against our family both astonishes and sickens me. But, surely, as a bastard, he cannot stand for Parliament?

Yours dyspeptically,

Percival Crupper

3.   Dear Sir Percival,

Balkwill, the attorney, declares that illegitimacy, tho' a bar to inheritance, is an impediment to little else; and that being a palpable bastard prevents one neither from standing for Parliament nor from subsequently sitting therein.

As the Election is to be contested, had you not better come down here?

Yours in perturbation,

Silas Dogsbody

4.   Pratt's Rooms
                                                      Piccadilly

Dear Dogsbody,

You know very well that my resolve not to allow my political perspectives to be warped by purely parochial considerations has never permitted me to visit Rotenburgh since my first election there; and, unhappily, a severe recurrence of the rheumatic gout I first caught on the field of Waterloo precludes my coming now.

You fuss too much, my poor dear Dogsbody! Rotenburgh has only a handful of voters and they are all in our pocket already.

Yours seigneurially,

Percival Crupper

5.   Dear Sir Percival,

It grieves me to drag back into your recollection events whose pain has obviously caused them to slip from it. Rotenburgh itself, as you know, has been a mere shell since the agrarian depopulation so touchingly chronicled in Mr Goldsmith's 'The Deserted Village'. It now has no electors at all. In fact, the only holders of the franchise are nine farmers – all once tenants of the Crupper Estate. I say 'once', because as a result of the loss of your unfortunate wager with the Prince Regent (as he then was) you were obliged to sell five of the farms to their sitting tenants for far less – once the long agricultural depression was over – than they were intrinsically worth. (You may recall that you bet the Prince that the Brighton Pavilion, which you damned as a 'monstrous carbuncle on the beloved face of Sussex', would be torn down by an indignant populace within a year of its erection. How rash – these soft Sussex folk are almost too inert and puddingy to breathe!)

I fear that these five farmers, no longer dependent on your whim, now assert that you have been the most negligent and rapacious of landlords. One of them declared in the tap-room of The Fleece the other day that he would rather vote for a gorilla than vote for you. To which another retorted that voting for you and voting for a gorilla would be one and the same thing. This unseemly sally was, I regret to say, received with gales of wild merriment by those who frequent this foul tavern.

Yours in deep embarrassment,

Silas Dogsbody

6.   Bacchante Club
                                                    Conduit Street

Dear Dogsbody,

I boil with rage at your tidings. But rage is impotent. Let us remain rational. We shall obviously have to *buy* one of these scoundrels. £10 should do it. Use your discretion.

Yours in direst dudgeon,

Percival Crupper

7.   Dear Sir Percival,

Alas, we are forestalled! The rogues have banded together. We must buy *all* their votes – or none. They demand £100 each.

Yours in extreme mortification,

Silas Dogsbody

8.   Semiramis Baths
                                                    Jermyn Street

Damn you, Dogsbody!

Your odious intelligence occasioned a return of the marsh fever I first sustained during my heroic exertions on the Walcheren Expedition in 1809. Only this stops my immediately coming down and, since I cannot now, it seems, enjoy the pleasure of personally evicting them, setting about the dogs with a horsewhip!

However, in sweating out the fever, I have devised a stratagem both to foil these grasping villains and to be revenged upon them. I enclose five promissory notes for £100, post-dated to the day after polling. See that one note is conveyed to each of these rascals. You will note that I have cunningly varied my signature to an extent that will enable you, when they are presented to you, as my Agent, for settlement, to denounce them as forgeries. I shall of course swear an affidavit that I never uttered them. Nothing will give me greater satisfaction than to learn that these blood-suckers have been taken up, tried, condemned and transported. They will have plenty of time to reflect on the Nemesis that inevitably overtakes dishonesty!

Yours righteously,

Percival Crupper

9.   Dear Sir Percival,

Calamity – we are undone! Somehow these fellows got wind of your wiles. Offering to discount the bills at £80, they presented them to Mouldering, your corn-factor. He has, as you know, never been quite right in the head since, as a beater, he accidentally strayed into your late father's line of fire during one of the grand old Rotenburgh pheasant shoots. The imbecile, without consulting me – and obviously thinking he was doing a shrewd stroke of business on your behalf – let the rapscallions depart with £400's-worth of your seed, feed and assorted livestock. They then hurried to the hustings and voted *en bloc* – FOR YOUR OPPONENT! It is my ghastly duty to inform you that you are therefore no longer MP for Rotenburgh.

I did not congratulate your nephew (as by your own account he assuredly is) on his victory, knowing that you will, with your notorious magnanimity, wish to do so in your own way.

Would that this were all! Alack, the fact that you never actually *were* at Waterloo – and never got further than Ramsgate on your way there – is now common knowledge. Also, that on the Walcheren Expedition when 'The good old Duke of York / He had ten thousand men / He marched them up to the top of a hill / And he marched them down again', you never even got to the top of the hill, being overcome by vertigo at the altitude of fifty feet. God knows how these things got out!

You can imagine how it afflicts my loyal quill to indite all this, but it is plainly my duty to apprise you of the universal contempt and execration in which your name is now held locally.

As a connoisseur of drawing, you will be interested in the enclosed – prints of which have been circulating in the constituency and exciting, I regret to say, much mirth among the lower orders.

Depicting you as it does, as a hairless baboon, with rather random excretory habits, it may appear to you a shade offensive in personal tone. However, you will, I think, agree that the artist (anonymous – but said to be our new Member) has secured a remarkable likeness; and it is altogether a minor *tour de force* that you will doubtless wish to add to your collection.

Trusting that this missive finds you in buoyant spirits,

I am, Sir Percival,
     Ever your most humble, obedient and attached servant,
                                        Silas Dogsbody

NOTE: He never received a reply to this letter, as on first perusing it Sir Percival went off in an apoplexy, aged only forty-nine. His passing is mourned in this extract from Creepey's Diary: 'That fat sot Crupper died in a fit this a.m. at the Beelzebub – *before* paying me the 600 sovereigns he lost to me at backgammon last evening. A swindling blackguard even in death! His brother Peregrine (*see Letter 2*) succeeded to the title, but was shortly afterwards pecked to death by a heat-crazed emu at Wagga-Wagga. *His* only issue, Horatio, could not of course, being illegitimate, inherit and the baronetcy was consequently extinguished. Nor did Horatio long sit for Rotenburgh, as it was one of the 143 seats disfranchised by the great Reform Act of 1832. However, in that year he was elected for a newly-created Staffordshire constituency – taking with him, as his Agent for the property he began rapidly to accumulate in that county, none other than Silas Dogsbody!

This transfer of allegiance supports the inference (shared, I am sure, by all close students of the correspondence) that Silas was playing a double game throughout. How else did the five farmers circumvent Sir Percival? The zeal and speed with which he and Lawyer Balkwill sold up all Sir Percival's local property (buying much of it in for a pittance themselves through nominees) suggests that he had, with the true Dogsbody instinct for keeping the Dogsbody bread buttered, sensed that the day of the Regency buck was forever over, and that the day of the Victorian entrepreneur was just over the horizon.

MARTIN FAGG

1836
The Alamo

LETTER FROM Captain Remington Dogsbody of the 13th Derbyshire Foot to Colonel Sam Houston. Preserved in the archives of the State of Texas.

                                                    as from The Rectory
                                                    Little Spreyton
                                                    Wiltshire
                                                    England
                                                    14 November 1836

Colonel S. Houston

   Dear Sir,

   I write as a visitor to your native country, not so very long ago a colony of my own, and I address you in your capacity as the apparent representative of the local army. It is this army which, so I gather, is proprietor of the out-of-town hostelry designated The Alamo. I wish, Sir, most strenuously to complain about the standard of attention I received during a recent stay at the place.

   I had travelled down the Chisholm Trail to Texas for some sun, and booked into The Alamo, which I thought charming, very much in the Spanish style, etc., after a preliminary recce. During this recce, I had some time earlier become mildly inebriated with a Mexican fellow called Santa Anna. He had with him a mass of homely peasants, all gaily dressed in their national uniform, and carrying ladders to and fro. Apparently – tequila is a most potent beverage – he had some grouse against The Alamo's staff, and it was from his lips I first heard of the place. The origin of his dispute was not clear to me, but I believe there to have been some anxiety that Mexico had accidentally been left out of the United States, and agitation that it could not immediately be designated Texico.

   Making my way through the Mexicans next day, I noted their strenuous labour (their hoes are very like English bayonets, and – their rain-dance being very similar to what we in England would call a soldiers' march – it looked for all the world as if they were preparing for battle, rather than tilling the fields).

   I staggered into The Alamo, my head reeling. At this point I must stress that the staff were most amenable, and happily accommodated my request to stay a week or more. The hostelry seemed a beautifully healthy place, its bedrooms open to the air, and – a delightful touch – there were bales of straw piled most carefully everywhere to ensure the security of the guests. The staff were apparently engaged in various refurbishments, and it was a time, I should guess, of holiday for women and children, for all were leaving as I arrived. Their affection for the 185 menfolk was most affecting. What they had done had their men been marching off to death, Heaven only knows! The men meanwhile repaired their wagons, the first necessity apparently being to turn them on their sides.

Further affability was to follow before the source of my complaint. This I wish to stress so that you may feel the full force of the injustice done to me.

Advised by the staff to watch our water – I perused my own with singular interest – we were nevertheless fed doses of rum nightly by Colonel Crockett, by all accounts the *maitre d.*, or 'wild frontier' as he was obscurely known. You may have heard of him. The cook, whose knives were admirably sharp, was a fellow called Bowie, who had invented a penknife to outfox a Switzer. A sumptuous feast followed during which I consumed portions of the Texan delicacy of dog, before falling into the perfect sleep of the dead, as the Alamese about me sharpened wits and implements for the next day's menus.

Now, Sir, imagine my sense of injustice when I awoke to find myself in a thoroughly deserted inn, shivering under a flimsy blanket, in a cupboard, and with no sign of the management anywhere. They had scuttled the place. And fouled it, Sir, too – there were traces of catsup on every door, and the unmistakable signs of barbecues having been left to incinerate themselves. All that remains with me as evidence of this sordid and fickle piece of American hospitality is a fragment of ballad left beneath my pillow, viz.:

> O rose of yellow Texas
> The musket Mexico
> From San Antone to Brownsville
> De-dum-de-dum-de-O.
>
> O Crockett Bowie Travis
> The prairie herds are fat
> O rose of yellow Texas
> The ol' ten-gallon hat.

I submit to you, Sir, as an officer and I hope a gentleman, that reparations need to be made if I am to regain my respect for the American way of life – one inferior, such is its duplicity, to the harmless style of the labouring Mexicans who are your neighbours. I was presented no bill, as such, but I believe I have offered sufficient documentary evidence to convince you of my having stayed at your army inn. A sum of your choosing may be sent directly to the address at the head of this letter, whence I am promptly returning.

I remain, Sir, as I hope you shall also be mine, your humble servant,

Remington Dogsbody
(Captain)

BILL GREENWELL

R EMINGTON DOGSBODY (1780–1836) *Served as a subaltern at Waterloo, and was afterwards seconded to Lord Raglan's staff upon the latter's succession to the peerage. Created Captain. An intrepid traveller, he preferred to leave his wife Maud, whom he married in 1810, at home. They had no children. He vanished on the way home from the trip of which he writes, having taken a short-cut through Cherokee territory.*

1840
The Death of Napoleon

NAPOLEON'S REMAINS WERE brought back to Paris in 1840. Thomas Hood's description of this event has unfortunately been lost, except for one verse, inscribed by the poet in Alfred Dogsbody's autograph album:

'Who lies within this coffin, pray,
  You now bring *à la carte*?'
'A Corsican,' they answered, 'but
  Naught but a boney part.'

JOYCE JOHNSON

1840
The Introduction of the Penny Post

ALTHOUGH GERARD MANLEY HOPKINS had left his poems to Bridges, one remained in Max Dogsbody's possession. It is of interest as showing Father Hopkins's joy at the long existence of Sir Rowland Hill's Penny Post (it lasted well into the twentieth century), and his troubles with the local postal service:

I met this morning morning's postman, riding
    Over the bareback down; how manfully his meddling,
    Perusing privately my post, coloured his pedalling;
His saddled guilt impelling all his gliding,
His cycled glide and guilt; for him no hiding
    His reading of my mail, my curious mail, my riddling
    Mail, whose dear, whose abstruse news, near to unsaddling
Him, baffled him, oh, him almost with me colliding.

Oh, the curses that broke then from him, the spoken oathing –
    Worse curses than verses span can: 'For one penny!'
His cry; 'Fast fly I, die I, degged my clothing
    For no fruit, meed, boot, need, none; save one penny, not any;
Under rain's pain, lightning's rod (ah God!) and I an old man!'
'Praise to Sir Rowland Hill still!' I cry; 'his ways uphold, man!'

PAUL GRIFFIN

THE SPORTING ORDER OF THE BOOT (19th century): Augustus Dogsbody, M.P., undergoing initiation into the Sporting Order of the Boot, a convivial club of devotees of fox-hunting. The lady is Catherine 'Skittles' Walter, 'the girl with the swansdown seat', celebrated fox-hunting courtesan and doyenne of the 'pretty horsebreakers'. The initiate had to drink a magnum of champagne from Skittles's boot while bearing the charming equestrienne on his back, thereafter performing several leaps that demonstrated her perfect seat. The insignia of the order was a diamond fob seal in the form of her boot. Sketch signed on the reverse by John Leech and dated 1843.

1844
The Factory Acts

THIS LETTER ON the headed writing-paper of Dogsbody Cotton Mills, the noted textile firm, was discovered, along with an assortment of items, in a strongbox marked 'T.D.', presumed to have been the property of the educationalist Thomas Dogsbody. Doctor Tom (as he was known, although there is no record of a doctorate having been awarded to him by any British university) did not himself participate in trade, but it was with a substantial loan from his brother George (later Sir George), the noted philanthropist, that he founded the Dogsbody Academy of Learning.

It is from such hints as this letter that we learn that even the happiest of families have their difficult moments:

Dear Tom,

I write to you in gt distres and must embaris us boath by askin you to fowad to me the capittle and intrest I loned you as I am on hard times it would greev me to hav to take you bifor the beak for this triflin sum but beleev me brother I need the moneys. I got done in court over thees new laws whose side is the goverment on? I mean they talks about national wealth with one hand but with the other they passes inhuman laws wich makes it impossible to make a descent profitt. I mean with kids now only aloud to work 6½ hours a day – and hows kids goin to earn enough to live I ask you? I mean wear am I goin to find enough kids if they can only do halfshifts? I ask you. Any way I got done. After the regretted accident of little Elizabeth Robertson wot got stuck in the machine and lost her hand, I paid her parents 4 weeks money compensation for her full wage but they still complained I mean what could I have done more? You tell me. The inspectors come in – thogh what they knows with there hairs and graces I dont know – never had to scrape for a living like some – anyway I told the kids to tell the inspectors they done 6 hrs but they tells them 12 hrs wich is a flat lie cos they gets ten minutes for their dinners at the bench and five minutes for the lav. Any way they done me and I got the wrong judge (old whiskers was ill) so I asks you fer the money by the first of next month at the latest. Otherwise sorry but its the bailiff. My name looks very good on the George Dogsbody Ward at the Cottage Hospittle its in fancy copperplate.

Regards to Fanny your wife and from my own Hilda.

Is the kids doin all right at that nobby school?

> Yore affectionate brother,
> *G. W. Dogsbody*

GERARD BENSON

1846
The Repeal of the Corn Laws

IT IS KNOWN that young Charles Dickens, in his time as a journalist, reported debates in the House of Commons. What is not known is that he refers, in his report on the debate concerning the Repeal of the Corn Laws, to one Dogsbody, a Member of the House. There is, in fact, no reference to any Member of that name in the annals of Parliament, and A.L.L. Growse, in his surly way, claims that Dickens invented it. However that may be, this fragment of early Dickens is lovingly preserved in the Dogsbody archives:

As mobs go, it was an exemplary mob, a united, well-intentioned sort of a mob. Not one man, woman, or gleeful child in that mob but was firm on one holy principle: the Repeal of the Corn Laws.

Aged fathers of over-large families shouted for it; slatternly aunts shouted for it; ragged young rips shouted for it, or something very like it. It was true that the fathers, coming newly upon the word 'Repeal', had convinced themselves that it had some connection with Sir Robert Peel; it was true that the aunts had a hazy belief that the Corn Laws were connected with the licensing of chiropodists; it was true that the young rips knew nothing, and cared to be told nothing, so only that they could add their voices to the din that was currently shaking the very foundations of the Mother of Parliaments; nevertheless, here was the voice of the people, which, we are assured, is the voice of God.

There was not wanting one to echo that divine voice within the august chamber of the Commons. Dogsbody M.P. was on his feet and in mid speech. He could hear the chanting of the mob, and he well knew what they were chanting. It had cost him enough to arrange, in all conscience; if the word 'conscience' is appropriate.

Dogsbody knew exactly what it meant, this Repeal of the Corn Laws. It meant a great number of things, all but one of which he was listing to the House at this moment; it meant liberty, fraternity, the divine principle of *laissez-faire*, and so on. What he omitted to mention was that it meant money for certain friends of Dogsbody M.P., money some of which might conceivably contribute to the upkeep of Mrs Dogsbody and the little Dogsbodys.

It is a privilege to observe the noble process of government in our great country. The mob shouted: 'repeal the Corn Laws' and behold, the Corn Laws were repealed. Who could doubt that the fingers of Dogsbody M.P. and his colleagues were firmly on the pulses of the People?

Sloven that I am, I almost wrote 'purses'.

PAUL GRIFFIN

1848
Sir Richard Burton

Lady D. Goes for a Burton

EXTRACT FROM THE private memoirs of Euphrosyne ('Phryne'), Lady Dogsbody, which were discovered in manuscript in thirty-four exercise books in an attic of Kennelworth Manor, a Dogsbody country seat:

It was in India that I became acquainted with the future Sir Richd. Burton the Famous Explorer and Discoveror of the Sauce of the Nile and Congoo etc, *notorious* for his transallation of the scandallous amusing Thousand and One Knights! a *Grate Flame* of mine in '48 at Chupattipoor a desalate young Relict, newly Widowed and staying with my dear Brother-in-Law the Very Revd. Septimus, Bishop of Poppadumabad.

Lieutenant Burton 18th Bombay N.I. as he then was, wicked wicked hansome fellow and no wonder he became an Explorer! was engaged in rendering into English a fascinating naughty Hindoo Love-Treaties called Karmasootra in which larned task I gave him he said most valuable matereal assistence and a deeper understanding, for on larning of my interest as a Devotey of Physacal Cutlure (with *Professional Experiants*) and Oryentall Dance, he besought to read portions of the book to me for to assertain whether some of the Poses and Altitudes etc etc was Humanly *possable*!

Practicing the positions before the cheval-glass in the Privicy of my room I found that only by discarding almost *every stitch* was I able to perform the realy *advanced* excercices! and when later with many a virtuous Blush I assured the eager Inquiror that thus all of the Poses was indeed possable, but only to one possessing the suppleness of Youth allyed to experiants of Gymnasticks, he positively implored me *on his Knees*!!! to demonstrait them!

Being by now far from Insensable to his many *Manly Charms* which not surprising had awoke again in me certain warm Emotions unmentionable by a Lady, that had laid drowned in Grief since my poor dear veneerable Professor Dogsbody expired in my very arms ere our Honeymoon was half over! and moved too by that *Vanity* which is weak Woman's herotage from our Mother Eve, I consented to display to my importionate Admirer that I truely was Mistress of *all* the Karmasootra postures however difficult, daring or even Indelicate! But since this could not be done in the dear Bishop's Residance it was decided I should go on holiday to Cashmeer and stay in a houseboat on the Lake, while he would take leave there too but pretending to go to Persia.

And thus, 'twas done!! – Never can I forget those magicall nights of Romance, amourous enchantment, wine and Passion! What carefree voluptuous jollity too – what *gails* of Laughter puncturated the shrieks of grattified Desire!! when my dear Burton or Dick as I called him, swum the half-mile from his houseboat to mine and we there accumplished in *outragous* intimite detail all the Karmasootra notions. With daring varations from his knowlige of other Rude writings and what he called my Wit, invention and infinit variaty we plummed the hights of lovers' Rites, and Burton declared we had far exseeded the Original and that the Pupil outstript the Master! though as I said,

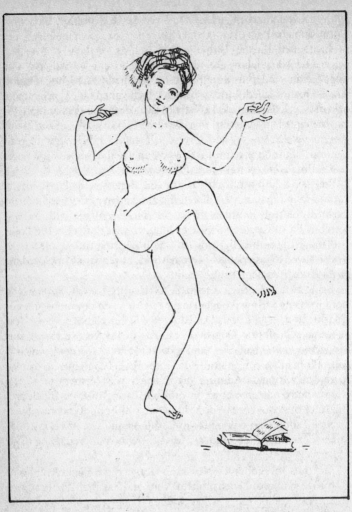

LADY PHRYNE DOGSBODY STUDYING THE KAMASUTRA: Inscribed 'Mme PD' and initialled 'JDI 1848'. Sketch for a portrait-study attributed to Jean Dominique Ingres.

off-stript would be a truer word!! Notwithstanding all my youthfull agilaty and his athalettism I would never have *imagined* the exstreams of conubeal contortions that was attaned! Burton was deeply intrested too, to larn how my dear horsey 1st husband the Professor proved with my help that 'twas Quite poassable, just like Legends tell, for Atiller and his no mad Anciant Huns to be so at home a-horseback as not to dismount even for what he politley termed pocreation. Infortunately the small Cashmeeri hill-ponys was not well enough scholed nor up to the combined *weight* like dear Prof. Dogsbody's heavy hunters was, so R.B. had to take my word for it. Neverthelass many and often was our Raptures and we vowed etarnal Fidelity despight his burning ambition to visit Persia and Arabia etc etc and make a daring pillgrimige to Meckah before returning to my arms. But alas for Man's piecrust promises and frail Woman's sackrefised *Virtue*! he departed for Scinde and Beloochistan and came not back, leaving me an Aching Void to be feebly consoled by calloh Subaltens until later comprensively filled by my dear Cousin-in-Law Captain (afterwards General SIR!) Hercules Dogsbody. But it is certain that had R.B. married *me* and not that moralistickal sangtified Isabel Arundell, *I* would NEVER have burnt like *she* did, his last grate sensational book nor his wonderful Private journals neither, some of which he showed me and on which I based my own in which I have wrote here below a *risquey but charming* poem he sent to me at Chupattipoor after I returned there from Cashmeer. It is enscribed: *To the beautiful and accomplished E. from her devoted R.B.*

> My Phryne now doth daily choose
> The Kamasootra to peruse,
> And o'er it doth intently pore
> To cull its esoteric lore.
>
> At times she calls on me to teach
> Some practice that the Vedas preach,
> Till she each convolution knows
> Of every oriental pose.
>
> She vows that love will be renewed
> With each athletic attitude,
> In variations unsurpassed,
> Each more exotic than the last.

Each Hindoo god's emphatic charms
Include at least three pairs of arms:
Should Phryne *all* their scriptures heed,
'Tis not, I think, spare arms I'd need.

W. F. N. WATSON

EUPHROSYNE ('PHRYNE'), LADY DOGS-BODY (1830–1915) *Shapely, sprightly only daughter of Sam Phillpot, ex-jockey, groom, tipster and circus-hand, and Jinnie née Belcher, known as Flossie. The future Lady Dogsbody had little informal, and less formal, education. 1838, child street-tumbler and singer; 1842, circus equestrienne; becoming consummate horse-woman and Beauty, engaged 1845 at Astley's Amphitheatre as Mlle Euphrosyne ('Phryne') La Fesse, World-famed Equestrienne Ballerina. Married (i) 1847 Professor Bedlington Dogsbody (died 1847 sans issue); (ii) 1850 Captain (later General Sir) Hercules Dogsbody (one son, two daughters). 1868, first lady M.F.H. (Backwater Hunt); 1914, raised Dogsbody's Own Girls' Mounted Ambulance Squadron (DOGMAS), nicknamed the Bitch Brigade. Died of wounds, Loos, 1915. R. S. Surtees, the sporting author, said of her: 'She had the finest seat in the English hunting world,' adding, 'on or off a horse.'*

1849
The California Gold Rush

Dear Silas,

It is with heavy heart that I write to tell you of the sad demise of my little Clementine. She will always be 'little' to me, despite the fact that latterly the size of her feet obliged me to contrive shoes for her from herring boxes.

News travels slowly here, brother, and it was the best part of a year before we heard tell of the publication of Mr Marx's infamous tract, the 'Communist Manifesto'. Young Percy Montrose rode over to tell us of this threat to all honest folk who seek only to be rich and ruthless, and my little Clem, on hearing what he said, started up in horror from the river's edge, pan in hand. Well now, I always did have trouble with splinters in those tarnation herring boxes and – how can I tell you of it, brother? – she gave a shriek and hopped on one foot and next thing, she was in the river and going away from us, head down and boxes up. We got her out at Blasted Creek and gave her a decent Christian burial with Edie Grimstone very moving on the harmonium. Young Percy was that touched, he said he would write a song in memory of the sad event. Maybe so, if the Lord wills.

This finds me more cheerful as I panned a good nugget this morning and don't reckon much to this fellow Marx after all. Communism won't catch on, not while there's gold to be got.

Your loving brother,
Ezekiel Dogsbody

ALISON PRINCE

EZEKIEL DOGSBODY (1800–1878) *Brother of Silas of Rotenburgh. Emigrated to America to join Gold Rush. Married 1830 Hominy Gritz; one daughter, Clementine.*

1849–83
The Journal of John Brown

THE KISS-AND-TELL memoirs of Queen Victoria's famous Scottish retainer. From Hannah Dogsbody's collection:

Leaves from the Journal of My Life in the Highlands
by John Brown

Balmoral, March 1849: Now that I have been taken on as Her Majesty's Gillie (which means being her servant, factotum and general Dogsbody) I have resolved to keep a diary. If I keep my eyes and ears open I may be able to pick up a few bawbees by selling court gossip to one of the popular Sunday newspapers.

(NOTE. The more interesting entries in John Brown's Journal begin after the death of Albert, the Prince Consort, in 1861, when the relationship between the royal widow and her faithful gillie began to raise Establishment eyebrows.)

23 September 1863: As I was leading her pony up a steep mountain path H.M. looked round to see if anybody else was around, then whispered in my ear: 'Do you know there is a lot of ill-natured gossip about you and me?'

I pretended to be surprised.

'I don't know what my dear Albert would have said,' she continued.

'I expect he would have said there's nae smoke without fire,' I said.

9 September 1865: An informal picnic on the grouse moors. H.M. and family: Vicky, Alice, Louise, Bertie, Alfie, Helena, Arthur, Leopold and Beatrice, plus a skeleton staff of ladies-in-waiting, servants, footmen, valets, maids, nurses, governesses, beaters and pipers. I expect Albert was looking down on us, too. There's no getting away from Albert. After the meal everyone was given permission to retire, leaving H.M. and myself alone.

I read her some love poems by her favourite Rabbie Burns. She was much moved. 'He had a wonderful way with the lassies,' she said with a sigh.

'Aye,' I said. 'We Scots are a' the same.'

'Why have you never married?' she asked.

'I've ne'er found the right woman,' I replied. 'Till now,' I added after a long pause.

'What can you mean?' she said.

'Och, nothing,' I said. 'A cat may look at a king.'

'Or a queen,' she said.

Just then two reporters crawled out of the heather and began taking photographs.

'Now we'll be in all the Sunday papers,' she said.

21 August 1868: H.M.'s *Leaves from the Journal of Our Life in the Highlands* has just been published. I might publish mine one day, but it would have to be well after she's dead and gone. I get mention on almost every page of her book. 'Brown as usual on the box of the wagonette'; 'Brown caught some excellent trout'; 'Brown attended me at dinner.' Brown did this, that and the other. A guid thing she never mentions the other.

STANLEY J. SHARPLESS

The following verses are assuredly in John Brown's large, awkward hand. Whether the relationship they adumbrate is one merely of wish-fulfilment – yet more evidence of the grandiosity that grew in Brown concurrently with his influence over the Queen – or whether they trace the lineaments of an actual liaison is a matter for each reader's private judgement.

28 September 1869:

To My Ain Wee Mousie

Luve is like a golden tassie –
So drink thy fill, my Royal Lassie!
Tho' nae realms I can impairt,
    Nor orb, nor crown,
I give thee *mair* – a Hieland Hairt,
    My Empress Brown!

Tak' nae heed o' pious prattling;
Courtiers feed on tittle-tattling.
All blood o' Hieland veins evinces,
    Fu' well I ween,
Higher claims than Highborn Princes
    To snare a Queen.

Dinna fear that dear dead Albie,
Snugly stowed at Frogmore, shall be
Unco fashed. He wi' our welding
    Wouldna quarrel –
Nor wish his girlie served by *gelding*
    At Balmoral.

Come then, Vicky, why sae flighty?
(Braw tha maun look in thy nightie!)
It's whisht to a' expostulation –
    Sae hush thy blether;
And hurry on our consummation –
    I' the heather!

MARTIN FAGG

29 September 1869: After dinner H.M. invited me up to her room to see her etchings. We spent a long time admiring these. Then she started up about Albert again.

'With the greatest respect, Ma'am,' I said, 'it would be a great pity to spend the rest of your days in mourning. You owe it to your subjects now to discard your widow's weeds. After all, you are still in the prime of life.'

'I shall never marry again,' she said, giving me a look.

'A man's a man for a' that,' I said.

'We shall change the subject,' she said. 'That's a fine kilt you are wearing. Albert promised to show me what a Scotsman wears underneath his kilt, but he was always too busy planning exhibitions.'

I enlightened her. Crept back to my room about 3 a.m.

7 October 1874: Mr Gladstone arrived at the castle. H.M. always in a bad temper with everybody when he is here. It's 'Brown, the venison is tough'; 'Brown, tell that piper he's flat.'

How different when it's time for him to go. 'Brown, help Mr Gladstone pack his bag so that he can catch the first train back to London.'

When Mr Disraeli comes she is as sweet as apple pie. 'You can have the evening off, Brown. No need to hurry back.'

2 March 1883 [last entry in Journal]: H.M. very concerned at my worsening health. Musn't let her think I'm at death's door, otherwise she'll want me to take a message to Albert.

This morning she brought me my breakfast in bed. 'I cooked this haggis myself,' she said. 'Get well soon. Whatever should I do without you?'

'Well, Ma'am,' I said, 'you would have to get another gillie – willy-nilly.'

She was not amused.

STANLEY J. SHARPLESS

1850
Victoria and Albert

QUEEN VICTORIA'S LITERARY productions are usually recalled with the smile evoked by Disraeli's oily 'We authors, Ma'am'. However, there was a slightly less artless side to the Queen as authoress – expressive of her frank delight in the more monumental aspects of male architecture. The following effusion was filched from a secretaire at Windsor by that most ferrety-eyed of royal servants, Hannah Dogsbody, during the high noon of the Queen's marriage. Reading these lines, visitors to Osborne will no longer be puzzled by the sheer acreage of joyful nudity on its frescoed walls.

In youth I oft in Palaces
    A host of sculptures viewed;
Scanned many a massive marbled thigh
    And many a buttock nude,
Delighting in the shapely sight
    Of drapeless genitalia
(No timid fig-leaves e'er should mask
    A man's most proud regalia!)
And oh! the girlish graphic zeal
    (This matron now remembers)

With which my nubile pencil limned
   Mountainous male members.
Such splendour of the virile form
   I long adored – the more so
When I at last beheld unclad
   My Princely Albert's torso.
Oh manliest of all thy *Saxe* –
   I'd blithely swear on oath, a
More potent *Coburg* never primed
   A more insatiate *Gotha*!

MARTIN FAGG

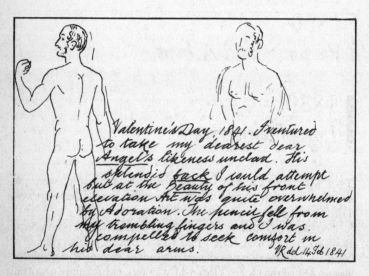

Valentine's Day, 1841. I ventured to take my dearest dear Angel's likeness unclad. His splendid back I could attempt but at the Beauty of his front elevation Art was quite overwhelmed by Adoration. The pencil fell from my trembling fingers and I was compelled to seek comfort in his dear arms. VR del 14 Feb 1841

QUEEN VICTORIA'S SKETCH OF PRINCE ALBERT: Among Queen Victoria's multitudinous sketches, only two depict her adored Albert. It has been suggested that, considering him such a paragon of male beauty, she felt unequal to, or unworthy of, so noble a subject, but her note on the sketch filched by Hannah Dogsbody sheds an entirely new light on the matter. It also arouses interesting speculation on the coincidence of the date on the drawing and that of the birth of the future King Edward VII on 8 November of that year.

HANNAH DOGSBODY (1820–1904) *Born in Rotenburgh, one of thirteen children of Silas and Rachel née Goodfarthing. Renowned for her infant piety, being able to recite the Pentateuch word-perfect at the age of 5. Entered service at the age of 14, at Balmoral, through the good offices of Horatio Fitzcrupper, and spent her entire career in royal service – at Windsor Castle, Buckingham Palace, Balmoral, Osborne, etc. Used entire trust placed in her by the Queen to accumulate a unique collection of papers, given even greater value by Edward VII's holocaust of his mother's letters and diaries in 1901. She never recovered from her mistress's death in 1901 and herself succumbed to a severe intestinal chill at Hampton Court (where she enjoyed a grace-and-favour residence) in 1904.*

1850
Lord Palmerston

THE FOLLOWING VERSES, of unknown authorship, were preserved by Hannah Dogsbody, who was at that time walking out with Lord Palmerston's valet.

They refer to Palmerston's many amorous adventures both up- and downstairs, which endeared him to the British public but not to Victoria and Albert (it was alleged that he had attempted to ravish Mrs Brand, one of the Queen's ladies-in-waiting), to his failure to consult the Queen and the Prince Consort over matters of foreign policy during his time as Foreign Secretary, and to his famous four-and-a-half-hour speech in the Commons in defence of a claim for damages by one Don Pacifico, whose house in Athens had been set on fire by rioters and who, although a Portuguese national at the time, had been born in Gibraltar and could therefore claim British citizenship when it suited him.

The Great Lord Pam

What was he doing, the great Lord Pam
  With the cook in the dusk in the bushes?
Scattering seed with the zest of a ram;
Replete as a wasp in the strawberry jam;
Discretion dismissed with a nonchalant damn –
  Modesty frankly blushes.

What was he doing, the Whig Grandee
  In the boat-house down by the river?
From flower to flower like a fickle bee,
Pollening ladies of low degree,
The sturdy nymphs of the scull-er-y –
  Seemly matrons shiver.

What was he chatting, this statesman spry
  With the tweeny? (Rather rum.)
Was he explaining, with twinkling eye,
Exactly how the shifty sly
Don Pacifico could cry:
  'Civis Romanus Sum!'?

What was he doing, the great Lord Pam
  With the nursery-maid up in the attic?
Discarding his ministerial cares,
Describing the various subtle snares
Bestudding the path of Foreign Affairs
  To an audience quite ecstatic?

MARTIN FAGG

c. 1850
The Creation of a National Inspectorate of Schools

ISABELLA DOGSBODY (1812–96) *Daughter of Parson Joseph of Woddlestone, Dorset, and sister of the Rev. Richard Dogsbody of that parish. Headmistress of Woddlestone Village School from 1832 until her death.*

PRESUMABLY PEOPLE HAD Freudian fantasies before Freud. It certainly seems so from this fragment of Matthew Arnold's, which was found on the staffroom table of Woddlestone Village School in Dorset:

The Forsaken Inspector

Come, dear children, let us away;
    Down and away below.
Here am I, all dressed in grey,
Hearing the stuff your teachers say –
    Little of me you know.
I heard the expectant hum:
'Mr Arnold has come!
He's an Inspector of Schools.'
Oh, fools!
That is not *me*.
I am King of the Sea.

Children dear, was it yesterday
I heard your school bell over the bay,
    The far-off sound of your silver bell?
And I knew it was time to go my way,
    All dressed up like a swell,
To visit the school where, day by day,
You sit and long for your luncheon box
And idly twiddle your golden locks
And shake your head, for there's nothing in it;
You haven't listened for half a minute
To the beautiful things your teachers say;
Children dear, was it yesterday
I heard the waves? and I thought: 'Oh, Lord!
I've been sent by the Educational Board
To see that your teachers treat you fair,
Not to look at your golden hair.'

And even anon there drops a tear
From my clouded eye as I dawdle here,
Writing reports that couldn't be worse,
For they fall into curious ways of verse.

Come away, little girls; time passes
    And midnight comes, sooner or late,
When out on the beach in his glasses,
    Mr Arnold is willing to wait.
Out of the reach of the Rector,
    Where Managers manage no more,
Behold a forsaken Inspector,
    Alone on the shore.

But though on the headland,
The dull and the dead land,
I spend all my daytime
Making notes on your teachers,
You pitiless creatures!
You never spend playtime
With me,
The King of the Sea.

PAUL GRIFFIN

1851
Mayhew: *London Labour and the London Poor*

THIS EXTRACT, omitted from the final published version by Mayhew, was in fact found among a pile of screwed-up scraps of paper in the British Library Reading Room:

London Labour and the London Poor

compiled by Henry Mayhew

OF THE CHARWOMEN

The charwomen for the most part are elderly, and many of them have sunk from a more prosperous life as bar-maid or kept woman, have lost their looks and are forced to this occupation to keep themselves from the workhouse. Coming out of the imposing front and down the grand steps of the British Museum I met one such called Nelly Dogsbody, whose protector had helped her start a lodging-house, but the depression of the last decade made it impossible for her to make it pay. She is a big hulking woman with a heap of untidy hair, dyed red, and she is very round-shouldered. She wears the dull grey shapeless dress of her class and the black sacking apron with the big pockets filled with dusters and rags. She carries a mop and pail. The charwomen have to find this item necessary for their work themselves. She was very ready to speak, indeed to burst out into the story of her life.

'I'm better off than most because I've got the lighter work of cleaning the desks and dusting the books and a little mopping, not that some of us like Maggie Drabble and Aggie Carter didn't get Library Lung from it and succumb coughing up paper dust. You wouldn't think you'd need to clean this big room with the top-'at [as she calls the Dome of the Reading Room] more than once a week, there being no real work like fish-gutting or eel-pie making going on 'ere, but there's always the spilt ink and the bits of paper and all sorts of flotsam that the reading gents leave – there's one seat that I clean

NELLY DOGSBODY (*c.* 1801–64) *Born in Bethnal Green, daughter of Arthur Dogsbody, costermonger, and Hetty née Clegg. 1808–16, worked on family stall; 1816–20, barmaid at The Quill and Pen; 1820–26, kept woman of Richard de Vere; 1827–47, lodging-house landlady in Wood Green. Common-law marriage 1840 to Harold Hastings, former butler, who died in 1846 from alcoholic poisoning. 1848–60, charwoman; 1860–64, inmate Frinton Street Workhouse. Died of pneumonia.*

which is always covered with 'airs, from a beard, and big coarse ones they are, and always the same colour, and you think this gent, 'e's married to 'is seat and like many an 'usband 'e treats it something awful – the legs of the chair is all kicked and 'e gouges out bits of the desk with 'is pen knife, and 'airs, 'airs everywhere.'

'Well, sir, during that big storm we 'ad there was a leak in the top of the 'ouse and some of us were called in out of our regular time to mop up and we 'ad to walk in among the gents and I keep my eye out for this gent and it's like what I thought – there's this foreign-looking gent with a beard like a sweep's brush and 'air like a dray 'orse's mane and 'e's moving about 'is chair discomfortable like and I'd say there was something wrong with 'im like boils or carbuncles as my old pa use to 'ave 'em and fierce it made 'im, and 'ard.'

'So Annie Fraser and me was walking back after cleaning up the water what dropped from the leak and she was whining, in a whisper, like a mosquiter, sayin 'er legs and bunions and 'aricot veins were killin' 'er and she couldn't take it – she'd give up and be a pauper tomorrow, says Annie. "You can't be a pauper, 'ave some pride, girl, it's an 'ard 'ard life, there's no denying like what they sing at The Star" – that's an 'all, Sir, where we go to get sung at – [sings]

> 'When it's not rainin cause it's snowin,
> All of us, we're all knowin',
> It's the work'us of the world, tonight –

'Lovely song, it makes yer cry buckets – anyway this wrigglin' gent pushes back 'is 'air and says, "Vat you say?" and I, feeling a bit cheeky, whispers, "Work'us of the world, tonight," and 'e stares – not at me, just stares in the air and writes something down – and we got out and Annie says 'er 'aricots are so bad she should get 'er legs cut off, and I said, why not, you've got nothin' to lose but your veins – and we go out, not without a word from one of the library gentlemen to 'old our noise. Annie says: "Nelly, that funny-looking man, 'e write down what you say, and 'e should give you somethin'" – thank you, sir, much obliged – I said, no, 'e was poor too, 'is coat all darns and not even good darns neither but lumpy ones. 'Is wife needs a talking to – so we went off for a porter and a stout.'

Books read & Débris left in The British Museum within 24 hrs.					
Reading Material	**Weight gmmes**	**wt. lbs**	**Débris**	**Weight gmmes**	**lbs oz**
Books	891202.	1963	Paper	2662.	5. 14
Periodicals	109868	242	Hair	224.	0. 8
Blue Books, Reports.	61290	135	Scurf etc.	168.	0. 6.
MSS.	12258	27	Ink	196.	0. 7.
			Fluff from clothing	252.	0. 9.
TOTALS	1074618	2367		3502	7. 12

REM BEL

1854
Florence Nightingale

P ATIENCE DOGSBODY (1851–80) *Only daughter of Nestor Dogsbody and sister of Jeremy, the watercolorist. A prolific if unsung writer of hymns, but perhaps better known as a writer of Christmas card greetings.*

LETTER FROM Miss Patience Dogsbody to her friend, Miss Florence Nightingale:

> The Rectory
> Trimmer
> Hampshire
> 1 December 1854

Dear Florence,

Thanks for your p.c. Of course I need to worry – you left these shores to cross the sea in such a dreadful hurry. I know you went to ease the plight of the Scutari sick, but do you think it was quite right – I've quite a nervous tic – leaving your loved ones here to grieve – your Mother's got the bile – could you not grant us a reprieve and come back for a while? Papa says prayers for every lad on our side in the war; but though you'll think me slightly mad, I don't know what it's for. They say we're helping out the Turk to tame the Russian Bear. But are we cut out for the work and is it our affair? Forgive my ignorance, dear Friend, in Providence I trust to see we come through in the end, as all believers must. The Crimea seems so far away, though it is on the map. I've purchased some new lace today and cashmere for a wrap. About your thoughts on Cousin Roddie's marrying Abigail – I'm proud to be a Dogsbody as you a Nightingale. My Cousin Roddie doesn't drink more than a sportsman should; your Auntie Abigail is plain, although her figure's good. I'm sure you'll see this our way when you get home to your people. We've a sale of work on Saturday in aid of the new steeple. Your mixing with so many males makes people talk, I fear. But the oil in *your* lamp never fails, as I tell the folk round here. If this letter reaches you – enclosed some scented soap – it brings my Christmas greetings, too, and my fervent hope that you'll be back with us, my dear – the family hopes so too – safe and sound in the New Year. We're all proud of you. Everybody sends their love and their congratulations on your good works. May Heaven above protect you!

> Much love,
> *Patience*

P.S. I'm writing a new hymn I hope will be of use to you. I've finished one for the Reverend Pym, The Mission, Timbuctoo.

NOTE: Letter returned unopened, possibly due to the exigencies of war.

MARGARET ROGERS

1854
The Crimea

LETTER FROM THE Vicomte le Corps de Chien, who was touring Europe, to his mother.

La Crimée
le 24 octobre 1854

Chère Maman,

Je continue mon voyage, qui est assez intéressant. Par exemple, aujourd'hui j'ai remarqué de mon compartiment un grand nombre de soldats, glorieusement vêtus, qui galopaient très vite parmi des feux d'artifice.

J'ai demandé à un employé du chemin de fer de faire arrêter le train, pour mieux voir, mais il m'a répondu que c'était impossible. 'En effet,' a-t-il dit, 'c'est magnifique. Mais ce n'est pas la gare.'

Ton fils,
Henri

W. S. BROWNLIE

HENRI, VICOMTE LE CORPS DE CHIEN (1836–82)   *Last scion of the ancient family, who could trace his ancestry back as far as the eleventh century to William le Corps de Chien.*

1854
The Charge of the Light Brigade

EXCERPT FROM a letter written by Rokesby Dogsbody to his father:

My duties at Balaclava – a small Crimean town which takes its name from a type of English woollen helmet – consisted of arranging the supply of 'army comforts' to entitled personnel. A popular item was the locally distilled plum brandy and it was dispensed in the field from a cask fitted to the back of a common soldier while another common soldier poured the tots. It was chargeable and the common soldiery had, of course, to 'pay on the nail', but credit was allowed to the commissioned officers.

The British and Russian armies faced each other over flatlands and, although there was desultory firing from both sides, neither was prepared to make a frontal attack owing to complete lack of shelter from artillery. I was supervising the plum brandy issue to a group of senior officers and, notebook in hand, requiring them to indicate whether or not they proposed to pay me then. Lord Raglan, the General Officer Commanding, was approached and, after he had been served, I enquired: 'Cash or credit, sir?' Owing to a sudden blast from a Russian gun his reply escaped me and I repeated the question. 'Charge, man, charge,' he roared, and a second later the Earl of Cardigan, accompanied by his second-in-command the Earl of Lucan, with a detachment of dragoons behind them, was galloping madly across the plain offering Ivan excellent target practice until his ammunition was exhausted.

The losses were heavy, about 700 of all ranks having taken part and rather less than 200 returning. A number of the casualties were officers; most of them owed considerable sums of money on their plum brandy account and I anticipate the utmost difficulty in recovering this money from their estates. It has been a very great disaster.

T. L. MCCARTHY

ROKESBY (later SIR ROKESBY) DOGSBODY
(1830–98) *Only son of Rokesby Senr., Lieut.-Colonel
(Retd.). Married 1855 Hetty Boxer; one son, Daniel, later Lord
Dogsbody of Rannoch. In his youth he served as a canteen manager of
the newly formed Navy and Army Institute with the family regiment,
the 13th Berkshire ('the Unlucky Berks'), and, indeed, detractors say
that this period saw the foundation of his immense fortune.*

1857
The Indian Mutiny

THE INSISTENT DEMAND of the public that the Poet Laureate
should comment on every conceivable event seems to have brought
this, perhaps mercifully unpublished, offering, presented to Jeremy
Dogsbody by his friend Alfred, Lord Tennyson:

> Now fades the last long streak of blood
>   Where Indian mutineers held sway;
>   Would I be just as bad as they
> Were I to stand where once they stood?
>
> Would I have done, were I Hindu,
>   The things they did? I cannot guess.
>   My public calls me, none the less
> To read *The Times*, and hear their view:
>
> 'Blow out, wild guns, to the wild sky;
>   Blow out the sepoys into dust,
>   Blow out the bad, blow in the just!'
> Blow all, they said; blow that, say I!
>
> Well, each event with other fits
>   And hastens to some perfect state;
>   It must be the decree of Fate
> These Indians shall be blown to bits.

I ask what brought them to this pass,
 What passions caused them all this pain;
 The answer is not very plain:
Something to do with grease, or grass.

I have to leave it to the Lord
 And do the work for which I'm paid:
 A piece about the Light Brigade
And 'Come into the garden, Maud'.

PAUL GRIFFIN

1858
Edward Lear on the Railways

RICHARD DOGSBODY, M. A. (1820–1900) *Vicar of Woddlestone, Dorset. Brother of Isabella and son of Parson Joseph. Occasional contributor of light satirical verse to literary magazines. Published a book of sermons.*

LEAR SENT THIS limerick to his friend, the Rev. Richard Dogsbody:

An old fellow who rode in a carriage
On the railway said, 'This is like marriage;
 You think you're in clover
 Going to Dover
Then suddenly wake up in Harwich!'

MARGARET ROGERS

1859
Darwin: *Origin of Species*

FROM THE Max Dogsbody Collection of Ephemera. Sticker seen in the back window of a hansom cab in 1859 and noted down by an unknown Dogsbody who thought it amusing:

DARWIN DOES IT WITH ANIMALS

V. ERNEST COX

1863
The Wedding of Edward VII

AN EXTRACT FROM the daily journal of Parson Joseph Dogsbody. It is wonderful to see the old man, his faculties and his loyalty unimpaired, joining, in his quiet rural way, in the day of national celebration.

10 March 1863

Fine Blustery day. Breakfasted on half a dozen scrambled eggs, a couple of rashers, a brace of Euphemia's home-made sausages and a black pudding, present from a parishioner. There is much disloyal talk in the parish about the Royal Wedding – the history (I had hoped buried) of the Prince of Wales's conduct toward Amelia Twistle, my grand-niece, during his visit to Woddlestone's pottery last summer was on the lips of everybody, even the womenfolk. Amelia has developed a taste for oysters but is otherwise unharmed. Her son is to be Christened on Sunday next. It is perhaps regrettable but I did not hear her complain when a diamond bracelet arrived by messenger at

Christmas, nor did she say: 'No' to the excellent vintage wine with which H.R.H. was so generous on his visit. Notwithstanding the gossip, which in my opinion is quite unfounded, I composed an ode to the occasion, a copy of which I despatched to Balmoral Castle for Her Majesty's later perusal. If I can find a tune we will sing it in church on Sunday, at Evensong, after young Edward Twistle's baptism. It here follows:

Ode on the Nuptials of H.R.H. the Prince of Wales and Princess Alexandra, 10 March 1863.

by Joseph Nehemiah Dogsbody

The day has dawned, let bells be rung
　　From ev'ry tow'ring steeple,
And rousing roundelays be sung
　　By ev'ry sort of people,
For Edward, Our Edward comes to church
Nor leaves his Alexandra in the lurch.

Across the sea his fair Bride came
　　All in a sailing vessel
And flew t'her Groom with faultless aim
　　In his strong arms to nestle,
For Edward, Our Edward loves his Bride
Nor will he ever stray from by her side.

Then let the heliograph flash forth
　　O'er Land and Sea the Tidings
And steam trains send 'em, South and North
　　On main lines and in sidings,
For Edward, Our Edward sware the vows
Which makes his Alexandra his sweet spouse.

Now gently falls the Eventide
　　Let's leave the pair together
T'enjoy love's rites, now they are tied
　　By Matrimony's tether,
For Edward, Our Edward now may seal
His Alexandra's lips in conj'gal zeal.

The composition took me the better part of the afternoon and I pride myself it is as good as anything ever achieved by my remote cousin, D. G. Dogsbotti, and a good deal more masculine. I am still not happy about the last line which does not scan in the manner that my old tutor (God rest him) would have approved. 'Holy zeal' might do but is misleading, and other possibilities are indelicate, and in one case downright ambiguous. Amelia was up here with her brat. Why she wants to call him Edward I do not understand. There have been no Edwards on our side of the family, and none mentioned in any record I know. I sat down to a pleasant supper while she gave suck, of boiled beef, some cold ham and veal, a glass of warm milk and some apple dumplins. She partook as heartily as I and there was nothing left on the plates save a little Norfolk mustard. I was taken with a little flatulence before bedtime (this March weather affects me). 'In mute appeal' sounds better in the Ode but does not make much sense. I shall leave it as it is.

GERARD BENSON

1863
The Gettysburg Address

EXTRACT FROM A letter written by Sylvanus Penn Dogsbody, a reporter on a Philadelphia newspaper, to his cousin, Parson Joseph in Woddlestone:

Tomorrow I return to Philadelphia; and from there I go soon to Gettysburg to report the formal dedication of the great new cemetery for those killed in the battle in July. Never will the events I witnessed then – such bravery and suffering as can never have been exceeded in the whole history of the world – never will the memory of these things depart from me as long as I live. There will be a great gathering and the famous Edward Everett is to give the oration. He is said already to have been preparing it for many weeks; and it will, we all hope and expect, be as rich and classical a performance – and as loaded with pertinent allusion – as Mr Everett's speeches customarily are. It is not certain yet if the President is to be there: he is so little valued or regarded by the governors of some of the states that it is rumoured that they did not, at first, think to invite him – or at least carefully 'forgot' to do so! He is a great man and a great American, but his greatness is not in his appearance or his manner, both of which tend to the ungainly and awkward. If he does come, perhaps he too will speak – though he may prefer not to risk an anticlimax after the sublimities of Mr Everett!

With the love and gratitude of all of us in America to all of you in England. Perhaps one day we may meet?

Your affectionate cousin,

Syl

MARTIN FAGG

1865
The Assassination of
Abraham Lincoln

A PIECE BY Sylvanus Penn Dogsbody, by then Drama Critic of the *Philadelphia Courier*:

The play was going along quite nicely, with some convincing acting by the principals. Then a ridiculous piece of what I think is called 'audience-participation' took place.

A character who had not even appeared in the action up to that point emerged from the wings, produced a pistol, and fired several blanks at one of the boxes. Here a clumsily made-up man, obviously planted by the theatrical director, pretended to be hit and actually to die. His acting was so overdone and amateurish that only the most naive and inexperienced spectator would have been convinced by it.

Yet, even had he been a master of his craft, and had he put up the best performance of his career, the episode would have remained a pathetic flop, for it had no possible connection with the dramatic action, and was imposed upon it in the most superficial and artificial manner.

A truly gimcrack trick, were the words that instantly came to mind.

Greatly disappointed that what might have been a pleasant evening had been spoiled, I left the theatre at once.

Reflecting later, I could think of no single word with which to label the regrettable affair, and therefore coined one, based on my immediate reaction. Whether or not my word will achieve currency, I do not know, but I at least will always think of the event as a 'gimmick'.

W. S. BROWNLIE

1880
William Ewart Gladstone

JASPER DOGSBODY (1834–1902)   *An attractive ne'er-do-well, he worked as a stage-hand at the Savoy Theatre during the palmy days of the D'Oyly Carte Company. He married, beneath himself, so they said, Carrie Buttercoop, who daily cleared W. S. Gilbert's waste-paper basket and handed Jasper any interesting rejects. Carrie always swore that she was the original of the buxom bumboat woman in* HMS Pinafore. *They had two sons, Max and Tancred. After his death an old tin trunk was found, containing letters and other objects which he had clearly collected during his years at the Savoy.*

W. S. GILBERT SATIRIZED the House of Lords in *Iolanthe*, and Oscar Wilde and the Aesthetic Movement in *Patience*. Did he, perhaps, plan an opera about the House of Commons, satirizing the Liberal Party and, in particular, Gladstone?

The P.M.'s Song

My father was in Parliament; his instincts were colonial;
The antecedents of my wife were perfectly baronial;
At Eton and at Oxford I was rich without vulgarity;
Alas! for these advantages do not bring popularity.
As a speaker I've no equal; I'm a pattern of propriety;
A Cabinet or Budget I create without anxiety;
On sundry State occasions I preside with proper dignity;
And yet the public treat me with the uttermost malignity.
For why? my love of harlots, which is noble and devotional,
Is thought by the illiterate to verge on the emotional.
In short, my truest sympathy is turned to something sinister!
I am the very model of a much-maligned Prime Minister.

They say the noble Pericles was captured by Aspasia,
But I am not an ancient Greek! No notion could be crazier.
I live with Mrs Gladstone in a marital security
That makes all other friendships of unquestionable purity.
Oh, it is true I love my whores, despite their frequent pettiness,
But never do my sentiments degenerate to sweatiness;
I try to keep them off the streets; what object could be civiller?
Yet constantly I'm treated as a lecher and a driveller.
I fear without my labours my beloved fallen women'll
Fall yet again and turn their thoughts to matters that are criminal;
And though I'm on the Left I am not consequently sinister;
I am the very model of a much-maligned Prime Minister.

PAUL GRIFFIN

1881
W. S. Gilbert's Own
'Nightmare Song'

THE FOLLOWING ITEM from Jasper's trunk, clearly never meant
for performance, shows that Gilbert was not above attempting to
rationalize his own problems in his verse:

When your partner's a bore with a character flaw,
For composing works sacred and serious,
You get quite out of sorts and your patience aborts,
And you chide in a voice quite imperious;
For you're ready to stage, D'Oyly Carte's in a rage,
Making threats in a tone of severity,
There's an outstanding bill, and a theatre to fill,
And you're seeking a place in posterity;
When you strongly insist it is time to resist,
Such a calling so high and ethereal,
And your worldly concerns he disdainfully spurns,
He considers such stuff immaterial;
In the end you degrade with a fearsome tirade,
Giving vent to your sharp irritation,
You condemn him outright with harangues which indict,
His unmannerly procrastination –
You're a regular scold, giving insults untold,
And no wonder you're fraught, when your plans come to naught,
And you've pains in the head, and you wish you were dead,
And your worries gyrate, and your psyche's in straits,
And your burdens increase, for there is no release,
From the follies of Man, which one Adam began,
But you cannot blame *him* for another chap's whim,
That deprives you of peace and contentment;
But there's darkness no more, when he fashions a score
Whose felicitous charm can so quickly disarm –
You forget your egregious resentment!

TIM HOPKINS

1886
On the Death of Mary Jane

MRS CYNTHIA DOGSBODY (1841–1916) *Poetess,
Madame and landlady of a certain house in Drury Lane.*

On the Death of Mary Jane

We're mourning for my Mary Jane,
Black laces in our stays,
And golden rings filled with the hair
She lost in her last days.

I taught her many little ploys –
She changed for every guest.
She'd take a bishop's gaiters off,
While he was getting dressed.

She lay with tender Eton lads
At play on the chaise-longue
Throughout the afternoons until
Cook rang the dinner-gong.

Arnold of Rugby came each week;
She'd bring him in his cane.
Although he thwacked my oldest girls,
He'd not hit Mary Jane.

In politics, my little pet
Was like the Vicar of Bray –
On Thursdays she chose Gladstone's arms,
Then Dizzy's knees next day.

The Palace servants tempted her.
John Brown brought in rich sweets –
She'd search for them beneath his kilt
While he caressed her teats.

She died in childbirth in my bed.
But Fate was not unkind –
I've something to remember her –
She left ten pups behind.

Mr Gladstone was a friend of Cynthia Dogsbody. Although the verses
that follow, found in her accounts drawer, belong chronologically to
1906, the year of her death, they nevertheless describe her therapeutic

work among the deprived in her heyday some twenty years earlier, when her co-operation with Gladstone was in full flower.

FIONA PITT-KETHLEY

c. 1890
The Rise of Socialism

WHEN TANCRED DOGSBODY became a Fabian Socialist he found the strain of associating with people monosyllabically called Shaw and Webb too much for him. He developed a strong inferiority complex. His furious debates with Chesterton and Belloc were doomed from the start by the fact that he was a teetotaller and came from a county with neither high hills nor the sea.

When I am living in the West Country [he writes]
    Where you can't find decent tea,
I long for the streets of Ealing
    And the Park of Osterley,
And the blokes that were blokes when I was a bloke
    In the glorious T.U.C.

Oh, the lads that live in Middlesex
    Are wiser than those in Devon;
They're thirstier than any lads
    That live this side of Heaven;
They start on their elevenses
    Ages before eleven;

And they argue like philosophers
    In the colonnades of Rome,
For a man can see in a cocoa mug
    The world in polychrome
Before he takes a kindly Tube
    Back to his Hounslow home.

TANCRED DOGSBODY (1870–1930)   *Fabian Social-*
ist. Son of Jasper Dogsbody and younger brother of Max.
Unmarried. Conscientious objector in First World War 1914–18.
Devoted life to struggle for the workers, and against the intellectuals
of whom, unknowingly, he was a prime example. Stood unsuccessfully
for Parliament twice during the 1920s. Died of TB contracted
during the General Strike.

> O the hallowed lands of Hounslow
>   And the hallowed halls of Staines
> Are home to us Fabian fellows
>   On the happy Underground trains,
> Who hope that the day is dawning
>   Of release for a world in chains.
>
> So spoke our Marxist Master,
>   Whose mighty stratagems
> Were made in the B. M. Reading Room
>   On the Middlesex bank of the Thames;
> And when I come to perish
>   My soul will ne'er lie still
> Till I rest in God's own county
>   By the Master, on Highgate Hill.

PAUL GRIFFIN

1897–1901
Daisy Dogsbody's Diary

DAISY DOGSBODY (1891–1943) *Daughter of*
Luther Dogsbody of Dogsbody & Dogsbody, antiquarians and
auctioneers. A precociously observant child, she was fascinated by the
adult world of the late Victorians, and kept a diary from the age of 6.

22 June 1897: Today is the Quean's Dimond Joobylee. I arsked Aunt Ethel wot this ment and she said it ment that sixty years ago to the Veriday, Princess Victoria came down in the middle of the nite in her nitegown to meet sum important gentlemen. Transparently she was now the Quean of England, so they bowed very low and she promised to be good and they kissed her hand and went out-backwards without bumping into anything. When *I* come down in my nitegown in the middle of the nite I'm told I'm norty. Next time I'll promise to be good and see wot happens. I would like to see Uncle Fred bump into something.

1 March 1900: I hurd the groan-ups torking a lot about the releef of Lady Smith. I lissuned hard but cuddunt make out why she was releeved and wot of. Praps Lord Smith was one of these Bores who got killed, and so she dussent have to lissun to him any more, like when Uncle Timothy tells us long stories about the Bore War. He says the Enmy dussent stand in red rows to be shot at any more but wares muddy looking uniform insted, and sum men disguys themselves as gorillas.

23 Janury 1901: The Queen died yesterday and we all have to ware black. After the funeral she is going to be laid in some linoleum beside the Prince Concert in the Albert Hall. People don't know how to go on making a new King as the last time they did it was so long ago, and I expect the Thrown has got very dusty by now.

JOYCE JOHNSON

1900
The Relief of Mafeking

WILLIAM (BILLY) DOGSBODY (1879–1901) *Illegitimate son of Nelly and brother of Percy and Millicent. Died in South Africa of enteric fever.*

LETTER RECEIVED BY Millicent Dogsbody of Walthamstow in May 1900:

Dear Milly,

Dont spose you spected to hear from your luvving brother shut up in pore old Maffyking – well to tell the truth old gal this Seeje is a Farse – if it goes on like as at present shant mind being Beseejed for the rest of my natural – Johnnie Boer is not reelly trying to take the town – far too busy with his baccy and his brandy the idel drunken devil – every morning after brekfust he lobs over a few shells – jist to keep us on our toes – but we is far too well dug in in our erth shelters to get urt – tho sumtimes the cashulties is shockin – a chicken killed last Friday and the major's terrier slitely grazed – grub is plentiful – grog too – the nobs sat down to thirteen corses at Crissmus – and even we Other Ranks got seven – the nigs is starving of corse – but they is used to it.

Everyone here is keepin their peckers up remarkable – but the life and sole of the Seeje is old Baden-Powell the Guvnor – he is a Wonder – a reel Card – like a big jolly boy what has forgotten to grow up – on the go from morn to night getting up sports and entertainments – just as well Johnnie Boer keeps mum in the arfternoons – and lets us have a nice long shut-eye – we should be eggsausted else.

But the thing the Guvnor is keenest on of all is Concert Parties – he does most of the turns hisself – juggling – yodling – conjuring – patter songs – and what not.

Well old gal I hope you are in the pink – if you are having as many larks as we are here then I know you must be merry and bright – the only thing we dred is that some busybodies will come and Releeve us – then it will be back to reel Soljering and no mistake!

Your luvving brother,
Billy

MARTIN FAGG

EXCERPT FROM a letter home written by Rudyard Dogsbody:

Mafeking
January 1900

Dear Mother,

I thank Divine Providence that I volunteered in time for a deucedly good 'scrap'. I have already been present at the reliefs of Ladysmith and Mafeking (pronounced 'Maffy King', by the by) and am proud to boast that in the process I have given at least a score of Smuts's contemptible scum a taste of cold British steel.

I have made the acquaintance of Baden-Powell, and mean to model myself on him. Some of his ideas are thought a little queer, but here is one I am thoroughly taken with. He envisages troops of young lads – to be known as 'scouts' – being trained in the manly virtues of warfare, patriotism and clean living. They would shun the company of the female of the species and live by the law of the jungle – an admirable preparation indeed for our future politicians, captains of industry, etc.

PETER NORMAN

1908
The Scout Movement

MAJOR RUDYARD DOGSBODY, D.S.O and BAR (1878–1928) *Son of Maj.-General Timothy Dogsbody and Ethel née Bracket; brother of Georgina. Writer, adventurer and fanatical imperialist. Even by late Victorian standards his rabid masculinity was unusual. At Eton he was celebrated for taking cold showers before, after and sometimes even during breakfast. Decorated for insane acts of valour in the Boer War, he later joined Baden-Powell in founding the Boy Scout movement. Married 1907 Amelia Twembling; one son, Ernest. Disillusioned by what he called 'the spread of this rank weed, democracy', he finally died by his own hand as a protest against Universal Women's Suffrage.*

RUDYARD DOGSBODY TELLS how he was in at the beginning:

> Brownsea Island
> Dorset
> June 1908

Dearest Mother,

At last our dream has come to fruition! In this remote part of Poole Harbour B.-P. and I are conducting an experiment with young minds and bodies which, if successful, may yet save our nation's manhood from enfeeblement by the vile socialist and pacifist scum proliferating in our midst.

You may recall that, whilst at the Cape, B.-P. and I visited a remote islet named Robben Island, and it was this that planted in our minds the suitability of an island setting for our experimental camp. Thus you find me here on Brownsea with our small band of 'scouts', who are learning the value of true comradeship and clean living by bedding down together under canvas, roasting red squirrels over an open blaze and arm-wrestling to the very limits of human endurance. Plucked from their genteel homes and the enervating influence of mothers, sisters and aunts, our young charges swiftly lose any traces of incipient effeminacy and are at one another's throats like wolves!

While my profound admiration for B.-P. continues unabated, I cannot deny that I am perturbed by some of his ideas for the future of scouting. To sit in a circle chanting 'dib, dib, dib' when one could be learning to lash an enemy to a tree or disembowelling a squirrel looks to me a dangerously *louche* activity; moreover B.-P.'s draft scouting code has much to say about whistling but does not even mention the perils of self-abuse. Already lavatory paper has appeared in the latrines and loose talk of warm water during ablutions has gone totally unpunished. Worst of all, under the pernicious influence of his sister Agnes he proposes to set up a parallel 'girl guide' movement for young females. If this corruption of our original intention to breed a new race of noble young Spartans continues I fear I may have to withdraw my support and go in search of more manly adventure.

By the by, Mother, in her last missive my sister Georgina declared that she had 'more than a shred of sympathy' with Mrs Pankhurst and her dastardly ilk. May I have your assurance that this was nothing more than a girlish prank, a foolish attempt to provoke her stern brother with an outrageous show of sedition? I need hardly add that if *any* member of my family were to be mixed up with that coven of harpies that call themselves *suffragettes* I should be forced to consider myself no longer a Dogsbody.

Yr son,

Rudyard

PETER NORMAN

1909
A Poet's Inspiration

QUEENIE DOGSBODY (née TINKER) (1881– 1965) *Wife of Percy, the Downing Street messenger. House- keeper to the Kiplings for a number of years. A lively and incorrigible gossip with the gift of total recall, her reminiscences of life among the literary lions were recorded by the BBC but were considered for the most part too 'spicy' for the radio.*

FROM 'Turn-of-the-Century Tweeny', the reminiscences of Mrs Queenie Dogsbody:

Very reserved he was, Mr Kipling – and the mistress – she guarded him like he was the Crown Jewels – wouldn't let no one near him hardly. That morning though – seemed he was at a bit of a loose end – stood there watching me dusting the dining-room – wonderful wood it was – took a polish lovely it did. Mistress must 'ave told 'im the trouble I was 'aving with Percy 'cos he asked about 'im. So I told 'im what I'd told Perce: 'If you can't learn, my lad, to 'old your liquor and stop be'aving like a drunken swine, you'll find that I shall up and leave you quicker than gipsies filching washing from a line.' 'Would you mind repeating that, Mrs Dogsbody?' Mr Kipling 'e says – so I did, and *as* I did he sort of beat time in the air. 'It's the rhythm, Mrs D.,' 'e says, 'it's the rhythm I want.' Anyway, I told him quite a bit more and 'e said: 'There seem to be a lot of "ifs" in your life, Mrs D.,' 'e said. 'Well, sir,' I said, 'that's what life is, ain't it? One big If.' 'Well, Mrs D.,' 'e said, 'you may be right at that.' And then 'e buzzes off back into his study and starts scribbling away as usual.

MARTIN FAGG

1914
The Start of the
First World War

AN EXCERPT FROM a letter written by H. H. Asquith, the Liberal Prime Minister, to his young mistress, Venetia Stanley, and entrusted to a Downing Street messenger, one Percy Dogsbody, who, on his way to the Stanleys' residence on a hot afternoon, failed to pass the door of 'The Beagle and Ferret'. The letter nestled unopened in the pocket of the jacket which Percy, who never sought other employment after his dismissal next day for insobriety, did not wear again.

PERCY DOGSBODY (1877–1921)   *Born in Peckham, the illegitimate son of Nellie and brother of William and Millicent. Married 1900 Queenie Tinker. Always troubled by drink and never found work again after his dismissal in 1914. Died of DTs in 1921.*

Sunday, 28 June 1914

My Most Adored and Beloved,

How difficult it is for us humans, in the dust and clangour of our days, to sift that which is important from that which is trivial almost beyond belief. Millions think of me as the Prime Minister of the world's richest and most powerful nation. Only you and I know that the only thing of any true significance in my life is my feeling for you. Who can measure the heart's proportions or trace the contours of the soul?

A bizarre piece of news just received. The heir to the Austrian throne and his wife have, it seems, been shot and killed by a Slav nationalist somewhere in Bosnia. As the Archduke is said to have been heartily disliked by his uncle, the Emperor – and indeed by almost everyone he ever met – the Austrians will probably feel the Serbs have done them a good turn, though bound to make a bit of a fuss about it on the surface . . .

MARTIN FAGG

1914
The Defence of the Realm Act

TANCRED DOGSBODY's struggle for the workers continued during the Great War, when he was of course a conscientious objector. He worked in a factory making shells, and from time to time emitted a blast, in the manner of whatever poet happened to be fashionable at the time. He was particularly angry about the Acts passed from 1914 onwards, aimed to divert attention from the incompetence of the politicians and generals. In 1915, this resulted in the introduction of the licensing hours from which the nation still suffers, in order to stop munitions workers spending their time in pubs. Here are two of Tancred's poems:

> 'Good morning, good morning!' the Minister said
> When he joined us last week in 'The Marquess of Wells';
> Now he's telling us lads we're to blame for the dead,
> By drinking all day when we should have made shells.
> 'He's a cheery old card,' grunted Jack in my ear
> As we carried on downing whatever was near.
>
> But he did for old Jack when he locked up the beer.

*

> What closing times for us who live as cattle,
>   Feeding the monstrous fodder to the guns?
> Only the brainwashed public's wretched prattle
>   Prolongs the murder of the wretched Huns.

·231

Let working lads from trench to earthwork call out:
  'Suspend the massacre! withhold the shells!'
Then let the great conflicting armies fall out
  And run in gratitude to ring their bells.

But now, these men by whom we are defended
  Pass laws to make our tribulations worse;
Losing the wits to which they once pretended,
  They turn upon our labours with a curse;
And, to excuse slack fingers on the helm
Make us their scapegoats 'to defend the realm'!

PAUL GRIFFIN

1915
Rupert Brooke:
Posthumous Sonnet

GEORGINA DOGSBODY (1884–1942)   *Spiritualist medium and secret supporter of the suffragette movement. Younger sister of Rudyard. After his suicide in 1928 she began to receive a number of violently angry messages from 'the other side' to the effect that he had discovered her sympathies and strongly disapproved.*

THIS POSTHUMOUS SONNET was dictated by Rupert Brooke to Georgina Dogsbody shortly after the poet's untimely death in 1915 at the age of twenty-eight:

Now that I'm dead, think only this of me:
Some corner in the field of English Lit. –
Great War poet – will mine for ever be;
(My 'Soldier' sonnet was an instant hit).

I also used to write of Love and Laughter,
Of Life and Youth and Wind and Sea and Sun,
Although in fact what I was really after
Was pretty girls – and boys – and having fun.
    Then everything turned sour; I felt unclean,
    But cheered up at the prospect of a war;
    Came August, Nineteen-Hundred-and-Fourteen;
    God! Just the moment I'd been waiting for;
    Though actually I never had to fight,
    I died in bed from a mosquito bite.

STANLEY J. SHARPLESS

1915
Tin Helmets

Proceedings of a court of enquiry held at Bercy Les Deux Magots
on 18th June 1915
for the purpose of examining the cause of wounds
sustained by No. 403079 Pte Dogsbody J.
The court having assembled at 0900 hrs
proceed to take statements

No. 4029607 L/Sgt. Rasp, states:

'On 28th May when I issued No. 4 Platoon with the new helmets, steel, Private Dogsbody said to me, begging the Court's pardon, he said: "These here bleeding basins, tin, hand-washing, will not stop no ruddy bullet." I replied: "Replace your head-dress forthwith Private Dogsbody. You are improperly dressed on parade." He became excited and shouted: "Right, Sergeant. I will put on this tin jerry and I will show you as how it is no use." He replaced the said helmet, steel, jumped up on the firestep and presented his bent head above the parapet. Thereupon two bullets, sniper's, enemy, struck the helmet simultaneous, and Private Dogsbody fell back into the trench. Upon examination, it was seen as how one bullet had struck the side of the helmet and ricochetted off, thus proving Pte Dogsbody's opinion incorrect. The other bullet had struck centrally and pierced the helmet, thus demonstrating Pte Dogsbody correct, but dead.'

Nos. 403068 L/Cpl. Bunn and all members of his No. 13 Section corroborating, the Court was closed at 0917 hours.

Signed B. L. Montgomery, Lieut.
President

W. F. N. WATSON

1917
Life in the Trenches

Basingstoke
January 1917

The Editor
The Times

Sir,

It has been reported in your organ that on 25 December last a species of 'friendly' ball game was played between our serving men in Flanders and their Hunnish counterparts, in the area popularly known as no-man's-land, in direct contravention of the unremitting state of hostilities that exists between our nations. It has even been suggested by milksop clergymen and the like that this unwarranted fraterniza-tion was some sort of noble gesture, expressing man's essential humanity and so forth.

What tommyrot! These men are in clear dereliction of their duty as British soldiers and if I were their commanding officer rest assured that every man jack would have been before a court martial the following morning. As it is I wish to place on record that I have sent a crate of white feathers to the front for distribution to every faint-heart involved, and urge all like-minded patriots to do the same. This noble war will never be won by misguided tommies, infected by who knows what wicked pacifist claptrap, kicking around an inflated bladder with their nation's sworn enemies.

> Yrs faithfully,
> *Rudyard Dogsbody, D.S.O., Maj. (Retd.)*

PETER NORMAN

1922
La Vie Parisienne

L T. BRUNO DOGSBODY (1896–1969)   *Lifelong aesthete and traveller. A staff liaison officer in Paris during World War I, he stayed on in Europe, subsequently occupying British Council posts in Mediterranean and Aegean locations.*

AN IMPRESSION OF the *vie de Bohème* in post-war Paris:

4 August 1922

Dear Pater,

It's awfully hard to believe that the big show started four years ago today. It was a job well done, though of course hard on the poor chaps who never made it back to Blighty. And of course everything's been shaken topsy-turvy. You'd never believe what's going on here.

The blessed place is full of Americans, and half of them have some cock-eyed notion of being artists. I confess I've been slumming a little (shush – don't tell Mater) and have run into some frightfully queer coves. There's a fellow called Hemingway, for example – looks like a prizefighter, speaks out of the corner of his mouth, that sort of thing. Actually he's a reporter, but I've seen some of his 'stories' (he lives over in the Place Contrescarpe, quite a hike from the Crillon, but I can take in the Louvre on the way). They're all done in a kind of baby-talk, no point to them at all except they preach defeatist rot about the war. I didn't have the heart to tell him that he should read O. Henry if he wants to learn how to spin a yarn! What's more, the 'tough guy' act is pure bluff; apparently he's a doctor's son from some cosy suburb (Chicago, I think).

Still, he's a good fellow in the tavern and I've met some of his chums. One was Dos Passos, sort of a dago type. He's also written one of those pro-Hun novels that are all the go. Funny, it's always the educated ones who turn traitor – seems Dos Passos was at Harvard. Then there's a whiskered poet called Pound. Quite potty. Apparently he's helping some other chap write a great long poem that's all made up of things he's read. Something to do with 'imagism', but I call it plagiarism. I suppose after the late unpleasantness we should expect such upheavals, but it's all dreadfully faddish. Funny, the Huns have a word for it: *Kultur-Bolschevismus*.

But the oddest American of all is a woman (I can't call her a lady – quite frankly, Pater, she's one of nature's mistakes) who has a big place in the Rue de Fleurus. She holds a kind of salon there, and woe betide anyone who doesn't take her word as gospel. I think she could knock the stuffing out of Hemingway. She has a mousy little companion and the walls are covered with 'modern art', i.e. stuff done by people who can't paint for toffee out to shock. '*Épater la bourgeoisie*' seems to be the motto, and the worst daubs of all are by some barmy Spaniard who doesn't even understand perspective. Anyway, this creature (Gertrude something or other – a Jewish name) really lords it over her coterie. Can't help thinking of 'The Emperor's New Clothes' – and by the by, how is darling Nanny?

I suppose sooner or later all these odd fish will swim off and the world will get back to sanity. All the Yanks are filthy rich of course, that's half the trouble, and when I hear them boasting how they won the war I really have to count to ten, as you taught me. Luckily Paris has its compensations (no names, no pack-drill, eh?) and on the serious side I have my Aristotle – the one you bought me in my final term at Harrow. There's a fellow who knew what art was about!

Please give my love to dearest Mater. I still do *The Times* crossword in the Crillon lounge – jolly reassuring to know that some things don't change.

> Your loving son,
> *Bruno*

BASIL RANSOME-DAVIES

PORTRAIT OF A LADY WHO MAY OR MAY NOT HAVE BEEN VIRGINIA WOOLF: By the talented amateur portraitist Dora Dogsbody. The interrelation of astringence and sumptuous curves in the artist's Analytical Neo-Cubist Baroque style, influenced by Rubens and Picasso, admirably reflect both the unyielding internal realism and sensuously fluid rhythms of the sitter's work, and the emphatic mental suffering of both women.

1924
John Betjeman on the Tomb of Karl Marx

WHAT DO KARL MARX and John Betjeman have in common? Answer: the North London suburb of Highgate. Marx, ironically enough, was buried in that eminently bourgeois locality; Betjeman was born there. This poem was confiscated during prep. by Rudyard Dogsbody, then P.E. Master at Marlborough School:

Death in Highgate

Shades of early Fabians gather
To the sound of Highgate bells:
Ramsay Mac, the Webbs, Keir Hardie,
G. B. Shaw and H. G. Wells.

Haunting still the grave where tourists,
Taking pictures, stand and stare,
Left and Right opinions flying
Briskly through the Highgate air.

'Guess he ranks with Freud and Darwin,
Lenin, Einstein and – all those;
That's what I think. What do you think?'
''Fraid I'm one of the "don't knows".'

'Marx rewrote the whole of history
As the story of class war.'
'Should have shipped him off to Moscow.'
'Got a lot to answer for.'

'Everything he said was gospel
From the Commie point of view.'
'Ever read *Das Kapital*?' 'No,
Never managed it. Have you?'

'Look what monsters he inspired:
Trotsky, Stalin, Mao and Co.'
'Just a stirrer-up of trouble.'
'Ssh. *De mortuis*, you know.'

'Wonder what he would be doing
These days, if he were alive?'
'Should have thought that's pretty obvious,
He'd be head of M15.'

'Where are Groucho, Harpo, Chico,
Weren't they all his kith and kin?'
Underground, the skull is grinning
Its unchanging, private grin.

STANLEY J. SHARPLESS

1926
The General Strike

St John's Wood
May 1926

Dear Mother,

I have just completed the most invigorating week I have spent since the glorious days when we booted Johnny Boer all over the shop at Cape Colony! At last I have found a task which combines physical action (and an exhilarating dash of violence) with a sense that one is doing one's duty as an Englishman. If I tell you that I have spent the week at the wheel of an omnibus you will think that your poor Rudyard has finally lost his noodle, but no! Strike-breaking is indeed the most glorious and heroic enterprise. I had feared that the modern world was embracing perdition, to the disgusting strains of a negro 'jazz' band, so wholeheartedly that there was little a man of my advancing years could do to stand in the way of regress; I confess I had even, God forgive me, entertained thoughts of the noble Roman solution. But now I find myself filled with energy and hope.

Our day begins at dawn: we meet at a pre-arranged spot and make our way to the depot. Despite the hour, there are always numerous villainous-looking 'pickets', prodigiously scarved and capped, with faces like whippets, awaiting us. They shout incomprehensible cockney abuse and sometimes attempt fisticuffs but we are more than a match for them, especially when the Metropolitan Police weigh in with their truncheons. A cracked head is a wondrous pacifier of your average communist agitator! Indeed I sometimes wish these contemptible fellows would put up more of a fight, for it is many years since I have had an opportunity to practise my garrotting skills.

We are a mixed bunch – a professor of philosophy, a barrister, a captain of industry and a Fleet Street editor – all united in our determination that the honest English working man shall not be persuaded to question his lot by the socialist scum. Let the malcontents get a foothold now, mother, and I venture to predict that if, God willing, we wage a further war against the Hun, there will be rumblings of dissatisfaction in the ranks and, who knows, a socialistic government to follow. The thought is too horrible, I know, but we must face facts.

You might ask my sister what *she* is doing to preserve civilization as we know it – pressing for voting rights, no doubt, even for unmarried women, who would be bereft of a man's guiding hand and would be an all too easy prey for those who would raise the red flag in our land. Faugh – my gorge rises and I can write no more!

Your son,
Rudyard

PETER NORMAN

'OUR GALLANT MAJOR "RUDDY" DOGSBODY BLASTS THE BOL-SHIES': This drawing by ex-temporary Captain 'Fruity' Curmudgen, late Poona Light Horse, of Major Rudyard Dogsbody bursting through a picket-line of strikers while manning a London bus during the General Strike was printed in their bus depot's *Strikebusters Bulletin*.

1929
Pavlov's Experiments

LETTER FROM Ernest Dogsbody to his mother, with whom he corresponded in secret.

Dearest Mama,

Without wishing to lament my lot, I must confess that working in Dr Pavlov's laboratory has its irritations. While Klaus and I are cleaning out the kennels, the doctor stumps about tetchily, watching us at our work and endlessly eating chocolate, of which he keeps a large stock in the pocket of his white coat. This becomes increasingly irksome as lunchtime approaches, and this morning I observed to Klaus that the very sound of tearing silver foil made my mouth water.

The doctor whirled round at once. 'Dogsbody!' he roared, 'you will never make a more significant remark in your life!' I have no pretensions towards intellectualism as you know, dearest Mama, but I feel that the remark was unnecessarily belittling, and contemplate asking for a transfer to rats, as it seems unlikely that I will ever make a lasting contribution to science in my present post.

In some depression, I remain your loving son,

Ernest

ALISON PRINCE

E RNEST DOGSBODY (1908–   )   *Son of Rudyard. A scholarly boy, averse to all forms of organized physical activity, he left home at an early age to avoid the military career which his father somewhat forcibly desired him to adopt. Shortly after the date of this letter he left Pavlov's laboratory to take up a similar post with a Dr Frankenstein. Details of his career after this are vague.*

1934–9
Government Papers

M ONTAGUE   DOGSBODY,   M.B.E.   (1900– 1980)   *Joined the Foreign Office in 1922 and worked there in junior and intermediate grades until his retirement. An honest and faithful servant, he felt that the reward of a minor honour failed to make up for the regularity with which his memoranda, many of them written during the critical years of the 1930s, were ignored by his superiors. Defiantly, he preserved copies for posterity.*

---

3 August 1934
The minister should be made aware that, with the death of President Hindenburg, a power vacuum impends in Germany. Herr Hitler has united the offices of President and Chancellor, but this measure

betrays his weakness and will not hold the Reich together. It is imperative that H.M.G. opens negotiations with the Kaiser, letting bygones be bygones. The monarchy is the only rallying-point for Germans, who as a race are deeply traditional.

17 March 1935
Hitler's repudiation of the Treaty of Versailles and its disarmament provisions establish beyond doubt that he is a political gambler with exceedingly poor judgement. A peace-loving nation such as Germany will not support such an outright transgression of binding agreements. We may expect the forced resignation of the Führer at any hour, and H.M.G. should prepare to recognize a Social-Democratic government that will express the political will of its people.

12 July 1936
Hitler's guarantee of Austrian sovereignty is yet another concession wrung from him by a stronger and more stable state. It is vital that attention be paid to the overwhelming possibility of an Austrian invasion of the Reich, which would lead to a dangerously aggressive regime of professors and literati. H.M.G. should back the large and influential Protestant element in Germany that is the only hope of resisting a Catholic takeover. I can take no responsibility for the outcome if this advice is neglected.

28 October 1936
The Rome–Berlin accord must be seen as a cover for joint Italo-Austrian designs on Germany which Hitler, in his vanity, has failed to foresee. The way is potentially open for a mighty new European empire stretching from the North Sea to the Adriatic, controlled from the Vatican and the Austrian chancery. Events must now be seen as having developed to the point where a radical answer is needed. I strongly recommend that H.M.G. contacts the leaders of Kommunist Partei Deutschland who, with Stalin at their back, may prevent this dire threat.

1 October 1938
While it is gratifying to know that the P.M. and M. Daladier have squashed Hitler's ambitions with the small and derisory award of a troublesome piece of Central European territory, I fear that this humiliation may rebound by delivering Germany into the hands of

Soviet subversives who have been waiting for their chance. There is no doubt that the most urgent need is to stiffen Poland, whose strong, reliable government may exert a moderating influence on the anti-Hitler forces in Germany.

2 September 1939

A profound emergency must now be recognized. Polish provocation has lured Hitler into a foolhardy attack, and we may expect a quick penetration of Polish forces towards the Rhine, possibly assisted by Belgian intervention from the west. When Hitler's fragile position crumbles, H.M.G. will be faced by an expanded and hostile Polish state. Steps must be taken at once to forge an alliance with Switzerland.

BASIL RANSOME-DAVIES

1937
Auden on the Spanish Civil War

KARL ENGELS HERZEN KROPOTKIN DOGS-BODY (1900–   )   *Born in Sunderland. Served in International Brigade on Republican side in Spanish Civil War. Severely wounded while fighting on the Ebbro. Became a dominating figure in Labour Party politics in the North-East after 1945. Named Karl Engels Herzen Kropotkin by his passionately* engagés *parents, he could, with such a rich baptismal endowment, hardly have avoided enlistment in the International Brigade at the outbreak of the Civil War in Spain, to which he travelled at much the same time as W. H. Auden.*

WE ARE INDEBTED for the following MS. to Alderman K.E.H.K. Dogsbody of Sunderland. The verse letter (of which the exact date is unknown) came into Brigade-member Dogsbody's possession in Barcelona in circumstances that this veteran Soldier of the Left cannot

now, in his late eighties, precisely recall. It appears to be addressed to
Stephen Spender, one of Auden's closest friends.

> *Stephen Dear* – it's me again,
> To let you know I'm ditching Spain,
> And shortly coming home – by train.
> These verses (tersely) must explain.
>
> I find (it's rather hard to write)
> I have no stomach for a fight;
> But, fright apart, I find that war
> Is (literally) a bloody bore.
>
> Though difficult, I know, to plot
> An intellectual's proper lot,
> Of this at least I'm sure – it's not
> Fortuitously getting shot.
>
> Rushing trenches may be grander
> Than rushing out the propaganda,
> But being (probably) unread
> Beats being (definitely) dead.
>
> Admittedly, the boys are choice:
> With them at least I can rejoice
> In sex's sublimated anger,
> Dwindling down to lovely languor.
>
> What *really* drives me to the brink –
> THERE'S NOTHING DECENT HERE TO DRINK!
> I'm so pissed off with getting pissed on
> Hellfire *fino* – *Love from Wystan*.

MARTIN FAGG

1939
The Outbreak of the Second World War

AN UNPUBLISHED POEM by Ogden Nash, given to Emily Belle Dogsbody:

1939

I remember the invasion of no land
As clearly as I remember the invasion of Poland.
I had been seeing one of those Thin Man films I never tired of
    seeing –
Though thin was what Myrna Loy could hardly be accused of being.
To a boy she was a dream girl, curvaceous, centrally-heated,
Round-faced, round-bosomed, and round-seated –
Not Mae West-like but companionable, desirable,
The sort of girl who might really be acquirable,
A decent girl, a pal. It made me howell
To think of her being wasted on William Powell.

I was coming out of the cinema, in among the Studebakers and
    Packards,
When I saw it on the placards:
DECLARATION OF WAR BY BRITAIN.
Now what? I thought. Twice shy, once bitten.
It's no use looking for someone unattainable, resembling
Dear Myrna. There are other sorts of girl that get me trembling.
I'd better give my attention to them an'
As for this war business, the answer is a lemon.
Not so. In war there is much you can do with impunity;
War offers opportunity.

But when I look back on those wartime girls I realize they all looked
    as if they'd been skimped on,
In the manner of Twiggy, and Jean Shrimpton.

Grey-headed now, I still feel like a young boy
And long for Myrna Loy.
Now, where was I? Ah, yes, the war.
Well, it was girls I really valued it for.

PAUL GRIFFIN

1940
A Pioneer of Aviation

HERMANN HUNDEKÖRPER (1919–40) *One of twin illegitimate sons of Private Sam (Chunky) Dogsbody (1900–1919), Pioneer Corps, of Barnet, and Helga Hundekörper (1902–87), of Nuremberg. He was conceived during a fifteen-minute meeting, two days after the Armistice, at Aachen. This brief encounter encompassed an informal introduction, the act of congress, an exchange of addresses and the sad farewell. Little is known of Sam, except that he played the tenor saxophone rather badly and had Marxist leanings. Helga, who never married, was housemaid to Anthony Fokker from 1936 to 1938 – undoubtedly a contributory factor in Hermann's career in aviation design.*

Hermann Hundekörper was a pioneer in rubber-powered aircraft. He invented the Hundekörper Blitz, a very light bomber, constructed of balsa wood and powered by six giant rubber bands. It had two ten-foot propellers, fitted one above the other, the upper screw being mounted on a turret fixed to the pilot's cabin. When the upper propeller operated in a clockwise direction, tightening the bands in sequence, the lower one turned anti-clockwise, propelling the plane. This sequence alternated throughout the flight, power also being generated by a series of nose-dives when the plane had attained a certain height.

Hundekörper undertook to pilot his prototype bomber, carrying a six-pound incendiary device, from Frankfurt to London in June 1940.

Unfortunately the main rubber band broke through the balsa casing, strangled Hundekörper and ignited the device, causing the aircraft to catch fire over the North Sea.

Although many attempts were made to revive interest in rubber-powered aircraft, the Luftwaffe considered that the saving in fuel was more than offset by their low carrying capabilities. Hundekörper's last flight marked the end of an interesting concept.

> From *Hermann Hundekörper, Werk und Mensch* (1948)
> Eng. trans. Russell Lucas

RUSSELL LUCAS

1940
Dunkirk

A Letter Home

2 June 1940

Dear Mother and Father,

I am forbidden by the military censor to say where I am or what I am doing but I can tell you that it's no picnic. (Sorry about the stain at the top of this page but I dropped my lump of Brie and in brushing the sand off it I spilt my mug of Beaujolais.)

I am not in any real danger apart from being dive-bombed by Stukas and raked with fire by short-sighted RAF chappies.

I am not allowed to divulge how many there are of us here, but you do have to wait an awfully long time to bat in 169,000-a-side beach cricket.

PRIVATE PETER ('Pete') DOGSBODY (1920–   )
Born in Walsall. Joined South Staffs. Regiment in 1938. Married Ethel Olivier. After the cessation of hostilities, Peter and Ethel Dogsbody and Ethel's cousin Josie formed a comedy trio, 'Pete and the Puppy-Fats', which toured Number Two theatres with some success for several years.

I hope to be home shortly if the weather keeps nice. The sea is so calm at present I feel I could swim the thirty miles back to Dover.

My pal Ginger caught it in the leg yesterday (he was standing far too close at slip) and was evacuated this morning by a two-man troopship called the 'Ramsgate Municipal Boating Lake – No. 27'.

Our sergeant has just spotted a fleet of hollowed-out tree trunks approaching – this could be our turn! I shall be glad to get the stink of cordite and garlic out of my nose.

Hope to see you soon,

> Your ever loving son,
> *Pete*

Pete was able to deliver this letter to his parents by hand on 5 June 1940 after the glorious success of the planned tactical withdrawal from Europe by the British Expeditionary Force.

V. ERNEST COX

c.1940
Dylan Thomas

TERENCE DOGSBODY (1912–44). *Elder brother of Peter (of 'Pete and the Puppy-Fats' fame).*

THIS POEM, WRITTEN by Dylan Thomas c.1940, was given to a pub acquaintance the night before he (Terence Dogsbody) joined the RAF. It turned up recently among Terence's papers.

> Why did I stay daft in the draught-dank pub,
> The liquor bitter on my honey tongue,
> Broth of a doubting boyo Thomas; life
> Stretched out war to war?
> Drenched I was, bard-being, every evening;
> Hung over each morning bay for drying out.

I would lord it over my tenant words unliquored,
But people need their poets drunk as lords,
And I must wet my whistle to perform;
Not shanty on soda water;
And I must watch folk watching me watch them
And hang upon their chapel hat-peg eyes.

The wormy womb of Wales, dragon-begetting,
Feeds fat on water winey with lush weeds.
No other wine I wanted: but words sown
Would not spring fully-armed
Without the legend of my sodden ways
Winding out of Wales across the world.

MARGARET ROGERS

1942
The Head Girl of a
Grantham Grammar School

THE FOLLOWING EXTRACTS from a diary kept by Wendy
Spettigue (née Dogsbody) did not form part of the family archives,
but were submitted to the Editor direct soon after a note had appeared
in the *Bookseller* that this collection was in hand. In her accompanying
letter, Wendy wrote:

I suppose I had never taken the archives very seriously, a view that
was almost certainly reinforced as a result of my friendship with
Margaret Roberts. She was so kind to me, allowing me to carry her
books and open doors for her. 'These little jobs,' she said, 'will ensure,
Wendy, that you do not forget your lower-working-class origins.' It
was she who shaped my attitude to the archives. Maggie hated
bureaucracy and red tape. As for civil servants, I sometimes think that
Margaret had been bitten by one when she was a baby.

Wendy went on to say she was sorry that more of the diary had not survived the ravages of time. She had only found it when searching for some material she had borrowed from the archives when she was doing a course with the Open University. However, enough remains to give us some idea of how our first woman Prime Minister handled power for the first time.

Here are some typical entries:

21 June 1942: Margaret told me that the Head had asked her to be head girl next year. 'Did you say: "Yes"?' I asked. She said she had agreed in principle, but wanted some rethinking done about beginning each day with an act of worship. 'But, Margaret,' I said, 'so many girls don't believe in God any longer.' 'It's not Him I want them to worship,' she said. 'It's me!'

1 July: The Head announced Margaret's appointment to the school. The news was not universally popular. During her first year as a Prefect, some third formers had christened her 'Bossyboots' and these went round shouting: 'Heil Hilda' and making a salute which was a mixture of the Hitler salute and the V sign.

16 September: Margaret has begun her year in office by putting forward plans to privatize the school tuck-shop, and getting outside firms to sponsor the school choir and the orchestra as well as the drama society, but has been overruled by the Headmistress, it seems. I met Maggie on my way to Eng. Lit. She was in a very bad mood. 'Still wasting your time on that second-class subject, Wendy?' There was no point in replying, so I just asked how her job was going. 'Not enough authority,' she said. 'One ought to have the power to sack the Head. She even expects *me* to address her as "Ma'am".' Irene told me the third-formers have made up a riddle about Maggie which begins: 'Why are we getting grosser and grosser all the time?'

2 October: There is to be a limited experiment in privatization and sponsorship. Clearly Margaret has been doing some hard work on the Head. She announced the plan after prayers at morning assembly. Margaret was very reassuring. 'Lacrosse is safe in my hands,' she told us . . .

Unhappily, this is all that remains of Wendy's diary.

However, Wendy also enclosed a copy of the school magazine dated July 1943 which contains a report of the Headmistress's farewell speech to the girl who was probably the most memorable head girl any school has ever had:

HEADMISTRESS'S FAREWELL TO
HEAD GIRL OF GRANTHAM GRAMMAR

The Head began by saying that she was delighted that so many pupils had turned up to say goodbye to Margaret Roberts. It was a happy day, both for the school and for Margaret, for was she not going on to higher things and new worlds to conquer? The Head was sure that Margaret would do her utmost to conquer them. Margaret had always tried very hard. She deserved Oxford, and, as a Cambridge graduate herself, the Head was certain that Oxford deserved Margaret. Her year as head girl was especially memorable and productive, despite some problems over, for instance, the sponsoring of the hockey team by a commercial firm making door furniture. It had been unfortunate that the slogan on the team's shirts had read: 'If you want the best knockers, we have them'. But no one could forget this year. The school would never be quite the same again, although she herself would be making some small readjustments in the very near future. To start with, the tuck shop would be de-privatized and Keynesian concepts would be restored to the Economics syllabus. The ceremony ended with a presentation to Margaret of a leather-bound copy of *Opportunities for Chemistry Graduates in the Far East*. There were cries of 'Heil Hilda' and 'Farewell, Snobby' as the meeting closed.

E. O. PARROTT

1943
Wartime Censorship

LETTER FROM Ethel Olivier (later Dogsbody) to her fiancé, Able-Seaman Peter Dogsbody. The censor has been at his necessary work of deleting anything which might prove useful to the enemy.

23 November 1943

My dearest Peter,

You have no idea how we all miss you, I most of all. ▆▆▆ is a terrible thing. Pray God it will be over soon! Here in ▆▆▆▆▆ we get about as best we can but in these dark months the blackout is 'very irksome' as old Mrs Ed▆▆ds used to say, God bless her. Rationing is very tough but we get a fair diet and are quite healthy (although Deirdre has got the ▆▆▆▆▆ measles). Josie and I put on a little show at the Church Hall – all proceeds to the Sailors' Comfort Fund. It was wizard! Josie's performance of 'We're going to hang out the washing on the ▆▆▆▆▆▆▆ ▆▆▆▆' went down a ▆▆▆▆; and Major Knott-Reilly played 'Colonel Bogey' on the trombone. (You know – the march with the funny words about ▆▆▆▆▆ has only got one ball – only no one sang it, thank the lord). In the second half I sang a medley of Irving ▆▆▆▆▆ numbers. Afterwards we all got on a number ▆▆▆▆ bus and went up west to celebrate. Josie sang 'There'll always be an ▆▆▆▆▆▆' and the landlord of the Duke of ▆▆▆▆▆ gave us a free round.

The twins have been evacuated – to ▆▆▆▆ in the county of ▆▆▆▆▆ not far from ▆▆▆▆▆▆ where Deirdre used to go with that peculiar friend of hers (the one that collected ▆▆▆▆▆). As to us we ▆▆▆▆▆ on somehow. My nephew ▆▆▆▆ was given a toy ▆▆▆▆▆ ▆▆▆ for his birthday and now he races round the house saying 'Dadadadada – you're dead.' Poor lamb. We've got a new ▆▆▆▆ for the guppies (you remember how the old one leaked!) and they look very grand now.

I saw in *The Times* that ▆▆▆▆ are ▆▆▆▆▆ out of ▆▆▆▆▆ ▆▆▆▆ and wonder if it has any effect on ▆▆▆▆. I'm sure you know what I mean. Brigadier ▆▆▆▆▆ told me at the bus stop that the ▆▆▆▆ will be over by Christmas. I do hope he's right.

Well, love to you, wherever you are. And remember ▆▆▆▆ ▆▆▆ ▆▆▆▆ ▆▆▆▆▆ ▆▆▆▆▆▆ with brass knobs on. I long to take you in my ▆▆▆▆ and give you a big hug.

Ever your loving
Ethel

P.S. The ▆▆▆▆▆ the ▆▆▆▆ ▆▆▆▆ ▆▆▆ the ▆▆▆▆ if you don't mind my saying so. Only joking! Love, E.

GERARD BENSON

1944
The Invasion of Europe

TERENCE DOGSBODY was in the family's tradition of failed poets. Though publication eluded him, manuscripts found after his death in Normandy reveal an acolyte of the Auden school. This is an example:

In Time of Worry

Agents in underground cells awaiting
The coded order, the signal for sudden invasion
Anxiously stiffen their mouths, all muscles alert.
The leader fastens his helmet, hopeful that now,
In winter, in gardens surrounded by railings,
In damaged suburbs, by the temporary roundabout,
On bridges where thought of life fails,
The masses will heed the urgent noise of transmitters.
Freed from neurosis at last,
They will strangle the dubious fathers,
The stockbrokers with death in their pipe-stems,
The prefects, the major-domos, the ladies at tea
On the doomed lawn talking of birth control.
The horrible recipe unfolds.
Fear jumps out of the escritoire.
Hundreds reach for the suicide pill.
Thousands march like tanks, comrades together awake now,
Crossing the mined frontier, tearing the wire
Away from the intrepid concrete
Till no sound is described but agreement
And treaties are signed, unanimous
On arterial road and in restful elaborate valley.

BASIL RANSOME-DAVIES

1945
Berlin – a View from the Bunker

Unterstrassenbahnliegendehauptführer
Hundekörper, H.,
Bunker 384 Z K,
Berlin
6 Mai 1945

Liebe Gretchen!

Ach, was ist das alles für eine Schrabbelkockhandelschaft. Meine
Socken sind mit Hollen, meine beste Uniform ist still nicht von
dem Kleiderklienern zurückgesauberwiedergedurchliefert geworden-
haben sein, und ich habe eine pudelfinstergedammte Kalt in dem
Kopf.

Mein Skoffträgenkraftwagen hatte aus Wasser gelaufen, und ich
habe drei flammende Kilometer hier auf meinen platten Fleischtellern
herzumarschieren müssen haben gehabt. Jetzt sagt der Oberstabs-
hauptbeschlagregierungsmeister, dass ich als Sanitätsplotscher in
diesem filzigen Bunker werken muss. Was ein Leben. Heim war
niemals wie dies.

SCHWALK.

Dein Leibbinde

Hans

P.S. Es ist nicht halb kalt, nun.

W. S. BROWNLIE

1945
The End of the Second World War

T. S. DOGSBODY (1885–1960) worked as the London corres-
pondent of one of the major American newspapers and was sent to
Cairo to cover the Second World War. The similarity of his initials to
those of another expatriate American persuaded him that he was both
a poet and an Englishman. This, the second of his *Two Duets*, suggests
that he was not even a good journalist:

Little Gadding

Whatever you may think, it is not
Much fun not much
Fun,
Writing and partly writing.
At moments in Shepheards, I admit
I shed tears in the Fernet Branca.
What, after all, had been happening?
There were Egyptians, certainly;
In Egypt this was, I can say, not uncommon;
But in the streets, men spoke English.
'What is the truth?' I asked them.
Careless talk, they said, cost lives.
That, I suppose, was their truth.
But who *were* they, with their ample supplies of explosives?
I would have asked the Countess and Mr Da Silva;
Only they were not there to ask,
And I was there not to ask,
But to understand,
To climb out from under my bed
And above all to report.
What, then, was there to report?

Later, life was permitted.
Something, it seems, had ended.
When I returned to London

Mr Beckenheimer called it peace.
Why did this make him so angry?
Was it, perhaps, a new kind of peace,
Rationed like sweets,
Strictly for the children?
Fleet Street looked just the same,
But my words were like the tired wind under the door
Out of spent reeds in a barren season.

After a little, nobody notices those rather fine bits.
One goes on of course, but it is not
Much fun not much
Fun.

PAUL GRIFFIN

T. S. DOGSBODY WONDERS WHAT HAS ENDED: This sketch by an unidentified sapper appeared in the VE Day edition of the *Sidi Barrani Bulletin*, one of the innumerable Service news-sheets that mushroomed during the Second World War.

1945
The Last Message from the Bunker

NOTE FOUND BY Major Bruno Dogsbody (then serving with British Intelligence) in a milk bottle outside Bunker 384 Z K, Berlin:

30.4.45

Dear Milkman,

Please cancel milk until further notice. Cream ordered for last Thursday not delivered. Please adjust bill and submit to C.-in-C., Allied Forces, Western Europe.

Thank you,

E. Hitler (Mrs)
×××

E. O. PARROTT

▌Editor's Note

And so we come, somewhat prematurely, to the end of our selection from the Dogsbody Papers. There was a great deal of even more contemporary material, but soon after our researchers began work MI5, backed up by SAS units and the police, in a series of dawn raids seized all post-war material, on the grounds that publication of this was not in the public interest and might be of use to a potential enemy, even though much of the material has already been serialized in the press in the Soviet Union and Australia. However, one item was subsequently retrieved from a public convenience in Westminster and it is included as an example of what the reader is missing.

SECRET MI5 SWOOP FIASCO: An artist's impression of the attempt by MI5 to prevent publication of the Dogsbody Papers. Owing to an error in communication, a force of armed police and SAS ordered to raid the Penguin Offices and arrest a Mr Parrott went to the Regent's Park Zoo. By the time they reached the significantly named Wrights Lane, they found that, to quote Chief Inspector Fowler, 'the birds had flown'.

There is no doubt in my mind that publication of this collection breaches the Official Secrets Act, and that both I and Viking are certain to be prosecuted in the courts. We shall fight for our rights tooth and nail, to the Appeal Courts and the House of Lords. However, this will cost a great deal of money (well, men of law have to make a living, though why this is I am not sure). However, a Fighting Fund will be needed and I earnestly ask all readers to contribute as much as they can.

Contributions, large or small, should be sent to me, E. O. Parrott, c/o Viking/Penguin, 27 Wrights Lane, London W8 5TZ.

1975
The Downing Street Plot

HORACE DOGSBODY (1940–   )   *Recommended by Sir Maurice Oldfield, when the latter was Head of MI5, as the 'most versatile and accomplished bugger in the business'.*

REPORT BY Horace Dogsbody, Accredited Audio-Engineer and Bugger, on his round-the-clock electronic surveillance of No. 10 Downing Street, and particularly the 'Kitchen Cabinet', suspected by Mr Cecil King and other similarly Right-minded citizens of being the prime British outpost of the Kremlin and/or KGB:

Sundry devices were planted and I record below the placing and performance of each:

1. *HP Sauce Bottle*   Unfortunately, this wholesome condiment was in such constant requisition at the Wilson supper-table that the consequential crackling effectively blanketed any traitorous badinage.

2. *Lady Falkender's Corsage*   Alas, the ultra-high level of atmospherics induced by her constant snubbing of everyone else in the room, including the P.M., totally drowned out any potentially treasonable dialogue.

3. *Mary Wilson's Verse Diary*   This device remained, unhappily (as a result of a phenomenon known in the trade as 'contextual sympathy'), absolutely inert and lifeless.

4. *Lord Wigg's Braces*   I regret to report that this device also remained wholly inactive during his sojourn at No. 10. It became 'live' only later that evening when the noble Lord was kerb-crawling down Edgware Road. The resulting conversational exchanges with various 'Ladies of the Night', though doubtless of some marketable *auditeur* interest, were not strictly material to my remit.

5. *Mr Wilson's Hot-Water Bottle* A dense background roar, reminiscent of a furious anti-aircraft barrage, was eventually diagnosed as the mere abdominal aftermath of Mrs Wilson's cooking. However, at 00.17 hours the following exchange occurred.

'What do you want for Christmas, Harold?'

'Anything from Marx and Sparx, Mary.'

Clearly, an open reference to the author of *Das Kapital* and a cunningly coded allusion to the infamous Spartacus uprising in Berlin in December 1918, led by the Red revolutionaries, Liebknecht and Luxemburg. An even more sinister dialogue was to ensue . . .

MARTIN FAGG

Acknowledgements

I WOULD LIKE to express my warm thanks to all the contributors for their hard work, patience and understanding. Many labour for little or no reward. Space is always limited and the pressure on it great. Unfortunately a few contributors failed to make the book at all.

My heartfelt thanks must also go to Father Ian Brayley, S.J., of Campion Hall, Oxford, and M. J. Rees of Havering College library for help in research; Mrs Tricia Chamberlain for typing the manuscript; and most of all to my wife, who toiled long and hard to ensure that no Dogsbody was omitted.

FOR THE BEST IN PAPERBACKS, LOOK FOR THE

In every corner of the world, on every subject under the sun, Penguin represents quality and variety – the very best in publishing today.

For complete information about books available from Penguin – including Pelicans, Puffins, Peregrines and Penguin Classics – and how to order them, write to us at the appropriate address below. Please note that for copyright reasons the selection of books varies from country to country.

In the United Kingdom: Please write to *Dept E.P., Penguin Books Ltd, Harmondsworth, Middlesex, UB7 0DA*

If you have any difficulty in obtaining a title, please send your order with the correct money, plus ten per cent for postage and packaging, to *PO Box No 11, West Drayton, Middlesex*

In the United States: Please write to *Dept BA, Penguin, 299 Murray Hill Parkway, East Rutherford, New Jersey 07073*

In Canada: Please write to *Penguin Books Canada Ltd, 2801 John Street, Markham, Ontario L3R 1B4*

In Australia: Please write to the *Marketing Department, Penguin Books Australia Ltd, P.O. Box 257, Ringwood, Victoria 3134*

In New Zealand: Please write to the *Marketing Department, Penguin Books (NZ) Ltd, Private Bag, Takapuna, Auckland 9*

In India: Please write to *Penguin Overseas Ltd, 706 Eros Apartments, 56 Nehru Place, New Delhi, 110019*

In Holland: Please write to *Penguin Books Nederland B.V., Postbus 195, NL–1380AD Weesp, Netherlands*

In Germany: Please write to *Penguin Books Ltd, Friedrichstrasse 10–12, D–6000 Frankfurt Main 1, Federal Republic of Germany*

In Spain: Please write to *Longman Penguin España, Calle San Nicolas 15, E–28013 Madrid, Spain*

In France: Please write to *Penguin Books Ltd, 39 Rue de Montmorency, F-75003, Paris, France*

In Japan: Please write to *Longman Penguin Japan Co Ltd, Yamaguchi Building, 2–12–9 Kanda Jimbocho, Chiyoda-Ku, Tokyo 101, Japan*

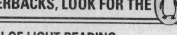
A SELECTION OF LIGHT READING

Imitations of Immortality   E. O. Parrott

A dazzling and witty selection of imitative verse and prose as immortal as the writers and the works they seek to parody. 'Immensely funny' – *The Times Educational Supplement*. 'The richest literary plum-pie ever confected . . . One will return to it again and again' – Arthur Marshall

How to be a Brit   George Mikes

This George Mikes omnibus contains *How to be an Alien*, *How to be Inimitable* and *How to be Decadent*, three volumes of invaluable research for those not lucky enough to have been born British and who would like to make up for this deficiency. Even the born and bred Brit can learn a thing or two from the insights George Mikes offers here.

Odd Noises from the Barn   George Courtauld

The hilarious trials and tribulations that George Courtauld underwent when he became a midwife on his wife's stud farm and found he didn't even know the difference between a mare and stallion. 'A cross between James Herriot and *Carry On Up the Haystack*' – *Daily Express*

The Franglais Lieutenant's Woman   Miles Kington

To save you having to plough through the classic works of literature, Miles Kington has abbreviated them and translated them into Franglais so that you can become acquainted with Thomas Hardy, Jane Austen, John Betjeman and many, many more in this rich and expressive language.

Goodbye Soldier   Spike Milligan

This final – for the time being – volume of Spike's war memoirs has our hero inflicting entertainment on the troops stationed in Europe, falling in love with a beautiful ballerina, and, finally, demobbed and back in civvies heading for home. 'Desperately funny, vivid, vulgar' – *Sunday Times*. 'He's a very funny writer' – *The Times Educational Supplement*